PRAISE FOR
UNEXPECTED DETOUR

"Lynn Marie Jackson's *Unexpected Detour* will dazzle readers with its authenticity and candor. This satisfying World War II tale explores the cost of war to a generation of patriotic young American men and women, who stood in harm's way on the heels of the attack at Pearl Harbor. It also reveals the depth of their patriotism, the threat posed by subversives who sought to undermine the war effort, the fragility of the human spirit, and the sobering reality that death notices could be served at anyone's front door.

Unexpected Detour is a worthy addition to the credible but limited collection of World War II home front novels. Highly recommend!"

— LAURA TAYLOR, SIX-TIME *ROMANTIC TIMES* AWARD WINNER

"Lynn Marie Jackson's detail-rich WWII novel about a young woman's decision to change the direction of her life and join the war effort places its readers smack dab in the middle of post Pearl Harbor paranoia. The racial prejudice that ensued reflected the moral dilemma Americans faced: to remain vigilant against an enemy threat from within while not turning their backs on loyal immigrants who had made the Unites States their home. We didn't always get it right, but there were a few strong women, like Faye Baxter Conner, who did. *Unexpected Detour* reminds us that the heroes of World War II included not only those who suffered and died on the battlefield, but also the millions of men and women back home whose efforts contributed to a victorious outcome."

— ANNA WILCOXSON, AUTHOR OF
*SECRETS AND PROMISES, THE STORY OF
AN ITALIAN AMERICAN FAMILY*

"Lynn Marie Jackson takes us on an exciting voyage through the World War II home front. From the fear of the unknown following the attack on Pearl Harbor to the violence that attended the victory celebrations (something history doesn't often talk about), her characters experience agonizing ups and downs. Jackson paints beautifully drawn and fleshed-out characters, mostly women who take on roles far beyond what they'd expected to vastly aid in winning the war. She addresses a war front not often covered in fiction that is equally important to the fighting fronts. Her women are gritty, determined, and willing to fight through adversity, overcoming systemic obstacles as well as emotional ones. A masterly crafted vision of what the home front was like and how the war was fought at home!"

— THOMAS M. WING, AWARD-WINNING
AUTHOR OF *AGAINST ALL ENEMIES*

"I read *Unexpected Detour* in three days because I couldn't put it down. This novel is especially remarkable because it stands out in quite a large field of recent books about women in wartime. A thoroughly enjoyable read from start to finish, *Unexpected Detour* is well-researched and beautifully written, and it reveals the rarely told story of WWII from the home front, through the eyes and heart of a young woman whose husband leaves for the war just after their wedding. The book immerses the reader in WWII-era San Francisco with lush descriptions, authentic language, and specific detail. Readers will root for the lovable heroine, Faye Baxter, both the girl-next-door and a gutsy dame, as she embraces the detour in her life as an independent career woman. In her new home of San Francisco, Faye and her friends celebrate shared triumphs and losses amidst a tapestry of 1940s fashion, music, food, and romance. The author deftly weaves in the more sobering aspects of a world at war, exploring the fears of reluctant soldiers and the loss of fallen heroes, wartime espionage, and racial prejudice."

— LAURA C. RADER, AUTHOR
OF *HATFIELD 1677*

UNEXPECTED DETOUR

Courage and Intrigue
in Wartime
San Francisco

LYNN MARIE JACKSON

Helping talented writers publish exceptional books

This novel is a work of historical fiction. Names of real people and events have been included to provide context. However, the characters and scenario are entirely fictional products of the author's imagination. Any resemblance of non-historical people and events to actual ones is purely coincidental.

Unexpected Detour:
Courage and Intrigue in Wartime San Francisco

Printed in the United States of America. For information, address
Acorn Publishing, LLC
3943 Irvine Blvd. Ste. 218, Irvine, CA 92602

www.acornpublishingllc.com

Interior design by Kat Ross
Cover design by Damonza

ISBN-13: 979-8-88528-106-5 (hardcover)
ISBN-13: 979-8-88528-105-8 (paperback)
Library of Congress Control Number: 2024910087

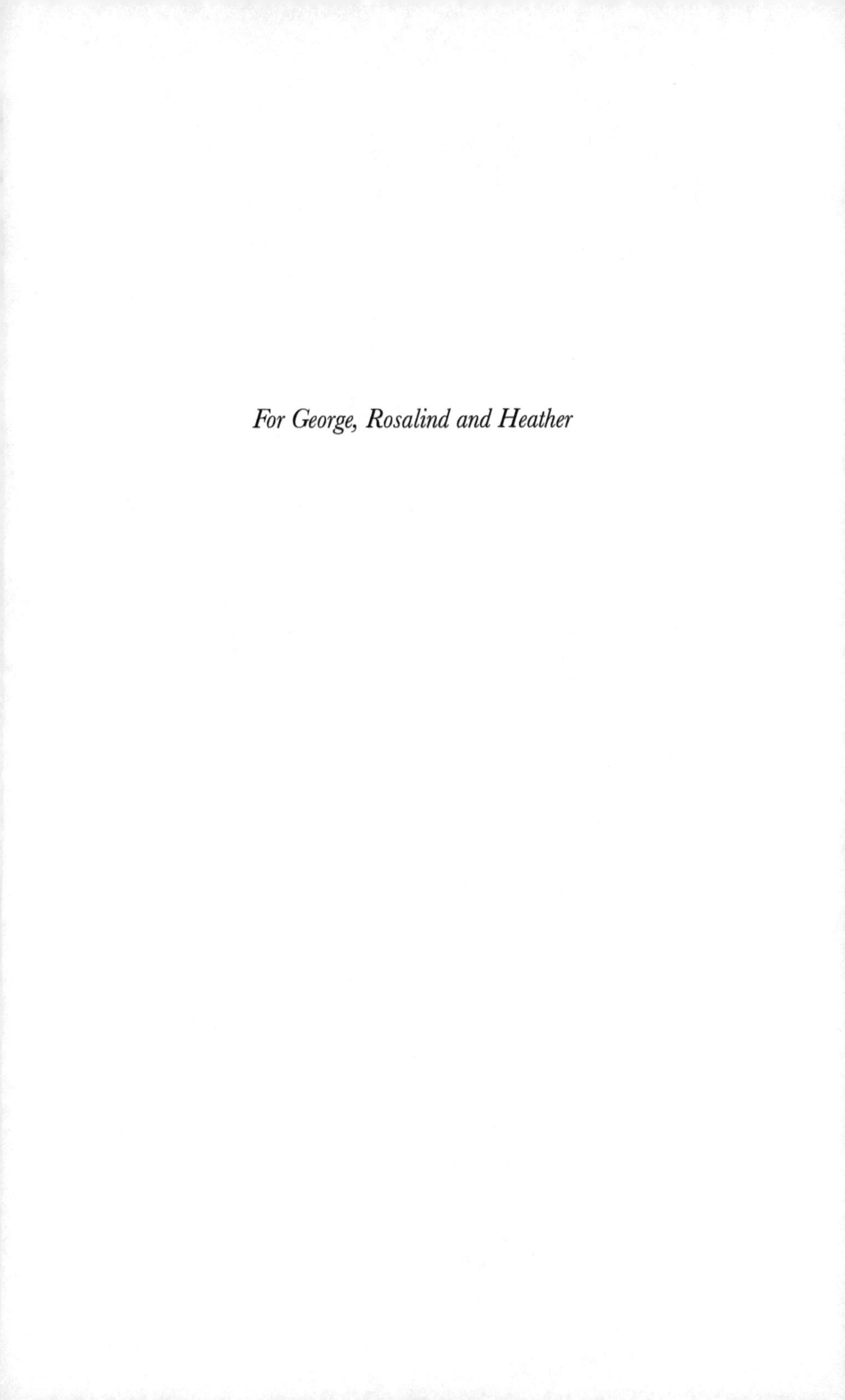

For George, Rosalind and Heather

FOREWORD

The Second World War thrust the San Francisco Bay Area into the international spotlight. Already the commercial and shipping capital of the West, the Bay Area became a point of embarkation for more than 1.5 million soldiers, sailors, marines, and civilians to war zones in the Pacific. Limited access and abundant resources made San Francisco Bay an ideal center for defense manufacturing.

In 1941, the US military was sorely depleted, due to years of isolationist sentiment in the wake of the First World War. As a result of persistent underfunding by Congress, its 180,000-man Army ranked nineteenth in the world—right behind Portugal. The Bay Area proved crucial to its ability to mobilize rapidly into an effective fighting force. Dozens of military bases were built or reactivated on the hills overlooking the Golden Gate and inside the bay, creating the "Fortress of San Francisco." Some eight ship-yards and numerous drydocks ringed the bay's shoreline, and the Ford Motor assembly plant in Richmond churned out jeeps, tanks, and armored personnel carriers.

The population of San Francisco increased by some 95,000 people during the war, due in large part to an influx of workers involved in the war effort. Among these were tens of thousands of women seeking jobs, adventure, a sense of purpose, and an opportunity to be closer to their soldier boyfriends and husbands. This is the story of one such woman as told through the lens of the 1940's.

Contemporary readers should remember that World War II was a time when misogyny and racial prejudice were rampant and well represented in news reporting. Feminism and civil rights would not become part of the American consciousness for another thirty years. Women had only gained the right to vote twenty-one years prior to the war's outbreak, and they still viewed their place in society as that of wives and mothers. That attitude shifted, along with countless other social norms, when the US entered the war and several million women took jobs previously held by men.

This is a narrative of women who followed their soldiers west, then worked for the war effort while they waited for them to come home. One such woman was Dorothy Watts, who would one day become this author's mother-in-law and whose experiences, although never shared in detail, inspired this novel. While the story is set against a framework of factual events with excerpts from newspapers and popular media provided for historical context, it is entirely a work of fiction.

1

Yesterday, December 7, 1941—a date which will live in infamy—the United States of America was suddenly and deliberately attacked by the naval and air forces of the Empire of Japan.

—Franklin D. Roosevelt, President of the United States

Address to Congress, December 8, 1941

It was a Sunday after church when word came.

Faye already felt on edge. She'd invited Steve Connor, her fiancé, for dinner, and she hoped to goodness there wouldn't be a fracas. Pops, a professor of mathematics, tended to be open-minded on all topics except one: the war in Europe. His experience in France during the Great War had left him scarred, and he vehemently opposed "sending our young people off to another fight on foreign soil."

Steve, on the other hand, brimmed with enthusiasm to "whup the Nazis," not at all afraid to voice his opinion.

Faye knew from experience that a casual comment had the potential to dissolve into a heated debate or, even worse, stone-cold silence. She always held her breath when the two men she loved most in the world were in the same room for any extended period of time.

Thank all the stars in heaven that the Big Game is this afternoon.

Of the many Big Games Faye could recall, this was the biggest. Both of Chicago's NFL teams would be locked in battle for a spot in the championship against Green Bay the following weekend, and all of Illinois was rooting for either the Bears or the Cardinals. Thankfully, while they remained far apart on the political spectrum, both Pops and Steve shared a die-hard love of the Chicago Bears. She figured they only needed to make it until kick-off and then she could relax.

"Use the good plates, please." Mother's instruction came *after* Faye had set the table with everyday dishes.

"But it's just Steve. He's practically family."

"First impressions are still important. You wouldn't want him to get cold feet, would you?"

Faye swallowed her aggravation and changed out the dishes.

No sense in adding more discord to the afternoon, she reminded herself.

As she filled the water glasses, she mentally strategized safe conversation topics, then rushed to answer the door when the bell rang. There he stood. Steven Connor, all six feet of him, a big smile on his face and a potted poinsettia tucked into the crook of his arm. He pulled her out into the cold of the vestibule and kissed her hard.

Golly, he feels good.

Faye had known Steve since their sophomore year at Evanston High. Even after all these years, he still zinged her strings. When he officially popped the question last Christmas, she marveled that this tall, handsome, compassionate, smart man had chosen her. His spontaneous kiss filled her heart, its sweetness lingering on her lips for hours.

Almost as gratifying was how edible the roast chicken was that Sunday. Even though Mother dedicated her life to keeping a hospitable home, she typically overcooked any form of animal or vegetable. The succulent meat and crispy skin that somehow emerged from the oven added to the general feeling of goodwill—to the point that the soggy green beans proved easier than usual to ignore.

Sticking to her strategy, Faye orchestrated the chit chat away from politics to less divisive subjects: Steve's upcoming graduation, next week's holiday party at the University Club, the new Alfred Hitchcock film, and the like. Steve veered into ominous territory only once with a mention that his cousin had enlisted, but quickly changed the subject when Faye poked him in the shin with her toe.

Dishes were cleared, custard pie sliced, coffee poured, and the dining room abandoned for the front parlor. Steve and Faye settled on the sofa while Pops tuned the Zenith to WGN.

Then, at 1:30 p.m.—right at the scheduled time for kick off—came the words that indelibly etched that moment in time: "*We interrupt this broadcast… Pearl Harbor…attacks on US military…*"

The brief announcement left everyone in the Baxter living room stunned. A muffled rushing sound filled Faye's ears, as if she stood on the platform at Union Station and watched her future whoosh by. She knew full well that an attack on American soil could only lead to one thing—the long-anticipated declaration of war. Her mind rushed forward into a pit of uncertainty. She noticed only Steve's tightening grip on her hand.

No, no, no. This is America! We're never attacked.

With the game coverage continuing as if nothing had happened, Faye tried to comprehend the magnitude of what she had just heard.

Thank goodness Steve is classified IIA. He might get called up at some point, but he's exempt while he's in college. Thank goodness, thank goodness.

Against the backdrop of the play-by-play, no one spoke. Tears pooled in Mother's eyes and slipped silently down her cheeks. The clock on the fireplace mantel ticked, the rocker on Pop's chair creaked.

I wish Pops would say something. This is going to be hard on him.

"I'd better go home," Steve said, abruptly breaking the silence and rushing for his coat.

"Shall I come, too?" Faye knew in her heart that, sooner or later, this war would take Steve away, and she wanted to be with him for every possible second. After all, they were a couple and should face everything together—the good and the bad.

He turned to her in the vestibule. "No, sweet pea, you stay. I'd better go talk to my mom alone. I'm going to sign up tomorrow."

Sign up?

Faye tried her best to quell her surprise. They both knew the high probability of the US entering the war and had talked about this—endlessly—and mutually decided he would stay in school until he was drafted. And now the man who wouldn't even buy a shirt without consulting her had made the decision to go ahead and volunteer?

"What about our plans for this spring?" She hoped the decreased volume of her voice masked her anxiety.

Their plans. They had discussed them again and again over the past year. Steve would finish his degree in May. They would get married and move to Texas for work in the oil fields. That's where the opportunity was these days—on the sunny plains of west Texas. She would have his babies and keep his house, and life would be long and sweet.

"Faye…" He hugged her close until her head fit perfectly against the curve of his neck. "Don't worry. This is just a little hiccup."

"You don't have to go right now," she whispered against his skin. "If you wait until you're called up, we could be married. Surely, they're not going to draft married men."

His sea-green eyes looked straight into hers.

"War is a sure thing now and our country needs me, Faye," he said gently as he cradled her face in his hands. "I love you so much, and I want to help make the world safe. For us. For our kids. For everyone." He kissed her forehead. "I'll call you later."

As she watched Steve get into his Model A and disappear into the snowy twilight, the reality of his impending absence began to sink in. He'd been her best friend for six years and, as the only child in an orderly household, Faye relied on his companionship. His large Scots Irish family, raucous and laughing, was like honey to Faye. She thought of him the instant she awoke each morning, and he always had a starring role in her dreams. Steve Connor had become second nature to her, and the notion of possibly losing him felt as dire as losing a limb.

Her thoughts were interrupted as a gust of freezing wind rattled the storm door.

Oh, good. A blizzard. Then she caught herself. *Get a grip, missy. It's just a storm, not an omen.*

As she checked the latch and retreated to the warmth of the front room, Faye wanted to turn the clock back a few hours to when life was tidy and predictable. For the first time in her twenty-one years, she felt irrelevant, held hostage by decisions she couldn't control or anticipate. She didn't like the sensation one bit.

2

No matter how long it may take us to overcome this premeditated invasion, the American people in their righteous might will win through to absolute victory.

—Franklin D. Roosevelt, President of the United States

Address to Congress, December 8, 1941

Those final few weeks of 1941 passed like a tornado off the plains—with just about as much upheaval. As promised, Steve enlisted. He assured Faye it was the best way to get a good post. He'd defer his final semester. With his college experience, he felt he had a good chance at Army Officers Training School. Or so he said. In the end, Faye decided she didn't want to spend what little time they had left arguing—something they rarely did when times were normal. He'd made a commitment. She'd show her support. That was what you did for someone you loved. But still, she didn't want the event to go unaddressed.

"I have to say, I was kinda hurt that you made this decision without me," she confessed as they cuddled in the Connor basement a few days later. "You signing up came out of the blue. I was just so taken aback."

"The last thing in the world I want to do is hurt you, Faye." His eyes softened.

Well, I guess that counts as an apology.

"I honestly surprised myself," he continued. "One minute we were listening to the radio, the next I just knew what I had to do."

Steve wasn't the only one. Boys from up and down the block, from high school, from church, from Pop's classes, from their extended family and circle of friends signed up in those first weeks after the attack. Pops thought it ironic that, only a month ago, many of these same boys wanted nothing to do with war. Now, everyone thought it would be a lark, better than hanging around their backwater home-towns with nothing going on.

"You mark my words, Faye. The excitement will end fast when people start dying. These idiots in DC will never be able to supply US troops across the ocean. They think they can fight in the Pacific *and* Europe at the same time? It's madness."

"But, Pops, you have to agree that fascism needs to be stopped," Faye countered. "It's a cancer. Look at Europe. Italy, Austria, most of eastern Europe, France—all gone. Hitler has bombed the hell out of England and occupied Paris. *Paris*, Pops. We can't just stand by."

"You're correct in thinking something must be done, but a war on foreign soil is sheer lunacy. And I say that because I've been there. I know what it's like to be stranded in a disease-soaked ditch, waiting for orders from someone far removed from the action, feeling like I'm fodder and no one really knows what's going on. We didn't start this war, Faye, and now it's supposed to be our fight?"

"It wasn't two weeks ago, but I think it is now," Faye replied calmly. "Even the America First Committee has disbanded and encouraged its previous members to support the war effort—and they were the loudest isolationist voices in the nation."

"I see where we're going to have to be involved somehow, but I'd rather focus on diplomacy and defense." Pops shook his head. "Our military is simply not strong enough at this point to be spread so thin."

Their discussions at the dinner table never resolved the father-daughter divide over the issue. While Faye disagreed with him, she didn't begrudge him his point of view. After all, he knew better than most the horrors of the battlefield and the scars the fighting men would bear for the rest of their lives.

Although she would never dare say it out loud to anyone, Faye felt a bit envious. Everyone had a purpose, and she felt like she was missing out. She longed to share that sense of allegiance to the Grand Cause now sweeping the nation.

In the wake of all the excitement, Faye's daily routine became more tedious by the minute. Despite her father's encouragement to pursue her education, she had chosen to go straight to work after high school. She was confident Steve would propose at some point and saw no sense in wasting the time in college. She'd worked at the local law firm of Ernest, Pierce & Begley for the three years since she graduated, starting out as a switchboard operator.

Last year, she received a promotion to the secretarial

pool for Stanley Pierce, and she was beginning to help with legal research. The work was tolerable–barely, but she often found herself wondering if contract law was where she wanted to spend her working years. In the end, it came down to rich people trying to get richer by suing each other. She always told herself she could tolerate the job until she married, even if it meant endless documents that needed to be amended—in triplicate.

Now, all the junior attorneys at the firm were leaving to enlist. Her weeks would consist of one inconsequential assignment after the next with no one to challenge or mentor her.

The whole world is changing, but sweet little Faye is staying right where she is. Eeegads. I might as well be embalmed.

The uncertainty she felt about her work situation impacted just about every aspect of her life. Plans for the wedding, the honeymoon in New York City, and the little house in Texas she was saving her $18.80 a week to buy all became more and more tentative. She'd be stuck in the hum-drum safety of Evanston, while Steve would be who knows where. Sometimes, she felt as if her chance to break away and really contribute was slipping through her fingers.

The night before Steve's departure, his folks hosted a going-away dinner in fine Irish style. Spirits were high with plenty of lamb stew, beer, whiskey shots, and boisterous talk about the exploits ahead. The Connor's basement was packed to the gills with young people, Big Band tunes blaring from the RCA Victor. Faye loved to dance, but that particular evening she couldn't shake the blues. She sat out "Boogie

Woogie Bugle Boy," sipping a beer and struggling to reconcile the optimistic lyrics with the reality of mobilization.

I wish Steve played the trumpet. Spending the war as a bugler sounds a lot better than slogging through swamps under fire.

She flinched as she felt a hand slip around her waist from behind.

"Hey, cupcake," Steve whispered against her hair. "I've been looking for you."

Steve's closeness spread like balm over her despondency, soothing and restorative. She relaxed into his body and, as the upbeat tune of the Andrews Sisters was replaced by Frank Sinatra's "Star Dust," she whispered, "Hey there, soldier. Wanna dance?"

Through one dreamy tune after the next, they clung to each other, enveloped in a cloud of tenderness that was theirs and theirs alone. Yet, as the evening turned to night, Faye silently tussled with a growing sense of panic. This boy, the only love she'd ever known, would soon be gone.

Well after midnight, once everyone departed, Steve and Faye found themselves alone in the Connor basement. She knew she'd have to put on a brave face at the station tomorrow, but right now the tears Faye had been fighting for weeks started to flow.

"Hey, sweet pea, don't cry." Steve gathered her into his arms. "I'll be back sooner than you can say Jack Frost. They're saying the war will be over by spring."

He took her chin in his hand and tilted her head upward, looking deep into her eyes. "You're my girl." As his kisses grew more intense, Faye could taste his desire, primal and tempting. In that moment, Faye knew she wanted to send him off with something they would both remember.

The next morning, Faye drove Steve to Chicago's Union Station. She watched as multitudes of young men crowded onto the platform, each with three days' worth of clothing in a suitcase, as instructed. Like thousands of other new recruits, Steve was headed for Camp Roberts in California for his basic training. Faye and Steve clung together as people rushed around them—families and sweethearts saying goodbye, one last kiss, one more minute in an embrace, one more promise to "be safe" and "write to me." No public tears. Only smiles for the courageous boys.

"Well, this is it," Steve said, holding Faye close. "I'll never forget last night."

"Me, either," Faye said, clinging tighter. *Do I look different?* she wondered. *Can people tell?*

She flushed as she remembered silently undressing, Steve's hands, his lips, his tongue, fumbling with a rubber, the briefest twinge of pain followed by the most excruciating sweetness. Like all nice girls, Faye had intended to save her first time for her wedding night. In the years she had been going with Steve, they'd perfected petting, but always stopped at second base.

"He won't pay for what he can get for free!" She remembered the cautionary refrain that circulated at slumber parties during high school.

While Faye had always valued her virginity, the war seemed to be changing just about everything she once held dear. Sex with Steve last night felt as natural a phenomenon as the sleet that was beginning to fall from the sky. And, to her delight, the intimacy they shared turned out to be wonderful.

"Don't you dare forget me." Her voice sounded muffled against his chest.

"Not a chance, sweet pea. I wish I could pack you up in my suitcase and bring you with me."

"Just stay safe and come back," Faye said. "I love you so."

"I love you, too, my Faye."

He kissed her hard, drew back, cupped her face in his warm hand. With his most endearing smile, he said, "You show 'em, kiddo."

Then, he was gone.

You show 'em.

As the train gained speed, Steve's parting words reminded her of the very moment she knew she loved him. It was at the end of their junior year at the Honor Roll Picnic. They had fallen into an easy high school friendship, as they shared many of the same classes. He sometimes joined their group at lunch, and he always walked her from Trig to Chemistry. He played both baseball and basketball, so Faye was glad when they were on the same softball team that bright June day in 1937.

Faye, one of the few girls on the team, possessed some sound *bona fides*. All those summer evenings of playing catch with Pops in the backyard paid off. She played second base for five innings, performed well, and hit a single in the third. But at the bottom of the ninth, her confidence wavered. The score was tied, bases loaded, and she was up. Mike McCann wanted to put in a sub, but Steve stood up for her.

"Hey, let her play. This kid's got a wicked swing," he declared, quelling Mike's objections.

Then, as he handed Faye the bat, he brought his face

close to hers and spoke as if she was the only person in the world. "You show 'em, kiddo."

For the first time, Steve's green eyes ignited a tingling in Faye that energized every molecule of her being and made her believe.

You bet your backside I'll show 'em.

She stepped up to bat, focused on the pitch and—*crack!*—hit a solid double that won them the game. That was the first time Steve kissed her and the moment she knew they were meant to be.

All these years later, as she watched her one true love disappear, she didn't have any idea what challenges were coming her way. But she resolved then and there to show everyone she could handle it and make Steve proud.

3

---

*We are now in this war. We are all in it—all the way. Every single
man, woman and child is a partner in the most tremendous
undertaking of our American history.
We must share together the bad news and the good news, the defeats
and the victories—the changing fortunes of war.*

—President Franklin D. Roosevelt

Fireside Chat, December 9, 1941

Each passing day brought new changes—more boys leaving, families divided, more uncertainty, talk of rationing, fear of invasion and lots—*lots!*—of rumors. German subs lurked off the coast of Long Island, Japanese bombers were headed for California, bombs containing "bubonic plague germs" were dropped in Oregon, Japanese soldiers hid in US sewer systems awaiting the command to attack, poison was found in crab meat packed in Japan. Paranoia seemed to tinge every conversation—at work, at home, among friends, and between strangers.

Families of German descent—and there were many in

Evanston—became targets of harassment, even attacks. In mid-December, an enormous Swastika and the words "Sieg Heil" were painted on the home of the Himmel family, who lived just three doors down from the Baxters. Word of the crime spread quickly around the close-knit neighborhood.

"Anyone who knows the Himmels realizes they're as American as apple pie," Faye said when she learned the news at Saturday breakfast.

"I saw Walter Himmel when I went out to get the paper. He told me seven families were victims of the same spree, and they all had German surnames," Pops commented.

"I can't believe it's happening." Faye shook her head as she buttered her toast. "The Himmels have lived here for at least three generations, and Josh just enlisted in the Marines."

"It's as if everyone has forgotten we are all immigrants," Pops responded. "Most of the Midwest was settled by German farmers, and practically everyone had some Teutonic blood running through their proud American veins."

Faye sipped her coffee. "Just think. If Grandpa had been German instead of Grandma, our name would be Hauptmann instead of Baxter. We'd be the very same people we are right now but labeled as enemies."

"As I've told you many times before, war is madness."

As soon as the breakfast dishes were cleared, Faye grabbed a loaf of fresh banana bread cooling on the counter and rushed to the Himmels to make sure they were all right. She wound up organizing a neighborhood brigade to help paint over the hateful markings.

Christmas that year became a footnote to the mobilization. All holiday furloughs were canceled as the armed services rushed to make up lost ground to build a battle-ready fighting force. Faye relied on the three national broadcasts a day for news of the war, which was not good. In late December, an American tanker was attacked by a Japanese sub just off the coast of California, feeding fear of a strike on the mainland. Merchant ships found themselves increasingly under fire as part of a strategy to disrupt Allied supply lines to both the Pacific and European theaters.

I hate to admit it, but Pops could be right about supporting two fronts abroad.

According to Steve's sporadic letters, he may as well have been on vacation in sunny California. He reported that training was physically challenging, but his tone was upbeat from beginning to end.

Everything here is just fine. I'm meeting all kinds of interesting people from all over the country. It's only January, and we already have fresh strawberries… There's nothing at all to worry about, the war will probably be over before I get to see any action. Be sure to write, my Faye…

As departures to the various basic training posts gathered speed, the wedding invitations began to arrive. A growing marry-your-man-while-you-can sentiment filled every city hall, county courthouse, and place of worship in the greater Chicago area with couples, including many of Faye's childhood friends, grasping for hope. Hastily planned ceremonies, borrowed gowns, church-hall receptions, then, with the "I dos" still fresh and unproven, the grooms shipped out and the new brides were left wondering what to do next.

As Faye witnessed a progression of ceremonies, her longing for Steve intensified. She could easily imagine it was Faye Elizabeth and Steven Sean standing up there instead of the couple-of-the-day. Their last night together replayed in her head with each set of vows exchanged.

I swear to God, I'd give just about anything to kiss him again.

Then came the phone call that changed everything.

"Long distance call for Faye Baxter."

"This is Faye Baxter."

"Go ahead, please." The operator clicked off and an unfamiliar voice came on the line.

"Hi, Faye, this is Midge Swanson. We met at the Tau Beta Pi Spring Mixer last year?"

Faye searched her memory and then vaguely recalled a curvy blonde girl in a print sundress clinging to the arm of Arnie Platt, one of Steve's classmates.

"Hello there, Midge. Of course, I remember you."

"I know this is kind of out of the blue, but I wanted to run something by you."

"What's up?"

"Arnie is stationed at Camp Roberts, and he wrote to me that he ran into Steve out there. I'm thinking of heading out to Monterey to see him before he ships out. My folks said I had to find someone to go with me if I'm going to do such a thing. So, I'm wondering if you'd like to come, too, since Steve is out there and all."

The very suggestion pushed Faye's pulse into high gear as she unleashed a barrage of questions. "When are you leaving? And how long will you be gone? Do you have a place to stay lined up?"

"I'd like to leave in the next few weeks, although they're

asking civilians to stay off the trains. I'm hoping to get a ticket. I'm not sure how long I'll stay, but I understand there's lots of war work in San Francisco. My aunt lives out there and has a spare room. Nothing's really keeping me here on the farm, believe me, so I might stay for the duration—to help the war effort and all."

As Faye stared at her desk, a pile of briefs to edit in front of her, an afternoon of endless meetings ahead, the pull became overpowering. To see Steve one more time before he shipped out was suddenly the very best use of her time Faye could imagine.

When I think about it, nothing's really keeping me here either.

"I can't thank you enough for calling, Midge. I'll talk to my folks this weekend, but count me in."

The talk did not go well.

"California! That's the next place they'll bomb," Pops railed. "Didn't you hear the president's warning the other night? It would be like visiting London during the Blitz."

Wow, Pops never yells. He must really be mad.

"But, Pops…"

"Besides, San Francisco is a den of sin and depravity. There are more bars than churches in that town, and I will not have my daughter out there on her own."

Now, Faye was irritated. She'd always been responsible —done well in school, went to church regularly, volunteered in the community, didn't smoke or drink—well, not to excess anyway, was helpful to her parents and faithful to her boyfriend. She could certainly handle a trip to California without sacrificing her well-honed reputation.

"Give me some credit, Pops. Do you think I'm going to

get off the train and turn into a floozy?" she shot back, surprising them both. She had never before rebelled against her parents about anything. She softened her tone a bit before she continued. "You raised me to have a strong mind and a compassionate heart. Right now, both my mind and heart are telling me that this is the right thing to do."

Pops just went back to his paper and, after a pause during which she wondered if she'd gone too far, Faye sat on the ottoman beside his chair. If outrage wasn't doing the trick, she'd try reason.

"Look, Pops," she said, assuming her most I'm-in-control tone of voice. "It's just for a month or so. I have plenty of money saved up. And Midge Swanson will be with me. She has an aunt who lives in San Francisco who has offered to put us up."

"I don't know Midge Swanson."

"Well, you'd like her. She lives on a big farm just south of Springfield. She goes with Arnie Platt, who's right at the top of Steve's engineering class with him. They're Methodists, just like us."

Faye didn't actually know if the Swansons were Methodists or not. In fact, now that she thought about it, she remembered Midge downing more than one beer at the mixer—very un-Methodist behavior—but she didn't care. If it would help build her case, she was just fine with a fib or two.

"We don't know them, Faye dear, and we certainly don't like the idea of you charging off into the unknown," Mother chimed in, the knuckles on her work-chapped hands turning white as she wrung her ever-present tea towel. The curls that escaped from her sensible bun began to tremble, which Faye found mildly irksome.

Has she ever had a gutsy thought? Ever?

"What would Steve say?" Mother continued, her voice beginning to quiver. "Surely, he'd want you safe at home."

Faye didn't know if she could hold out against a full-on breakdown with pleading and tears, so she raised her chin and looked away.

"Well, I'm twenty-one and the decision is made," Faye said with calm certainty. "I'm leaving on the tenth. Midge and I have already reserved a berth, and I cabled Steve this morning. I'm going with or without your permission. I just want you to know that I love you both, and I'd like your support."

With that, Faye marched up the stairs, closed her bedroom door and flopped on her twin bed.

Criminy, that was hard.

To defy her parents for the chance to see the man she loved: it wasn't quite Montague vs. Capulet, but it took all the moxie she could muster. Although committed to her plan, she felt at odds. The desire to please her parents, especially Pops, had always been a prime motivator.

Faye's relationship with her father was devoted and nuanced. A man of math and science, Professor William Baxter had raised his only child to appreciate the power of divergent thinking. Weekends were often spent on long walks in the woods or along the lake, sometimes with Michael Pennington from next door tagging along. Their discussions on topics like photosynthesis and the importance of mathematics—i.e. the key to the universe—fell into a Socratic pattern, the tutor challenging the student while encouraging debate and discussion. His calm voice and fact-filled discourse created a far deeper bond than any showy declaration of parental love could. She and Pops shared a connection she knew they would both miss once she departed. And yet, the pull to step out on her own and follow Steve felt stronger than a tide at full moon.

As she changed into her pjs and crawled into bed, she hoped to heck her little declaration of independence hadn't done any lasting damage. With so many changes in her life, she would hate to undermine the nurturing and encouragement she'd always known. On the other hand, it felt really good to make a decision all on her own.

It didn't take long for Mother and Pops to soften their stance.

"We raised you to be a sensible young lady," Pops announced at breakfast the next morning, while Mother attempted not to burn the waffles, Faye's favorite. "You are an adult, so we need to let you try your wings."

Wow, they must have been up all night talking this through.

"Here's a little something toward your travel fund." Pop's voice warmed as he slid a white envelope across the table to her, then rattled his newspaper as if to signal that no further discussion was needed.

Unable to contain her excitement, Faye jumped up from the table.

"Thank you so much," she said as she gave them each a quick hug. "I promise it's where I need to be."

She asked for a leave of absence from work first thing Monday.

"I have to say it seems rather an impulsive move,"

Stanley Pierce, Esq. opined, in his typical I-know-everything manner. "Be cautious out there. Sometimes it's hard to tell what's true and what's not. You've always struck me as being able to think for yourself, so I hope you continue to do so."

Not really knowing what he meant, Faye replied, "I appreciate your support, sir."

"Just do what you need to. You'll always have a job here. We'll have your last check ready on Friday—with a little extra as thanks for your hard work. Best of luck."

As she returned his handshake, the nervousness she felt in anticipation of the meeting morphed quickly into a sense of relief.

Now nothing's holding me back.

For the remainder of the week, off-work hours were spent planning and packing. Mother fluttered around trying to help. Faye decided to take only luggage that she could carry. No hat box, just a suitcase and a make-up case. Not knowing exactly how long she'd be gone, she rethought her wardrobe several times. In the end she decided to wear her suit, pack two dresses—one casual and one dressy—and be done with it.

It's sunny California, for criminy sakes. How many clothes will I need?

As Pops drove her to Union Station on February tenth, Faye knew he was struggling with his emotions. He was in full silent mode until the skyscrapers of downtown Chicago came into view.

"I hope you know what you're doing, Fifi," he said calmly, breaking the silence.

Pops only used her childhood nickname when he wanted her to smile. It always worked.

"I do, Pops. Steve is my whole life, my whole future."

"Just keep your head level, honey. Love is all very exciting, and Steve is a great guy, but war is terrible. It changes everything."

"I know. It's already changed my life in ways I never imagined."

"Remember, Mother and I have loved you longer than you've loved Steve."

"Thanks, Pops." She smiled and savored his reassurance for the rest of the ride, knowing she'd miss his thoughtful banter and their mealtime discussions even if it was only for a month or so. But as the familiar Chicago skyline grew larger with each mile, she felt a surge of anticipation, as if her life so far had been stuck in neutral and was only now beginning.

4

———————

Thirty-nine hours and forty-five minutes later, Faye and Midge stepped onto the platform at Oakland Pier. Suitcases in hand, they boarded the ferry for the final leg of their trip into San Francisco. The train journey was already a blur of packed cars, lines for the rest rooms, bad food, raucous laughter, and endless cigarettes. Civilians and soldiers alike sat on luggage in the aisles. The girls gave up their sleeping berth to a pregnant woman and her two young children, so they spent 1,850 miles in a crowded coach surrounded by sweaty, young, uniformed men in various stages of inebriation. Everyone seemed intent on cramming as much frivolity as they could into the trek.

Now the fresh breeze off the bay hit Faye's groggy face. She gulped in the crisp, briny air until her head was scrubbed clean of the dull ache caused by too little sleep and too many sips of whiskey from flasks of unknown origin. She was here, albeit rumpled and worse for wear. And, if all went well, she would be with Steve this weekend.

Despite the day being chilly by Bay Area standards, it was downright balmy compared to Chicago—crystalline clear verging on sweater weather. The sun was far too alluring for the girls to stay below in the passenger lounge, so they purchased cups of joe at the snack bar and headed to the upper deck.

"We did it," Midge said as they watched the deckhand cast off from Oakland.

"Yes, we did, sister." Faye sipped her coffee and took in the view. "And I may never go back. Look at this. The folks back home would be pea green with envy if they could see what I'm seeing."

The clear sky was reflected by the water, making the entire estuary a perfect shade of aquamarine. The bay was encircled by green hills, filled with moored ships and awash with activity. Ferry boats, military launches, merchant ships, and tugboats buzzed to-and-fro, leaving the bay choppy with their wakes. Several aircraft carriers were docked in Alameda, and a large troop carrier crossed just ahead of them, headed purposefully west.

The ferry passed under the Bay Bridge, which was bisected by a small rocky island. As they cleared the span, the city spread out before them. From the Ferry Building, with its iconic clock tower, the piers fanned out from the Embarcadero, bustling with people, trucks, wagons, and streetcars. Faye recognized Coit Tower and Nob Hill—so often appearing in movies, studded with elegant hotel buildings. To the west, the Golden Gate Bridge spanned the entrance to the bay like a lazy smile, as if to delude the entire nation that everything beyond would be just fine. Faye knew full well that these bright orange towers were the last glimpse of America for thousands of boys headed for war.

As they entered the shipping channel for the final run to the Ferry Building, a gust of wind lifted Faye's beret. In the split second she grabbed for it, her coffee went over the railing. Horrified, she peered down at a man sporting a splotch down the shoulder and sleeve of his well-tailored trench coat. He stared up at them, bewildered at first, then broke into a gradual smile.

"Sorry!" she yelled, then bolted down the stairs to the lower deck, Midge close behind.

"I am so sorry," Faye gushed to the victim as they emerged on the main deck. Midge, in the meantime, found her hankie in her purse.

"Allow me," she said. Not waiting for a response, she started to daub the man's shoulder.

"No worries, ladies," he said with surprisingly good humor. He handed Faye the empty coffee mug that had survived the fall just fine. "I'm sure it was an accident."

"It was really a comedy of errors up there," Faye said as Midge continued to daub. "My hat blew off, and before I knew it, my coffee just went flying."

"With a little more focus, you'd be excellent in the gun turret."

Well, at least he isn't angry.

It was only then she noticed how nice looking he was. Dark hair, gray eyes, a beautifully cut double-breasted suit under his overcoat, and a charcoal gray fedora set at a rakish angle. As she drank in every detail, she didn't quite know how to deal with the twinge of guilt.

Stop it. I'm not being disloyal to Steve just because I think this total stranger is nice looking. It's not like I'll ever see him again. What is that lilt in his voice? Does he have an accent? Never mind. Don't think about his voice. Or his dimples.

"Well, I've really made a mess of your coat. May I at least have it cleaned for you?"

"Not necessary. Your friend here…"

"Midge," Midge provided.

"Midge has done a superb job."

Is Midge blushing?

"Well, if you're sure…again, I am so sorry."

"Simon?" An icy voice sliced through the air as a woman with a beautiful mink coat draped casually over the shoulders of her fitted black suit came out of the lounge. Just beneath the little veil that descended from her smart black pillbox, her bright red lips turned ever so slightly down at the corners. "What's going on?"

"I've just been christened," he replied, gesturing to the splotch on his sleeve, "so I'm fully launched and ready to take on the day."

Mrs. Red Lips looked annoyed and eager to erase both Midge and Faye from her presence. "Well, we're pulling into the dock, so let's queue up. We're already running late."

"Of course." He turned, took Midge's hand and gave it a gentle squeeze. "Midge, it's been a pleasure. Thanks for your fine work." He then turned to Faye. "Midge's friend… *au revoir.*"

"That is one great big hunk of dynamite," Midge commented as the couple disappeared into the crush of passengers waiting to disembark.

"Well, dream on, sister. Remember, I'm engaged, and you have a boyfriend."

Midge shrugged. "Oh well. I wouldn't want to tangle with his lady friend, anyway. As I've heard it said many times in Charles Boyer movies, *c'est la vie.*"

"There she is!" Midge began to jump up and down and wave as soon as they walked down the gangplank and entered the Southern Pacific Waiting Room at the Ferry Building. "Aunt Liz! Aunt Liz!" She waved wildly. "Here we are!"

From the crush of people in the Arrivals area, a tall, big-boned woman emerged, blue eyes sparkling, arms flung wide for an embrace. Rosy cheek to rosy cheek with Midge, the family resemblance came through loud and clear. Her wool skirt, twinset, and sensible shoes reminded Faye of every housewife on her block back in Evanston.

"Well, Margaret! As I live and breathe." This is the first time Faye had heard Midge's given name. "You're all grown up!" The two women hugged and hugged. "It is so good to see you. I was thrilled to get your cable that you were headed out. Welcome, welcome, my dear."

When Midge stepped back, she took Faye's arm. "This is my friend, Faye Baxter."

"You are welcome, too." Liz leaned in and gave Faye a brawny hug, which felt awkward to Faye. Enthusiastic hugging among strangers was not part of her Baxter upbringing. "Consider yourself one of the family. Now, let's collect your luggage and get you girls home. I know you must want a bath and a good meal. I put a meatloaf in the oven before I came over. I hope you're hungry."

She led the girls through the crowded ferry terminal and out into the throng of people on the Embarcadero—so many uniforms, so many workers and businessmen, so many Asian people—all in a hurry. As they walked toward the streetcar terminal, Midge whispered to Faye that she had never seen an Asian person before in the flesh, only in Anna May Wong movies. Their tram was packed to the point that only Liz's sharp elbows and sheer aggression secured them some coveted standing room and a sliver of space for their bags.

Elizabeth and Henry Bosch lived in an area of the city called Cole Valley, a twenty-minute ride on the streetcar from the downtown area. The green expanse of Golden Gate Park was just three blocks away from their stately Victorian on Gratton Street. Henry managed shipping at the Anchor Steam Brewing Company, and Liz struggled with an empty house, her twin girls off to Los Angeles as of last fall, one to study nursing and the other to the teacher's college. Because civilian train travel was discouraged, the girls didn't make it home for Christmas and would stay down south for Spring Break, too.

Liz chattered away in a nurturing tone as she led Faye and Midge up the narrow staircase to the twin's room. As she opened the door to the twins' room, with its pink walls, ruffled curtains and matching single beds, she acted as if her own girls were home again.

"Here we are, lovelies. This is your room for as long as you like. I've cleaned out this dresser and half of the closet," she said. "The bathroom is the next door down the hall. Henry starts work at five a.m., so there's never been any competition for bath time. Linens are here." She gestured to a cupboard next to the bathroom. "I do laundry every Wednesday. I love doing laundry, honestly, I do, so just put yours in the hamper."

As Faye and Midge paused to glance at each other, as if to confirm that they both heard "love doing laundry" correctly, Aunt Liz chatted on.

"Now, let's eat, then you can both take baths and have a

nap if you like. I'm sure you're exhausted, and I know you want to head down the coast tomorrow."

Room and board plus laundry service? Did we ever luck out!

Camp Roberts, established for the sole purpose of training new soldiers, was isolated among the rolling hills about three hours south of San Francisco. The plan was to rendezvous with the boys in Monterey, a mid-point between San Francisco and the camp that offered hotels, jazz clubs, and promenades along the bay—all the makings of a fun reunion. Henry had insisted at supper that evening that they take the Bosch family's Buick.

"Liz and I won't be going anywhere this week, and we may as well give that sassy young filly some exercise before gas rationing kicks in. Besides," he added, "both the trains and buses are going to be too dad-blamed crowded to bear."

The girls set off in Uncle Henry's prized 1940 Buick Roadmaster convertible with a thermos of coffee, a bag of sandwiches, and Henry's warning to "stay off the bridges. I'm just waiting for one of them to be blown to smithereens by some Axis spy ring." Their destination: The Monterey Hotel, where Steve's cable promised the boys would be waiting.

As the morning fog retreated, the air grew lush with excitement. Midge drove, Faye navigated, and both sang along with the car radio as they passed mile after sunny mile of orchards just beginning to bud.

"Golly, it'll be great to see Arnie again," Midge mused. "I wonder if he's getting muscles from all the training."

Arnie was tall and reed thin, so the thought of him with biceps made Faye chuckle under her breath. And having observed Midge's flirtatious behavior on the train journey west, she wondered about how committed their relationship really was. She had seen the two of them together a few times on campus, but really didn't know if they were in love or had plans.

"So…are you two serious?" Faye asked.

"Me and Arnie?" Midge took a long pause to reflect, then spoke carefully. "I like him a lot, and we have tons of fun together, but serious is probably too strong a word," Midge responded. "My folks are pushing me to settle down, but I just don't know. Especially now with the war and all. I mean, look at us." She grinned. "Two single women out on their own with no father or husband telling us what to do. I kind of like it."

"Me, too," Faye admitted, "but Steve and I have been together for so long, I just can't imagine what life will be like without him."

"I've only been going with Arnie since last spring," Midge said. "He's fun, sure, but who knows what's going to happen next week, much less a year or two from now. I'm definitely taking a have-all-the-fun-you-can-while-you-can approach to life these days."

After a long pause, she added with certainty, "I know one thing. After being out here, I'm not going back to the farm, with or without a guy."

∼

Uncle Henry's directions took them south through the Santa Clara Valley to the farming community of San Jose, then through the hills to Santa Cruz and Castroville. There the orchards gave way to rows and rows of thorny plants that neither Faye nor Midge recognized. It was only when they saw a hand-painted sign advertising *ARTICHOKES 2 FOR A PENNY* that they made the connection. Faye had never seen an artichoke on the plant before but had eaten one once at the Drake Hotel in Chicago. The fibrous leaves drenched in melted butter bore little resemblance to these blue-green fields of thistle plants reaching out to the horizon beside the Pacific Ocean.

The farmland gave way to the charming streets of Monterey, postcard perfect on a bluff above the sea. They drove past neighborhoods of wood frame cottages, the sardine canneries along the bay, and the Spanish colonial adobes that ringed the town plaza. As they pulled up to the Monterey Hotel with its elegant arched windows, they noticed an abundance of single women, smoking and chatting, occupying every possible place to sit in the grand lobby. Midge must have noticed them, too.

"Guess we're not the only ones who missed our boys," Midge remarked. "My Lord, I have a feeling the Monterey Hotel will be rockin' tonight!"

Just as the sun dipped into the sea, the bus from camp arrived. So many men disembarked, identically dressed in Army greens—fitted tunics, long trousers, and cloth garrison caps. It was hard to distinguish one eager young soldier from the next in the waning daylight.

Is he here? Where is he? Where is he?

Then, out of the pack, a pair of arms emerged.

"I've dreamed of this moment every single night since I left home," Steve whispered into her hair. His embrace, something she'd craved for weeks, instantly validated her decision to make the trip.

She breathed in his scent—fresh and grassy, like the prelude to a spring rain. She knew she should greet Arnie and get on with their dinner plans, but all that could wait. She didn't want to move, only to stay right here in Steve's arms.

It wasn't the wedding Faye had dreamed of all those years. There was no church, no white dress, no Pops to walk her down the aisle…no aisle, for that matter. None of that was important. Steve and she intended to pledge their love and fidelity to each other. She didn't give a fig about anything else.

They made their decision to "go ahead and tie the knot" in a euphoric haze in a Monterey dance hall. After a leisurely dinner of local rock fish and the freshest salad Faye had ever tasted—*real spinach is nothing like canned spinach*—they wandered into the lounge for some dancing. Strong cocktails and intoxicating kisses flowed to the languid beat of a local band. Maybe it was the emotion of seeing each other again and wanting to cling to something familiar, but they decided then and there to take the plunge.

That is how they found themselves bright and early the next Monday standing in line with several other soldier-girl-friend couples at the County Courthouse in Salinas. Faye wore her travel suit with a gardenia corsage, Steve his uniform. Midge and Arnie, seemingly immune to the matrimony virus but more than ready to share the bliss, were there to serve as witnesses.

"Looks like they're geared up for a volume business," Arnie commented.

"It's 'grab your man while you can' in action," Midge quipped.

Steve squeezed Faye's hand. "Or in my case, 'grab your dream girl before you waste another minute.'"

Well said, soldier.

They filled out their paperwork, collected their marriage license, and waited for their names to be called. "Just like the DMV," Arnie took the opportunity to note. Then, they stood before a very practiced officiant, who wasted no time.

"Please hold hands and repeat after me. I, Steven Sean…"

"I, Steven Sean…"

In his uniform his eyes looked even greener than normal, Faye noticed, and his gaze seemed to penetrate to her core.

Can he see how much I love him? Can he see how scared I am that I might lose him?

"I, Faye Elizabeth…"

The sound of the surf stirred Faye from a dreamless sleep. As she lifted her heavy eyelids, it occurred to her that this was Wednesday, their last day. This evening at six, Steve would report back to base. He was scheduled to ship out next week.

She opened her eyes and looked around the little cottage by the sea. Leaving Midge and Arnie in Monterey, they'd driven over to Santa Cruz for a two-night honeymoon and found this resort set around a rose garden, not that it really mattered. Except for long walks on the beach and a few meals, they hadn't left this four-poster bed in two days.

She snuggled up against Steve's sleeping body. As she luxuriated in the sheer contentment of that morning, the stark reality that this was already Wednesday clawed its way through the bliss and planted itself front and center.

Knock it off, sister. You can't let tomorrow's sadness rob us of our joy today. This is it. We need to make it count.

She pressed herself closer to Steve's back, gently kissed his neck, then snaked her arm over his shoulder, across his chest and down his torso, warm from the sun that now streamed through the window.

"Are you awake?" she whispered.

"In more ways than one, Mrs. Connor."

"That's exactly the answer I was hoping for, soldier."

Exactly one week later, Steve was one of thousands of newly minted soldiers to ship out. As Faye stood on the dock at Fort Mason with what seemed like hundreds of other women, she somehow felt detached. She was oblivious to the waving, shouting, and, in some cases, tears that surrounded her, focused only on Steve as he stood in formation. He was one among hundreds of soldiers facing the *USS Hugh L. Scott*, gangway agape as if ravenous for the young men on the quay. One by one, as names were called in alphabetical order, soldiers picked up their duffels and disappeared into the hold. Faye's heart clenched as the segreant started on the Cs.

Don't you dare cry, Faye Baxter Connor. Tears will not keep him here.

"Cabot. Caddell. Cadiz. Cagan. Caggiano."

What if they just skip over him? That'd be a hoot.

"Centeno. Clement. Clinton."

Faye closed her eyes and held her breath.

"Connor."

She snapped her eyes open in time to see Steve pick up his duffel and make his way up the gangway. She waved wildly, hoping he'd see her. He paused, spotted her and, with a quick smile and nod of his head, disappeared into the cavernous portal. Gone. She stood frozen on that same spot, eyes dry and chin held high, until the troop carrier finished loading and the crowd thinned.

As the ship cast off and headed for the Golden Gate, Faye's mind gained a determined clarity. She knew for certain that she needed to stay in San Francisco. Mom and Pops might not like it, Steve might not like it, but that didn't matter. She'd get a job, find a place to live and do everything in her power to help end the war. And she'd be right here when Steve came back.

The wind gusted from the west. As she thrust her hands deep in her pockets to fend off the chill, she became acutely aware of the gold band on her finger. Hastily purchased mere days ago, it was clear evidence that she and Steve were now officially united—not just in spirit but by law. As she watched the ship clear the bridge and head into the Pacific, that fact was the only comfort she could find.

5

WOMEN IN WAR: DEFENSE JOBS FILLING

This war will not be won by men alone. The men must fight, but the women will do their part, too, not only on the home front but also on the industrial battle line.

By Zilfa Estcourt

San Francisco Chronicle, February 10, 1942

The job market in San Francisco that early spring of 1942 had surpassed hot and was well on its way to ballistic. With so many young men exiting the workforce for the military, employers clamored for qualified workers, which opened opportunities for women to hold jobs previously reserved for men. The geography of San Francisco Bay—a large, sheltered estuary with only one point of entrance/egress—made it a natural fortress and an ideal location for facilities such as shipyards, dry docks, munitions depots, and supply stations. People poured in from all over the country for the well-paying jobs created by mobilization.

Arnie Pratt shipped out a few days after Steve. Within hours of his departure, Midge found work as a switchboard operator at the Western Pipe and Steel headquarters at Broadway and Front Street, just a block from the Embarcadero. The contractor for the Grand Coulee Dam, the company had in recent years shifted its efforts to shipbuilding with a highly productive operation in South San Francisco. As a new employee, Midge was assigned the afternoon shift on the switchboard, which began at four p.m. and ended at midnight.

Faye's contract law experience made her a sought-after commodity among the corporate headquarters in the Financial District. After a whirlwind of interviews, Faye accepted a position as executive secretary to Mr. Raymond Dalton, head of operations for the west coast region at Gregor Corp, an engineering firm specializing in large infrastructure projects—hydroelectric power plants, airfields, highway improvements, and, most recently, maritime facilities all around the bay. Her salary of thirty-five dollars a week was beyond what she thought she would ever earn.

The apartment hunt proved more daunting. The influx of war workers to the Bay Area made decent housing almost impossible to find and most options just too hideous to consider. Even East Bay communities were chock full of war workers and their families, lured west by good paying industrial jobs. Roach-infested studios in the Tenderloin, shared rooms with two sets of bunk beds and three strangers, rooming houses way out in the Avenues—nothing seemed plausible. Faye received an offer of "hot bed" for ten dollars a month but passed. The idea of sharing a bed with someone who worked the night shift was just too far removed from Faye's midwestern sense of propriety.

"Just stay with us," Aunt Liz offered. "The twins won't be back home until summer. It would be a shame for a good bed to go to waste, and at least you'll know your roommate."

"Absolutely," Midge chimed in. "With my schedule, it'll be practically like having a private room—for both of us."

Faye was thrilled with the offer. Midge was turning out to be a good friend. Her gregarious personality and curvy good looks attracted people of all ages wherever she went. Faye admitted to herself that she enjoyed living life on the fringes of Midge's popularity.

Who would think that a fresh-off-the-farm girl would make such a splash in Baghdad-by-the-Bay?

With the housing issue temporarily resolved, Faye dipped into her savings and bought some new work clothes. The war had all but eliminated silk, wool, and cotton from the retail racks, but The White House department store was showing spring suits in the new rayon fabric. The shorter, slimmer skirts, narrower lapels, and single-button jackets, all in keeping with the new manufacturing restrictions intended to conserve fabric, accentuated Faye's tall frame and well-toned legs. She selected two suits: a warm gray tone, nice and neutral, and a classic black that could be dressed up or down, depending on the occasion. The sales lady clucked her approval and suggested a few complementary blouses. Silk stockings were nowhere to be found, so, like every other young American woman in 1942, Faye resigned herself to make do with saggy-baggy cotton or leg makeup. Two suits, three blouses, a slip from the sale rack, and a new pair of black patent leather peep-toe shoes came to $66.59.

Before Faye paid, she added in one more spur-of-the-moment purchase: her first pair of slacks—drapey taupe beauties that made her feel just like Lauren Bacall. She'd never dare wear them to work, of course, but the next day she appeared in full betrousered glory at Sunday supper. Aunt Liz raved about how sophisticated and modern she looked, but Henry only gave her what the folks back home called the "stink eye."

"Don't get me wrong," Faye said, staring at her reflection in the vanity mirror. "I think my bob is fine for Evanston, but I have a new job in a big city."

"You don't have to justify wanting a little spiff up," Midge replied, focused on the task at hand. "I've been itching to play with these locks for weeks!" She sprinkled the front of Faye's hair with sugar water, combed it through, and fanned it with a magazine to encourage it to dry.

Faye normally preferred a low maintenance style for her honey-blonde hair. She set it in pin curls at night and wore it brushed off her forehead in soft waves or, for dressier occasions, the sides swept back with combs. She never fussed much with her hair and makeup, but, like every other aspect of her life, that would also change.

"The last thing I want is to show up on my first day of work looking like Miss Midwestern Hayseed of 1942."

"Not a chance, sister. These Victory rolls are gonna put the diggity in hot diggity-dog!"

Midge talked around a bundle of pins in her mouth as

she patted and pinned. She backcombed Faye's hair from forehead to crown, combed it smooth, patted and pinned, then patted and pinned some more.

"There," she said, stepping back. "How's that?"

Faye looked at her reflection. Midge had divided the waves around her face into two sections, rolled them toward each other and pinned each with a big swooshy curl near the center part. The back section of her hair, which hung just past her shoulders, was rolled up and forward over a rat, a little net sack filled with fluff, and pinned securely at the nape of her neck forming a sleek chignon.

Moving her head from side to side, Faye liked the effect of the new updo. It made her feel refined—even powerful, feelings she had craved since she first entered the working world three years ago.

"Well, it looks great, but that took some time. I'm not sure if I can do this every morning."

"Then just do it once in a while for important meetings," Midge suggested. "Or you can just do the rolls in front and leave the back in loose waves."

"Will I be able to wear my hat?"

"Sure. See, it will sit on the crown of your head. Your navy pillbox and beret will work great, and so will that little porkpie number. I'm not sure your fedora will work, though."

"Let's try it!" Faye jumped up and grabbed her fedora out of the closet.

Midge settled the gray felt fedora at a flirty angle and gently pulled the brim over the roll at the left side of her face.

"Okay. Let's see if the rolls will hold when you take it off."

With that she gently lifted the hat off. The sugar-water

spray served its purpose and held the roll of hair firm and undented.

"Ta da!" They both cheered and laughed.

"I'm telling you, Faye, you look like a big boss lady now."

"Well, be that as it may, I'm just hoping to be accepted on the lowest level of the pecking order. I know there's a war on and all, but I'm sure there are no boss ladies at Gregor Corp."

Work settled into a pleasant routine. Faye would take the crowded streetcar downtown every morning, so she arrived at the Gregor Corp Building by eight. Her desk, just outside Mr. Dalton's sixth floor office, provided a view across the bay to the Berkeley Hills. She could see the ship traffic on the bay, including the steady stream of troop carriers as they set off through the Golden Gate.

Her day consisted of screening Mr. Dalton's phone calls, keeping his schedule, greeting his visitors, taking notes in meetings, and reviewing contracts that had already been approved by the legal department. Several times a day she would hear "Take a memo, Mrs. Connor" over her desktop intercom, and she'd sit in Dalton's office, steno pad on her lap and pencil flying, while he dictated communications. It was all well within her skill set, and she quickly earned the reputation as a competent, well-organized support resource.

The company employed several hundred people. Managerial roles were held by men who were either too old or ineligible to serve in the military. Most were well into their forties, uncommunicative—except to bark orders and dictate letters in monotones, overworked, and overweight.

Any male of draft age became the subject of rampant speculation. Was he an objector? Did he have a hernia? Was he light in the loafers? Although some of these young men felt compelled to make the reasons they were unsuitable for service clear, most held their secrets close.

The massive secretarial pool was entirely women, as was most of the bookkeeping staff. Faye rather enjoyed the chatty, spirited atmosphere of the break room, and she quickly expanded her network of acquaintances. Every lunch hour and coffee break was chock full of war updates, Hollywood gossip and romantic exploits, a combination Faye found both amusing and educational. She thought it rather ironic that *No Room for Rumors* and *Mr. Hitler Wants to Know* posters were displayed prominently on the break room wall, and she liked that the government's anti-gossip warnings didn't seem to deter the lunchroom banter. Besides, the thought of enemy agents among the Gregor Corp workforce seemed laughable, especially with an entire security department right in the basement and a guard stationed on every floor.

One of many civilian-owned industries dedicated to the war effort, Gregor Corp was a major government contractor that specialized in large-scale construction projects throughout the country. Mr. Dalton oversaw large maritime facilities and airstrips throughout the Western Region. With the outbreak of war, business boomed. He often traveled, so Faye learned quickly to rely on her common sense to manage the flow of business. Her days were long and busy, a welcome antidote to the nagging undercurrent of anxiety about the war.

Socially, San Francisco in 1942 was a whirlwind of parties, dances, teas, cocktails, and men looking for a good time. Midge often dragged a reluctant Faye on her club rounds, meeting friends at the Top of the Mark or the Roseland Ballroom. For something more casual, they stopped in at one of many bars. They particularly liked the Geary Tap Room, where the laughter and booze flowed and uniformed military officers swarmed—Navy men from the base on Treasure Island, GIs on leave, and airmen from across the bay in Alameda or Hamilton Field in Marin. They were all so young and handsome and polite, looking to share a drink with a pretty girl.

Faye was always hesitant to join the scene. Midge, who had no firm commitment with Arnie and seemed perfectly willing to play the field while he was away, incessantly coaxed and cajoled her.

"It's just drinks and dancing, and the girls are always way outnumbered," Midge emphasized. "No harm, no foul. If you sit home alone, you'll just get sad. Do you think Steve would want that? Besides, it's our patriotic duty to show these boys some fun."

Faye knew Steve would much rather she sit home, but she occasionally gave in to Midge's coaxing. The war changed the rules. She would never compromise her relationship with Steve, but Midge was right about being alone and feeling sad.

There's no harm in a few laughs and a little innocent fun. Is there?

After not hearing from Steve for weeks, several letters arrived from him in mid-March—all in a clump. He knew his unit was going to the Pacific Theater, but he didn't know where. Faye fervently hoped he didn't end up in the Philippines, where reports of fighting were particularly grim.

To get by the censors, Steve and Faye had worked out a code, based on the current US military presence in the Pacific. "Shark" would mean Midway Island, "dolphin" would mean Australia, "butterfly" would mean the Solomons, and "parrot" would mean the Philippines. His first letter was written in transit, so the news was of long hours at sea in the troop carrier, watching the flying fish, playing gin rummy, and wondering what was ahead.

Everything's fine here, I can't wait to hold you in my arms again, was the news.

No clues in the second letter, just more news about settling in at the base camp for extensive jungle training.

In his third letter, she found the clue.

I saw a dolphin in the bay this morning.

Steve was in Australia! Darwin had been bombed last month and was also in constant danger of invasion, but Australia sounded much safer than a dinky, enemy-infested island.

We're just waiting around for the action to begin, playing baseball and working on our tans. Everything is fine here. Take care of yourself and keep those letters coming. Please send socks, cigarettes, and chewing gum if you can. Dry socks are hard to come by and my toes look like albino prunes! I love you so much, my Faye.

6

Any news was bad news that spring. Everything in the Pacific was not fine, despite Steve's incessant reassurances. Battles raged on the Bataan Peninsula on the Philippine island of Luzon, where General MacArthur and 120,000 American and Filipino troops were getting pushed back to the sea. The fall of the Philippines to the Japanese invaders was imminent.

The Japanese also defeated a US strike force at the Battle of the Java Sea, and all of the Dutch Indies were now under Axis control. Japan consolidated its positions in New Guinea, and they appeared poised to launch an invasion on the Australian mainland. Battles erupted in North Africa. Allied casualties soared from air raids in Europe and the fierce fighting on the Eastern Front. Neither the newsreels shown at the Telenews Theater on Market, nor the thrice-daily national news broadcasts, contained encouraging reports.

As the days and weeks passed, in the quiet times, Faye acquired a new companion: worry. She lay awake into the wee hours of the night, fretting and hoping Steve was safe. His letters had begun to repeat the same cadence of, "I am fine. I hope all is well with you," without giving any real details. Was he really fine? Did he have enough to eat? Was he actively fighting and just not able to tell her about it? Would he come home to her safe and sound and whole?

After a litany of questions she couldn't possibly know the answers to, the what-ifs started. What if he's injured? What if he's captured? What if he's tortured? What if he's killed and doesn't ever come home? What if I never feel his cheek pressed to mine again?

The possibility that Steve might not come home drifted on the fringes of her consciousness and banged into the realm of possibility more often than she liked, typically when she was reading the morning paper or watching the newsreels. The bombing and destruction reported in the press fueled her anxiety and, like every woman in America, she lived in dread of the telegram man.

As the death reports began to trickle in, she spent her late-night hours imagining the worst, which was a very dark place.

I've always considered myself capable and resilient, but I'm not sure if I could cope. Please, please, please let him come home safe.

Fear of an attack on the mainland escalated. Shortly after Pearl Harbor, the Army designated San Francisco, with its many air bases, shipyards, training centers, munitions factories, supply depots, and corporate headquarters, a likely target area. The frequent blackouts and air raid drills were clearly intended for emergency preparedness, but also served as a constant reminder of the threat. Some 45,000

San Franciscans had signed up for volunteer positions with the Office of Civil Defense, and every neighborhood had an Air Raid Warden with Block Leaders to help enforce the lights-out policy.

Even though Mayor Rossi declared San Francisco "emergency-ready," talk around the Bosch dinner table began to reflect the growing nervousness about Japanese air and sea attacks, as well as espionage activities from the Japanese American community. The fear was fueled by the bombing of an oil refinery near Santa Barbara in late February, launched from a Japanese sub off the coast.

The Bay Area's enemy alien residents, primarily of Japanese and Italian heritage, had come under increasing ostracism since Pearl Harbor. Fishing boats were confiscated from the Italian American population in North Beach, the entire community subject to curfews. Even more severe, some 10,000 people of Japanese descent were ordered to leave their homes and businesses and evacuate the "military restricted zone," which included the entire west coast.

"You never know what those people in Japantown are up to," Henry commented one evening. Midge was working, so it was just Henry, Liz, Faye, and a bland tuna noodle casserole. "I say, good riddance."

Faye found his comments ironic, as Henry was himself of direct enemy lineage. His parents had immigrated from Bavaria—the birthplace of the Nazi party. Discrimination because of one's heritage just didn't seem right.

"No offense, but how are they different from your own family, or my own family?" Faye asked. "My grandma on Dad's side was full-blooded German, as were both of your parents. If we're relocating the Japanese, shouldn't we restrict Germans?"

The clatter of Henry's fork against the edge of his plate was followed by a full half-minute of silence. Aunt Liz's eyes rounded like saucers, as she sat speechless. Faye fully expected to be immediately tossed out onto the sidewalk.

Henry just stared at Faye, then said, calmly, "My family was fully assimilated within months of hitting these shores. They learned English, took pride in their homes and their new country, and mixed with other Americans right away. You can't say that about those shifty people in Japantown." He resumed eating. "There are many generations who still don't speak English. They stick to themselves and stay in their filthy little neighborhoods, just like the Jews back east and in Europe."

In Faye's mind, Henry's comments were disconcerting. She didn't know many Japanese people—in fact, she didn't know any—but she knew lots of Jewish people back home and didn't think Henry's characterization held water. It just didn't make sense. But Faye just nodded and smiled. As the beneficiary of Henry's hospitality, she wasn't about to push her luck.

"Well, it can't hurt to ask them to leave—just for the duration," Liz chimed in, obviously trying to diffuse the tension. "After all, the entire California delegation to congress voted in favor of the evacuation order."

"I'm sorry if I offended you, Mr. Bosch," Faye offered. "I see why we need to take precautions, but they're Americans, too. Where do you draw the line? I heard that Joe DiMaggio's parents might be evacuated from North Beach. Joe DiMaggio! Jolting Joe! You can't get more American than that!"

"Then they won't mind helping the war effort and doing as their government asks," Henry said with finality.

Well, that discussion is over.

As Faye picked at her congealed casserole, she longed for the spirited discourse her parents had always encouraged. Even though she and her father disagreed on many issues, the Baxters felt there was a place for debate among friends. It was clear that Henry Bosch was on an entirely different wavelength.

"He's like a lot of people I know back in Springfield. It's like they've forgotten that almost everyone was once a foreigner," Midge commented when Faye recounted the incident late that evening. Midge arrived home late from her shift, her commute that night especially challenging as the Bay Area had snow flurries—rare in coastal California—and the buses were all off schedule. "Let's not worry about it too much, though. It's an order from FDR, so I'm sure it's in the best interest of the country."

Faye's feelings on the issue became even more conflicted when she began to see Japanese families, from young children to grandparents, lined up to board Greyhound buses bound for relocation camps. *Closed* signs sprouted up on previously thriving businesses all along Geary Boulevard from the Tenderloin to the Outer Sunset. More upsetting were the *Out Japs!* and other epithets that were hastily painted across shop doors and apartment buildings, reminding Faye of the incident with the Himmels back home.

In the following weeks, newsreels of the austere camps surrounded by barbed wire and empty desert began to filter back. The flickering images showed a camp yard in Arizona as young children walked through the wind and dust to their makeshift school.

These aren't camps, they're prisons. I want more than anyone to end the war, but this just doesn't seem right. I hope FDR knows what he's doing.

As suspicion of Japanese Americans grew, displays of nationalism became part of life in the Bay Area. Easter Sunday was declared Army Day, and an Easter Army Day Parade highlighted the after-church hours. Soldiers, Red Cross workers, Scout troops, and nurses in gas masks all marched up Market Street from the Ferry Building to the Civic Center, flags flying from every window along the route. In a steady spring rain with thousands of other civilians, Faye watched the disciplined legions march, cheered on by spirited crowds. Even with her misgivings about forced evacuations, she couldn't help but join the cheers. Here was clear evidence that people of all walks of life could work together to support our troops, and Faye was 100 percent on board with that.

7

In April the shipyards put out the call for women workers. "Women, do something for your country. Go to the Richmond Shipyard and become a welder. Bring proof of citizenship. No experience necessary," the radio announcer read.

Already on the fringes of the shipbuilding industry, Midge jumped at the opportunity to get out from behind the switchboard and make some real dough. She set off to the Kaiser Shipyard in Richmond and came home a few hours later as a tack welder trainee. After a two-week training period, her salary would be $1.12 an hour, the same as the men in the tack welder category. That afternoon, Midge tried hard to persuade Faye to sign up, too.

"Plus, we get time and a half for overtime. Just think of the house you and Steve will be able to buy after the war," she prodded Faye, waving her new training manual. "Look, it's easy. I just showed them my birth certificate, took a physical, and—bingo—I was hired."

As tempting as the pay sounded, Faye decided she was

better off where she was. She was dedicated to helping the war effort, but not keen on working in a hot, dirty ship hull with sparks flying all over the place. Besides, Steve had been uncharacteristically quiet on the whole topic of her staying in San Francisco. She knew she hadn't consulted him—*fair play?*—and she wasn't sure he fully approved. A job in the shipyards might only bring added stress to a new marriage. She decided Midge could break new ground for women in the shipyard; Faye would do her part behind the scenes at Gregor.

The situation on the Bataan Peninsula in the Philippines, which deteriorated rapidly during March, only added to Faye's angst about Steve's safety. As the Japanese troops advanced, General MacArthur made a quick exit by boat to Australia, leaving his men under the command of General Wainwright. The outcome proved to be catastrophic. After weeks of pitched battle and no reinforcements, the Allied forces were exhausted and outnumbered. Wainwright had no option but to surrender. Tens of thousands of American and Filipino soldiers were captured and forced to march hundreds of miles through the jungle to prison camps in Japanese-occupied territory.

Word of the Fall of Bataan hit the Bay Area hard. Its large Filipino American community was well established. Several of the girls in the clerical pool and accounting were from Filipino families. They were hard-working, stylish, and mixed easily with the other girls in the break room.

"Poor things. Most of them have families back on some remote island and have no way of knowing how they're doing," Faye reported to Midge. "It's not clear what territories are currently occupied, and there's no communication from civilians. I see them standing in little clumps around the water cooler, weeping and looking miserable."

The defeat cast a perpetual gloom over San Francisco. The newsreel cinemas were packed with people seeking news of friends and family involved in the conflict. They sat in silence, searching the flickering black-and-white images for familiar faces as they soaked in the discouraging news—not just in the Pacific, but in North Africa, too, as Rommel made mincemeat of the British forces. The Allies just couldn't seem to catch a break.

Maybe Pops is right. Our generals really don't seem to know their elbows from their backsides.

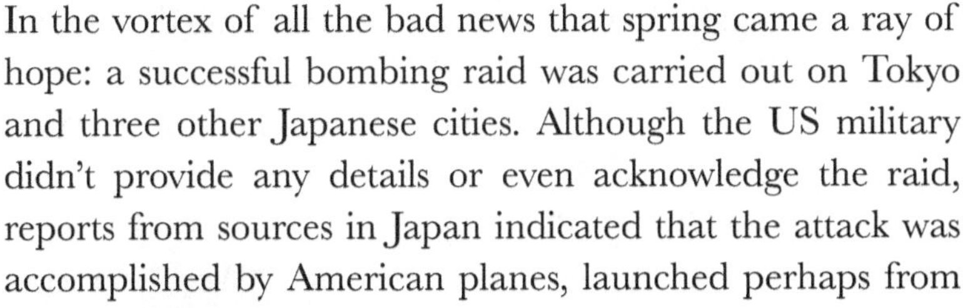

In the vortex of all the bad news that spring came a ray of hope: a successful bombing raid was carried out on Tokyo and three other Japanese cities. Although the US military didn't provide any details or even acknowledge the raid, reports from sources in Japan indicated that the attack was accomplished by American planes, launched perhaps from an aircraft carrier.

News was sketchy, but San Francisco was ready to celebrate. The raid occurred on a Saturday. That evening, Faye found herself with a group from work at The Yankee Doodle near Union Square, which was even more packed than usual. The cigarette smoke was so thick, it seemed as if the fog bank making its way across the Financial District had crept right into the bar to join the revelry. The juke box blared, but it couldn't compete with the lively talk and laughter.

Five girls from Gregor Corp were crammed into a

booth. Faye and Helen Beach, who worked on her floor, sat on one side with Becky Ross, Silvia Giametti, and Evie South all smushed onto the opposite bench. They sipped their weak highballs and rehashed every bit of news they had gleaned about the raid. Soon the men in uniform began to swarm, coaxing one or another of the girls to dance. They all offered a similar line: "I'm shipping out tomorrow and want to have a pretty face to remember."

Amid the din, Faye appreciated an opportunity to chat with Becky, who hailed from Hyde Park. Ever since learning that Becky's parents were on the faculty of University of Chicago, Faye wondered if they had any mutual friends.

"Did you play any sports in high school?" Becky asked, looking for connections. "I was on the tennis team."

"I did field hockey and crew," Faye responded. "Do you know Jean Bellach? She did tennis."

Becky drew a blank, so Faye tried another tract. "What church did you go to?"

"The KAM Temple."

That rang a very loud bell for Faye. "Well, you must know Rachel Stein and her brother Ben!" Faye hoped the brightness in her voice masked her momentary shock. With her light brown hair and blue eyes, Becky didn't look Jewish, but that was such a cliché. As fellow children of academics, they should be beyond stereotypes.

"I know them both. We were at JLO camp together."

"I volunteered at the Red Cross with Rach. I think Ben liked to hang around to flirt with all the girls knitting socks for refugees."

"Sounds like Ben."

"What sounds like Ben?" asked a silken baritone voice

as one of the few men not in uniform slid into the booth next to Becky.

"Simon, you meatball, will you stop eavesdropping!" Becky giggled, then smiled as she introduced him around the table. "Simon Miller, these are my friends Silvia, Evie, Helen, and Faye."

"Faye, as in Midge's friend?"

Stunned, Faye leaned toward the table to get a good look at the newcomer. *How could this be? The hunk of heartbreak from the ferry!*

"Do you two know each other?" Becky looked from Faye to Simon, then to Faye again.

"No," Faye said as Simon simultaneously said, "Yes."

They both laughed as the other girls at the table stared at them intently.

"Well," Faye explained, "yes and no. I accidentally spilled my coffee all over Mr. Miller on the Union Pacific Ferry when Midge and I first got off the train." Thinking about it, she flashed on the red-lipped woman he was with. Surely, from her demeanor, she was his wife. Yet, here he was, acting very much like he was fishing.

"As you can see, no permanent damage." He gestured to the shoulder of his trench.

He did have an accent. Was it French?

"Simon is working with our Canada group," Becky said as Simon leaned in to light her cigarette. "You've probably seen him lurking around our floor. He is working with Mr. Brooks on some power plants on the Niagara River. Faye, here, works for Dalton in the Western Division."

Ahh, Canadian. Could be from Quebec. That would account for the accent.

The mystery of the red-lipped woman was still just that —a mystery.

"I didn't realize you worked at Gregor Corp," Simon commented, his head cocked and dimples on full display.

"I didn't when we last met," Faye explained. "I started working in March, shortly after my wedding," she said, with a slight emphasis on the word wedding as she held up her left hand and wiggled her ring finger.

"Ahh," he acknowledged. "Life moves fast these days, never a dull moment." He took a drag on his cigarette. "And your husband is…"

"Overseas," Becky interjected. "All you need to remember is that she's married and unavailable, so put away that famous Miller charm. In fact, unless you're going to ask me to dance, quit flapping your lips and beat it. Your presence is cramping our action."

This ignited laughter, but no objections, from around the table.

"Sadly, I'm late for a dinner appointment, so must offer a rain check for that dance, Miss Ross." He stood up and tipped his hat to the table. "Ladies, a pleasure."

"Next time," Silvia said, flashing her most alluring smile.

"I look forward to it," he retorted, then, looking from Silvia back across the table to Faye, gave the slightest wink, and disappeared into the crowd.

Was that a wink? How dare he, when he knows full well that I'm married—and he's married, too! This war is really changing the game when it comes to propriety.

"And right before he left, I think he winked at me," Faye recounted later that night to Midge. "It's so inappropriate."

"Don't snap your cap, cookie. It's damned near impossible to say what's appropriate and what's not these days," Midge replied. She still wore her work clothes—grimy Levi's, flannel shirt, and steel-toed boots—as she wolfed down a midnight supper of bacon and eggs. Her hair remained tied up in a kerchief, revealing a recently scrubbed face, contrasting sharply with the heavy coating of soot that still clung to her throat from right under her chin to where it disappeared under her collar. It seemed that Midge was of the eat-first-shower-later school of thought when she finished her shift.

Midge appeared to be thriving in the environment of Kaiser Shipyard #2. The welding equipment was as familiar to her as her dad's John Deere tractor. The busy, noisy, gritty work seemed to give her even more self-confidence, which most often translated into bluntness. Faye noticed salty new phrases and swear words peppering their conversations recently. It was like Betty Boop had acquired the attitude and vocabulary of Bluto.

Faye reflected. "I'm just not used to married men flirting with married women, whatever the circumstances."

"You don't think for a dad-blamed minute that all these young men hanging out at bars and begging for dances are unmarried, do you?"

Faye hadn't really thought about it. They all seemed so sincere and polite.

"Oh, come on, Faye. I bet half of them are strictly from Dixie with a wife and kids back home in Arkansas or wherever and just want a thrill before they're under fire. This war is making one thing clear. Love and sex are two different things. And," she said after taking a long sip of her coffee, "given the war news, I can't say that I blame them."

〜

"Take a memo, Mrs. Connor."

Mr. Dalton's voice crackled over the desk intercom. It was a request she heard a dozen times a day when Dalton was in town, her cue to grab her steno pad and head into the corner office.

After she'd scribed a few mundane reminder memos, Mr. Dalton handed her a folder.

"I'd also like you to start helping me with this audit report," he said, and Faye was delighted with the challenge of additional responsibility. "Here are the receipts for bulk purchases of gravel we've made this month at our various projects in the Western Division. We just need to make sure they match up with the requisitions."

Faye looked at the figures, which were noted in tons. The deliveries amounted to thousands of tons each.

"Just to help me visualize, how much is a ton of gravel?" she asked.

"Good question," he replied in his most mentor-like tone. "A ton is equivalent to about 2,000 pounds. And that would be enough gravel to cover a space twelve feet by twenty feet with one inch of crushed rock. So..." He glanced around. "My office is twelve feet by fifteen feet. Just envision a space that's five feet longer."

Faye glanced at the far wall, then from side to side.

"Got it. That helps...a ton, so to speak."

"Don't worry about the figures being exact. There's often material that's lost in transit. With these volumes, we never worry about discrepancies under 2 percent. Just give it a crack, and I'll review your draft when I get back from Seattle on Friday."

"Very good, sir."

"You're doing a great job, Mrs. Connor."

Faye enjoyed the afterglow of Mr. Dalton's compliment for the rest of the afternoon.

As she dug into the receipts and records over the next few days, two things stood out. First, after she did some quick calculations, every delivery receipt was exactly 1.8 percent under what was scheduled—within the parameters of acceptable, but oddly consistent. And second, the company paid what seemed like an enormous amount to transport the materials to Gregor's delivery sites.

Hmm. Maybe there are opportunities for cost savings here. It'll be interesting to see if there are any long-term patterns.

8

It sounded too good to be true: a vacant three bedroom on Nob Hill, just off the Powell cable car line. Evie appeared at Faye's desk bright and early with the news—and an invitation to share.

"How can that be? A vacant flat right downtown?"

"I know, but it's legit. The landlord is a friend of my boss, so I have the inside track. I've already asked Helen Beach to share, but we need a third."

Helen, out from New York, had followed her boyfriend west, much like Faye. She was smart and tidy in her appearance with a much-admired wardrobe, so Faye was thrilled with the trio. As much as Faye would miss seeing Midge every day, she knew the Bosch twins were expected home for the summer and her days of rent-free-including-laundry were numbered. Her part of the rent would be twelve dollars a month for her own room. Faye knew if she didn't take it—sight unseen—it'd be snapped up by someone else in a heartbeat.

"Sign me up!"

The excitement of the new place was tempered by news from the Pacific. The horrible battle in the Coral Sea involved troops from both the US and Australia. Where was Steve? She hadn't received a letter from him for a few weeks. When Steve went silent, Faye instantly imagined the worst. The "what ifs" roiled in her brain long into the night.

What if Australia is attacked again? What if he's wounded? What if we can't have children? What if he loses an arm or a leg? What if he stops loving me? What if I never see him again? Jeez, Faye, get a grip!

Her anxiety was amplified when a few of the Blue Star Service Banners in windows of Cole Valley homes, which identified the family of a service member, were replaced with Gold Star Banners, indicating a family member killed in action. She would be forced to wait days—even weeks— for the list of casualties from the latest conflict to be published. During that time, it proved to be an unrelenting struggle to stay levelheaded and hopeful.

The move, as it turned out, was well timed. The twins would be home in a few weeks. And Midge had just received an offer to move into a house in Berkeley with some girls from the shipyard, a home base that would make her commute to Richmond much easier.

"It's just two blocks from the Shipyard express bus

stop," Midge informed her. "My housemates won't be nearly as fun to live with as you, but it'll be better."

"I hope you come to the city on your days off. I can't imagine navigating the Union Square bar scene without you."

"Roger-wilco, sister. In fact, you'd better have a nice big sofa in that place, 'cause I plan to freeload often."

"I'll miss you," Faye said, her eyes beginning to tingle as she gathered her friend into a hug.

"Now, don't you get sloppy on me."

"I wouldn't even be in San Francisco if you hadn't called."

"Don't sell yourself short, Faye. I have a feeling you would have found your way here anyway."

Faye's new flat was located on Fella Place, an alley off Powell Street between Bush and Pine. As she hauled her few boxes of belongings from the cab to the second floor flat, Faye still tried to comprehend her good fortune. This location was the "bee's knees," as Pops would say. It amazed her that Evie had snagged it.

The apartment itself was kind of quirky, the only residence that was accessed from the short alley. Their "neighbors" were the back sides of commercial buildings—a grocery, a florist, a church, and a small office building—so the alley was nice and quiet at night. Like most "shotgun" buildings constructed right after the 1906 earthquake, the rooms were arranged around a central light well with windows only at the front and back of the building. A small vestibule opened to a sizable living room with one adjacent bedroom overlooking the alley. The kitchen had a window to the light well, then the bath and two additional bedrooms overlooked a ten-foot space between the back of their building and the garden of the First Presbyterian Church.

Although rather dim in the morning light, the flat offered tons of space plus a hidden treasure: a small staircase behind the kitchen led to a roof terrace—and a panoramic view across the city and the bay to the East Bay Hills.

Holy mackerel! This is like a stairway to heaven!

Faye stood in the quiet of that May morning and drank in the view. She looked east to where the Bay Bridge touched down in Oakland and recognized the Campanile Tower on the University of California campus, easy to spot against the green hills. Beyond the elegant white tower and the imposing summit of Mount Diablo lay her past as a dutiful daughter and devoted fiancée. She turned west and gazed across Russian Hill to the Presidio and the fog bank that had just slithered its way back through the Gate. Steve was out there somewhere; her future was tied to him and the outcome of a horrendous war that enveloped the globe. As the breeze lifted the curls off her shoulders, it dawned on Faye that her life right now resembled an unexpected detour from the safe, predictable continuum of family and marriage.

Here I am—for the first time in my life, truly on my own. I never imagined I'd be here, but here I am.

She smiled as she remembered Steve's "you show 'em" parting words.

Well, Faye Baxter Connor, it's entirely up to you to decide just how and what to show 'em.

∼

A commotion down on the street brought Faye out of her musings and back to the task at hand. She dashed down the stairs to greet Evie and Helen, who had just arrived with the moving truck of furniture to supplement the smattering of pieces already there.

"Get ready for good times, girls," Evie said as she marveled at the size of the living room. "I can already picture some great house parties."

"Before we do anything else, let's get some music on."

As big bands blared from the radio, Helen directed the movers. Soon the girls were left with their furniture in place and a stack of boxes to unpack. They mopped all the floors and scrubbed out the bathroom. As they hung fresh living room curtains—fully lined for blackout purposes, a sharp knock sounded at the door.

Two men, one tall and thin, the other short and rotund, and both well past middle age, stood on the front landing wearing Civil Defense arm bands and helmets. Their sense of self-importance amplified the comical appearance of the duo.

"I'm Warden Bailey, and this is Warden Seabourn. We're your official block wardens," the short one said. "We both live in the next block over on Bush. Here is our contact information, in case you need to find us."

Helen took the contact card. "Nice to meet you, gentlemen. We'll keep this by the telephone."

The short one continued, "We like to have meetings once a month to discuss any issues for our area. Here are the rules for blackouts and procedures for incendiary bomb attacks…"

He handed Helen a thin printed pamphlet.

"Thanks, we're just hanging our curtains now," Helen responded.

"You'll need to pick up your ration cards at Washington Grammar School," Warden Bailey continued, all business. "I want to be very clear: We'll be keeping an eye out for blackout violations, so be sure to close your drapes entirely from the time the alarm sounds until you hear the all-clear signal. Remember—the alert is a modulated tone like this…"

"Aaaa-aaaa-Aaaa-aaaa-Aaaa-aaaa," Warden Seaborn demonstrated. "The all-clear is a steady continuous tone for two minutes."

"Thanks for the reminder, gentlemen," Helen said as Evie and Faye rolled their eyes and stifled their laughter.

"In case of a bombing raid, the disaster relief station for this section is in the basement of Grace Cathedral, just up the hill. And we will be counting on you to report any suspicious looking people in the area. All enemy aliens have been evacuated, but you never know."

"You certainly don't," Helen confirmed, trying hard to be serious.

After recording their names and phone number on a clipboard, the two wardens—in perfect unison—stepped back on the landing, saluted, then walked down the stairs and purposefully down the alley.

The girls, who managed to restrain their amusement throughout the brief meeting, dissolved into peals of laughter as soon as the door closed.

"It's so good to know that Tweedledum and Tweedledee are watching out for us," Helen said, "but I hope those two nosy Nellies don't cramp our style."

"Did you smell alcohol? I swear I smelled alcohol when he was talking," Faye said.

"Oh great. Surly *and* sauced."

The girls decided then and there to visit the Civil

Defense station and sign up for training. If there was a disaster, they wanted to be well equipped to take matters into their own hands.

With the curtains hung, the girls spent the afternoon unpacking, exchanging stories and getting to know each other.

As it turned out, Evie, a Midwesterner, too, came out to San Francisco from Michigan two years earlier to work for Gregor Corp. Her glasses masked beautiful brown eyes and gave her a bookish look, which was part of her strategy to be taken seriously in the workplace. She was single and just wanted to see the world after she graduated from University of Michigan in '39.

Helen, much like Faye, had come west after her boyfriend was assigned to flight school, which was located on the St. Mary's College campus across the bay in Moraga. She got engaged a few months ago and was busy planning a big Long Island wedding for after the war. Her flyboy, Rick, was currently based on an aircraft carrier, flying bombing raids in the South Pacific somewhere.

By evening, with the addition of some potted plants, throw pillows, and an area rug in the living room, the place began to feel like home. On the wall in the dining room, the girls tacked a map of the world, with pushpins to show areas of conflict and location of husbands, friends, and loved ones: Faye added a pin in Australia for Steve, one in New Guinea for Arnie, and one for her cousin Stuart, on a ship somewhere in the North Atlantic. The girls then tucked into a pot of spaghetti—Helen wondered if eating pasta could be considered a suspicious activity—and a bottle of cheap red wine, toasting their new place.

As Faye lay in her own bed in her very own room that night, she basked in the glow of her good luck, trying not to think about the old Japanese-language newspapers they'd found lining the pantry shelves.

It would be heartbreaking to think that we are benefiting from someone's misfortune. But Roosevelt himself signed the relocation order. It must be the right thing to do. We'll just have to figure out how to apologize to the Japanese American community when the war is won.

9

———————

A letter from Steve, forwarded by the Bosches, finally arrived the following week. "Everything is fine here." His refrain sounded rote. "We've been watching the dolphins in the bay every evening."

He must still be in Australia! Such a relief.

As news from Coral Sea trickled in, the battle seemed to be an Allied victory, but still sounded horrible in terms of casualties. To know that Steve remained away from the active front in Australia eased her mind.

Days ticked by filled with busy office hours and events almost every evening. Faye found the apartment, an easy ten-minute walk *to* the office, a lung-busting forty-minute climb on the way home. The most direct route from the Gregor Corp office took the girls through Chinatown, which Faye found fascinating.

Chinese and Japanese people looked pretty similar to Faye, yet there was a huge difference in public and political opinion. Until the beginning of the war, Chinese Americans faced widespread discrimination—politically, in the workplace, and in society-at-large. But since Japan invaded China in 1937, China was an ally of the US. People of Chinese ancestry enjoyed elevated status as they worked side-by-side with people of other ethnicities for the war effort. There was even talk of repealing the Chinese Exclusion Act, which had established strict quotas on Chinese immigration since the late 1800s.

San Francisco's Chinatown, with its iconic architecture, represented the largest such settlement outside of Asia. When the sun went down, these colorful blocks swarmed with servicemen looking for entertainment and mischief at the district's many nightclubs. Exotic women in form-fitting silk dresses with slits up the side lingered in doorways, looking for clients, Faye assumed. During the day, the streets took on an open-market character, with a wonderful variety of produce spilling out onto sidewalk displays. Roasted ducks, crispy bronze skin glistening with fat, hung by the dozens in shop windows. Tanks of live fish, crab, shrimps, and frogs—of all things—attracted shoppers who demanded absolute freshness. Groups of locals gathered on street corners and in tea houses, smoking cigarettes, playing something that looked like dominos, and chattering in their native tongue. All-in-all, Faye found the bustling streets of Chinatown titillating.

Equally alluring was their proximity to Market Street, located just a few blocks down the hill. No fewer than eleven movie houses, not including the newsreel theaters, were located tooth-to-jowl within a few blocks. The big "glamor houses," like the Orpheum and the Golden Gate, presented a double feature plus a live variety show—all for the price of a twenty-five-cent ticket. Faye and Midge went to the movies a few times a week, but they knew people who went every night. There seemed to be an endless stream of musicals—*For Me and My Gal* with Judy Garland and *Once Upon a Honeymoon* with Cary Grant and Ginger Rogers—and wartime adventures—*Spitfire, Flying Tigers, Casablanca*—coming out of Hollywood these days.

Just one block north of the flat was the top of Nob Hill, or "Snob Hill" as the locals who didn't live there called it. Surrounding the red stone Flood Mansion were hotels named for powerful industrialists of the last century: Mark Hopkins, The Hotel Huntington and the somewhat seedy grand dame of all San Francisco hotels, The Fairmont. This was also the location of Grace Cathedral, their disaster relief station, where all three girls signed up for civil defense advanced first aid training, which required classes two evenings a week for six weeks.

As it turned out, Faye, Helen, and Evie had all received their Red Cross first aid certification in the years leading up to the war. After a quick refresher and some additional training in procedures for air raids and gas attacks, they all advanced to the mid-echelon of the San Francisco Civilian Defense organization and were assigned to help oversee disaster preparedness at the Gregor Corp offices.

The Gregor Corp building, along with the Bank of America building and the City of Paris department store, constituted "safe buildings" in the downtown district, their basements deemed strong enough to use as bomb shelters. Under the trio's capable direction, the Gregor Corp Disaster Preparedness Committee stocked the basement with blankets, portable cots, drinking water, and first aid supplies and distributed air raid instructions to all employees. In case of an actual attack, people would pour in from all over the Financial District, and Faye's committee accepted the responsibility of preparing for any medical or logistical emergency that might occur.

"Thank goodness we won't have to cross paths with our trusty neighborhood wardens," Helen said one afternoon as they inventoried clinic supplies. "There's nothing worse than dealing with an incompetent person in a position of authority."

"As I well know," Evie guffawed. "I do that all day, every day."

~

Because the flat was located close to the action of Union Square and Broadway, many of the girls from the office began to use it as a changing stop between work and evening events. After the quiet rigidity of the Bosch household, Faye thoroughly enjoyed the steady stream of girls, primping and changing into their evening clothes, gossiping and giggling all the while. On weekends, there were always extra girls—Midge often among them—who slept over, much easier than crossing the bridge in the wee hours of a weekend morning. Thankfully, Faye noticed that the constant hubbub helped keep those niggling "what-ifs" in check.

~

It was early May and the apartment was abuzz with girls from the office putting on the glam for a house party.

Unlike most dinner parties of the day, which tended to be low key, this one required formal dress. Mrs. Herman Smith, wife of Gregor Corp's executive vice president of procurement, had cordially invited every female on the employee roster to serve as partners for a guest list of officers from Fort Mason. It seemed like they were now in every corner of the flat, stripped down to their girdles and painting their legs with makeup or trying to achieve perfectly slick victory rolls with the help of rats and pomade. Faye decided that the abundance of unattached women on the guest list would allow her to duck out of most of the dancing, but the mansion in Hillsborough would also provide an opportunity to see how Gregor Corp's upper tier of executives lived.

"Why do you have all of these gowns?" Faye asked as she gazed into Helen's walk-in closet with no less than twenty cocktail dresses and full-length gowns glittering on the rack. To Faye, who like most girls had a total of maybe six outfits to her name, the selection was remarkable.

"My uncle is a buyer for Saks back in Manhattan," Helen explained. "He gets first pick and a 30-percent employee discount and, fortunately, he's my godfather."

"And has exquisite taste." Faye marveled, grateful that Helen was nearly her identical size and offered to loan her a frock for the evening. Her own simple black dressy dress with the sweetheart neck was a classic, but she'd worn it so many times before. Helen's offer was much like having an entire luxe evening wear department at her disposal.

Helen suggested a satin cocktail dress with a wide portrait collar. The deep sapphire set off Faye's eyes. Faye added her own graduation pearls and black satin evening gloves and snagged a fox stole—inherited from her great aunt—that had recently arrived in her steamer trunk of belongings from Evanston.

Faye set her blonde locks with sugar water in pin curls all afternoon, then solicited Helen's assistance to pin the curls high on top of her head for an almost crown-like effect. She fastened the ankle straps of her black dress pumps and checked herself in the hallway mirror, turning to admire the low V back of the dress and to make sure the drawn-on stocking "seams" were straight. Although she still had two pairs of real silk stockings hidden away, she decided the leg makeup was just fine for tonight, considering the mid-calf length of her dress. One of the girls had brought over a leg liner contraption made from a springy C-strip of metal and a screwdriver handle. You simply inserted your eyebrow pencil in the holder, positioned the C around your leg, moved it slowly from ankle to just above the knee and presto—straight seam lines.

Well, take a gander at you, sister. Not bad. Not bad at all. Not a single hint of Midwestern hayseed anywhere.

She gave a twirl and admired the heavy satin as it floated and swished, enjoying the uptick in her confidence that came with the outfit.

So long, Country Mouse. Too bad Steve isn't here to see this!

With gas rationing in effect, Mr. Smith arranged for a hired bus to collect the girls and deliver them to his Hillsborough estate, located about a half hour south on the Peninsula. Spirits were high on the ride through town, thanks in part to the flask of cheap rum Helen discreetly produced from her silver beaded evening bag.

The setting was out of a fantasy. The Smiths lived in a massive Georgian-style mansion that occupied many landscaped acres. Set well back from the street, the main house opened onto a terraced motor court, where the girls disembarked. Faye half expected to see a fairy godmother lurking in the well-trimmed shrubbery.

Mrs. Smith had decorated the reception salon with dozens—quite possibly hundreds—of candles. The effect was full-on enchantment. The boys, all done up in their dress uniforms, greeted the girls in the salon and escorted them into what could only be a ballroom. A live combo in natty white dinner jackets played all the romantic tunes of the day with a lively jitterbug number now and then.

Faye had promised herself she would only allow one dance per boy. That way, he wouldn't think she was interested in anything more than a dance and chit-chatty conversation. She danced with an ensign from Virginia and one from South Dakota. Then, dodging a persistent young lieutenant from Oregon, she slipped onto the terrace to sip a glass of champagne as the sun began to sink behind the hills, turning the sky to flame.

The garden was captivating in the dusk of that late spring evening. Faye leaned against the terrace railing and sipped her drink, enjoying the tickle of the bubbles against her tongue.

Well, girlie girl, this is as close as you'll ever get to the Upper Crust. Better enjoy every minute.

"Why, as I live and breathe, it's Midge's friend, Faye."

She startled at the voice behind her and turned to see Mr. Simon Heartthrob Miller on a lounge chair, smoking a cigarette.

"You scared the bejeezus out of me. What on God's green earth are you doing here?"

"I'm considered a friend of the firm, one worthy of wining and dining. But I might well ask you, a married woman as I recall, the same question."

He rose from the chair to the full glory of his evening jacket and crossed purposefully to the railing next to her.

Holy crow, he looks better than William Holden and Clark Gable combined!

"I am doing my patriotic duty by dancing with some of our brave boys in uniform." Faye detected a note of rationalization in her own voice. "It's all quite innocent and anonymous."

"Really."

"Well, truth is, I wanted to see how the elite of Gregor Corp lives."

They gazed out over the manicured garden with its pathways and fountains, bathed in the evening light. As they stood there, Faye became aware of the strong allure that was slowly drawing her closer.

Why does he have to be so blasted manly?

Simon took a long drag and exhaled the smoke slowly. "We're not in Kansas anymore, are we?"

Faye chuckled and, hoping a bit of distance would short-circuit the energy she was feeling, shifted a bit to look back toward the French doors and the swirling couples inside. "Is your wife with you this evening?"

"Beg pardon?"

"Your wife. As in, spouse."

"As far as I'm aware, I'm not married."

"Really? I thought you were with your wife when we first met—on the ferry."

He wrinkled his brow for a minute, then remembered with a chuckle. "That was my cousin from Montreal, who needed an escort on the trip west. I was coming out for business, so the timing worked perfectly."

One mystery solved, but there was another. Faye knew that Canada had entered the war shortly after Germany invaded Poland in 1939. Why then, she wondered, was this striking specimen of a man not in uniform? She looked him in the eye. "So why aren't you in the military?"

"I'm in a civilian role essential to domestic defense," he said with a slight tinge of self-importance. "Or at least that's how Ottawa sees it. The higher ups have massive hopes that Niagara hydroelectric and similar projects in the Canadian west will lead to energy independence."

After a pause, he asked, "Any more questions?"

Faye shook her head, slightly embarrassed to be busted for giving him the third degree.

"Then I have one. Will Mrs.— What is your name now?"

"Connor. Mrs. Steven Connor."

"Will Mrs. Steven Connor do Mr. Simon Miller the honor of a dance? All quite innocent, of course." He stood quite close.

Jeepers, his biceps fill out the sleeves of his dinner jacket well.

"No dice, buster," Faye replied after a long pause, her voice bordering on sultry. "Unless it's absolutely anonymous, dancing is never really as innocent as people say."

"Quite true." He flicked his cigarette over the railing and turned to her, smiling. "Then I will, in my desolation, escort you back to the ball and turn you over to the anonymous hordes."

Rejoining the throng in the ballroom, Faye chatted with her friends and to various other boys as they nibbled their way along the buffet table. Mrs. Smith had evidently not heard about rationing. Mountains of snow crab claws, huge prawns, oysters Rockefeller, eggs in aspic, beef canapés, pyramids of fresh strawberries, platters of petit fours and lemon tarts…it was all magnificent. The champagne and laughter flowed. And, every once in a while, Faye noticed Simon across a room as he spoke with one or another of the Gregor Corp top executives.

He really is a first-class schmoozer.

Then, out of the corner of her eye, she noticed the lieutenant from Oregon making a beeline for her group.

Uh oh. Diversionary action required.

"Evie, I'm going to run to the ladies," she whispered, relinquishing her glass and ducking quickly into the crowd, hoping the crush around the stuffed mushrooms covered her escape.

She made her way stealthily to the second-floor guest bathrooms, both of which were occupied. She waited for what seemed like a reasonable amount of time for someone to finish up, then ventured deeper into the warren of second floor chambers, hoping to find another washroom.

After a few minutes of searching, Faye found an unoccupied powder room in a small anteroom down a dimly lit hallway. She took her time freshening up, hoping the persistent lieutenant downstairs would lose interest while she reapplied her lipstick. As she stepped back into the anteroom to rejoin the party, Faye's attention was drawn to the adjoining room—an enormous study.

She stepped through the doorway. This was the kind of room Pops could stay in forever. The library was more than two stories high with a frescoed ceiling and a balcony around the perimeter at the second level. Rolling library ladders on both levels accessed what appeared to be an enormous collection of books, many with hand-tooled leather bindings. A massive desk was flanked by tall arched windows. The walls not dedicated to books were covered in hunter green damask and showcased a number of paintings.

Faye walked silently across the dim gallery to the far wall for a closer look and stood stock still in awe.

Matisse. Van Gogh. Cezanne. Jeez Louise, is that a Picasso?

She had been to the Chicago Institute of Art innumerable times over the years, and she possessed a good knowledge of the Impressionists and early abstract art. She studied the technique and the signatures closely.

These sure look like the real deal.

Suddenly, she heard footsteps, then the sound of voices coming closer. Not wanting to get caught snooping, Faye instinctively ducked behind the velvet drapery and held her breath.

The lights in the study flicked on, then Faye heard a drawer open and close, some papers rustle, and footsteps retreat. All the while, a man and a woman were conversing in agitated tones. In German.

"Buck Rogers calling: Earth to Faye, Earth to Faye. Come in, Faye."

In the wee hours of the next morning, gowns were exchanged for pjs, faces were slathered with cold cream and tissued free of makeup, and the girls were all crowded into the kitchen sipping cocoa.

"Sorry." Faye had been in a fog since the incident in the study. She knitted her brows over her mug, asking, "Why would someone at the party tonight be talking in German?"

"What?"

"When?"

"Are you sure?"

"Yeah. When I went to powder my nose, I overheard a conversation in German. I don't speak German, but I recognize it."

"Just because someone speaks German doesn't mean they're sinister," Helen said. "Maybe someone's *grossmutter* insisted they learn her mother tongue. I can't tell you how many German families there were in my neighborhood growing up. Some of them spoke nothing but German in the home, even though the kids had absolutely no German accent as soon as they stepped off the front porch."

"Or it could be something more nefarious," Evie chimed in, clearly relishing the thought. "The Fifth Column, baby. The enemy within. Who knows where the sympathies of the Gregor execs really lie? It's not too far-fetched that they could be working secretly to enrich their own coffers and further their own ideologies."

"*Ooh.* The Fifth Column right here in our own back-yard," Helen commented in a tone of voice right out of *The Shadow*.

"Now, wait a minute," Faye cautioned. "There were two voices, a man and a woman. I've only heard Smith speak a few times, but I'm pretty sure this man's voice was much younger and a lot less phlegmy."

"Be that as it may, we need to look at who's got money. You don't think for a minute that the Smiths got rich without doing business with some Nazis, do you?" Evie challenged.

"What are you talking about?" Faye sounded shocked at the mere suggestion of collaboration with the enemy.

"Before the war, Gregor Corp had extensive dealings in Europe—and that included power plants and bridges in Germany," Evie explained, who had been with the company for just over two years. "Until we officially entered the war, a lot of American companies were doing business with the Nazis. GM, IBM, and Kodak, for example…and plenty of prominent people like Henry Ford and Charles Lindbergh were pretty vocal about being admirers of German production systems. I'm sure there are secret Nazi lovers all over the world, even in Hillsborough. And who knows what networks and ties may still be in place."

"Haven't you ever heard of the American Bund?" This from Helen.

"As in cake?" Faye suddenly felt clueless on every front.

"Bund, B-U-N-D, not bund*t*, silly. Bund. It was a pro-Nazi organization active here in San Francisco until last year."

"Come on…"

"No, really," Evie concurred. "There was a big scandal, because the German consulate here in San Francisco was kind of the center for organizing an espionage network. Two Counsel Generals got busted and thrown out of the country, I think it was in '41. It was all over the papers when I first arrived. I'm sure that, even though the leadership is long gone, there must still be remnants of the network left."

"That's a creepy thought."

Come to think of it, Faye read reports in the newspaper a few months ago of German spies being dropped off by U-boats on Long Island under a cloak of darkness. With all the German heritage in the land of the free, sympathies were certainly possible.

Faye sipped her cocoa, its creamy sweetness comforting after her agitation during their ride home. She savored it for a moment, then added, "It just makes me steamed that Steve and thousands of other boys are off putting their lives on the line and while some dad-blamed rich people are living high on the hog from money they made doing who knows what."

Soon conversation changed to a far more pressing matter. The White House department store was advertising a new kind of stocking made of rayon. Could they really be as sheer as silk?

10

───────

I have tonight issued a proclamation that an unlimited national emergency exists and requires the strengthening of our defense to the extreme limit of our national power and authority. The Nation will expect all individuals and all groups to play their full parts, without stint, and without selfishness, and without doubt that our democracy will triumphantly survive.

—President Franklin D. Roosevelt

Address to the Nation, May 21, 1942

The Japanese forces were stopped. Their attempt to widen their perimeter of influence in the Pacific failed. The Allied Navy had bombed the bejeezus out of their carrier fleet and sent them limping back to Tokyo.

The encouraging news only fueled Faye's concern for Steve's safety. A victory like this was just the thing to ignite revenge, and the warriors of the Rising Sun were nothing if not vengeful. She tried in vain to push the sense of fore-boding aside and focus on the Allied success.

The following Tuesday, right after lunch, Mr. Dalton's voice crackled over the intercom.

"Take a memo, Mrs. Connor."

Faye grabbed her steno pad and the sharpest pencil in her desk drawer, and took a seat opposite Mr. Dalton's massive walnut desk, poised and ready for the typical torrent of memos. She only suspected something was up when Dalton closed his office door.

"Are you comfortable driving a car, Mrs. Connor?"

Mr. Dalton, for all his seniority at the company, was unremarkable in his appearance. He was medium height and medium build with medium brown hair. He wore the same navy suit and white shirt to work every day, changing only his tie from solid to regimental on an alternating basis. But today, there was an intensity in his voice that commanded Faye's attention.

"Yes, sir. My boyfr—um, I mean, my husband—taught me years ago."

"Excellent. In that case, I am going to ask you to volunteer for service to your country. You need to be totally on board, so feel free to say no if you don't think you can commit fully. Should you decline, you will not be penalized in any way."

"Of course, sir. Being of service to my country is the reason I'm in San Francisco in the first place."

"It's fairly simple, but will require your complete confi-dentiality," Mr. Dalton explained. "Every so often, I will ask you to deliver a messenger envelope or a locked briefcase to someone. You will take my car, drive straight to the destination, make sure you deliver the package to the specified recipient. Not a secretary, not an assistant, but the specified recipient. On some occasions, you'll be asked to wait for a return envelope and bring it back to me. Complete secrecy is required. I cannot stress that enough."

A courier.

"What kind of communication?"

"Before we discuss this any further, I need you to accept or decline."

"Well, of course I accept," she said without hesitation. "I'll do anything I can to help end the war."

"Very good. In that case, I have a standard oath for you to sign."

He slid a piece of paper in front of her and offered her a pen. She scanned the brief statement printed on letterhead with the United States Office of Strategic Services insignia. It read:

> *I, Faye Baxter Connor*—her name was hand printed on
> a blank line—*do solemnly swear (or affirm) that I will
> support and defend the Constitution of the United States
> against all enemies, foreign and domestic; that I will bear true
> faith and allegiance to the same; that I take this obligation
> freely, without any mental reservation or purpose of evasion;
> and that I will well and faithfully discharge the duties of the
> office on which I am about to enter. So help me God.*

Faye bit her lip and reread the statement more carefully. The Bay Area was filled with volunteer opportunities for women on the home front: USO, Red Cross canteens and hospitality events, civil defense projects, the Win the War Committee, and oodles of church and school organizations.

But they seemed somehow beside the point—busy work to keep those at home occupied while the men in uniform took on the true task at hand. Now, here she was being presented with an opportunity to be directly involved with the war effort.

It's my duty to help. I'm proud to be selected.

She wrote her name firmly on the line and handed the paper back to Mr. Dalton.

"Welcome to the team, Mrs. Connor. Now, back to your question regarding the nature of the communication. It's best that you don't know specifics, just that it's of vital importance. In fact, in these instances, very few people know the whole story intentionally. We need to uphold the integrity of the projects and the safety of our people. You'll always know what you need to and nothing that could compromise the mission. Just be assured that the information is too important and too urgent to be communicated through regular channels."

"So, the OSS is in on this?" Faye asked, aware that the intelligence agency often worked with the FBI on matters of national security.

"The OSS is aware of the big picture but doesn't get involved in granular details. This is way below their radar. The oath is a formality. You will be a volunteer while in the employ of Gregor with no formal connection to the OSS. Your activity should be considered top secret and you are not to share your involvement with anyone."

"Is it dangerous?"

"My dear, everyone in America is in danger. That's why we're asking for your help."

Surely Dalton knows hundreds of people far more educated and experienced in these matters.

"So…why are you asking *me*?"

Dalton shifted and leaned back in his chair and paused to gather his thoughts.

"You have proven yourself capable, diligent, detail-oriented, and discreet. I have easy access to you. You have a husband in service, so are motivated to help end the war. You have no known connections to any suspicious group—we have checked—so I'm sure you are not on anyone's radar. I'm asking you because you are not likely to attract attention, and that is imperative. You are to tell no one of your involvement. All you need to know is that these communications are vital to the war effort and need to be made in a timely fashion."

"How often will I be asked to make these deliveries?"

"Most likely a few times a week beginning tomorrow morning."

"The other girls are sure to notice that I'm out of the office. What should I tell them?"

"Hmm." He thought for a minute. "Let's just tell them you're doing an errand for me."

"With all due respect, sir, they're going to want specifics. I know how the gossip mill works around here. Let's tell them I'm doing research for a special project over at the Bancroft Library in Berkeley. That would explain the use of a car, which believe me, they will notice."

"There...that's exactly why I chose you." Dalton smiled, obviously pleased with his choice. "I knew you'd be good at this."

The sense of elation that accompanied his words remained with Faye for the rest of the day.

Of all the people he could have chosen, he picked me.

The "special delivery" the next day went off without a hitch. At ten in the morning, Faye was summoned into Dalton's office and given a locked satchel.

"Here are the precise directions," Dalton said, handing her a large messenger envelope and a set of car keys. "There is no return message today. You will give this case to Commander Snyder. That's Snyder with a *y*. Wait while he removes the enclosed packet, then bring back the empty satchel. Got it? You should be back before noon.

"A few rules," he continued. "Always observe the Victory Speed Limit. And under no circumstances are you to pick up hitchhikers. Is that clear?"

Faye was disappointed at this last directive, as hitching was a popular form of transportation these days, especially for servicemen. It was considered patriotic to pick up hitchhikers, particularly those in uniform.

"Understood," she replied, conceding that the nature of her business required strict rules.

"When you return, please burn these instructions and the map. We don't want your whereabouts falling into the wrong hands."

"Of course."

When Faye slid behind the driver's seat, she opened the envelope and read her instructions. The delivery was to the Alameda Naval Air Station. Faye had never been to Alameda, but knew it was an island off the Oakland waterfront and home base to several fighter squadrons.

Following the hand-drawn map, Faye steered Dalton's hunter green DeSoto out of the Gregor Corp garage and made her way down to First Street. She turned right, and at the crest of Rincon Hill, there it was—the entrance to the Bay Bridge. The Victory Speed Limit, instituted to save rubber by minimizing tire wear, was just thirty-five mph, so she had a good view as she crept along with the rest of the traffic. All three eastbound lanes were bumper to bumper, and the stream of autos was scanned by armed guards stationed at intervals along the deck.

Completed just four years earlier, the Oakland-San Francisco Bay Bridge was an engineering marvel. Spanning more than seven miles, it connected the city to the East Bay communities of Berkeley and Oakland. While the Golden Gate Bridge enjoyed more fame, the Bay Bridge was a workhorse with thousands of cars crossing it on a daily basis. Faye had ridden the electric train on the lower level over to Berkeley a few times to visit Midge, but she had never driven on the top deck. The views of the East Bay Hills, just turning golden with the advent of warm weather, were well worth the drive.

After she paid her quarter at the toll gate, Faye followed Cypress Street toward the port, then cut over on Seventh Street to Harrison when she arrived downtown.

Goodness, I had no idea there was such a bustling Chinatown in Oakland!

She dodged produce trucks, gaggles of women with their market bags, and delivery men pushing crates of exotic-looking vegetables on her way to the Posey Tube, the tunnel that connected Oakland to Alameda Island. Emerging on the Alameda side, she turned north and made her way to the base.

The guard at the entrance to the base confirmed her appointment and gave her directions to Commander Snyder's office. After a short wait in his reception area, he appeared, a middle-aged man in his khaki uniform. They ducked into a conference room, he produced a key that opened the satchel, removed the sealed envelope and handed the empty case back to Faye.

"Thank you, Miss."

"Of course, Commander. Good morning."

As Dalton had predicted, she pulled into the Gregor Corp shortly before noon. That was it.

Mission accomplished. Easy as pie.

As she made her way to Dalton's office, empty case in hand, she passed dozens of co-workers: the crowd in the elevator, the line at the lunchroom, Evie on her way to a meeting and the sixth-floor secretarial pool—all without an inkling of Faye's assignment. Even though she didn't really know the scope of her role, she knew it was important. For the first time since Steve shipped out, she felt that her actions could directly help end the war. And it felt good.

11

The Gregor Corp secretarial pool buzzed about Lana Turner's scheduled appearance in the Victory Window at I Magnin. Faye adored her performance in *Ziegfeld Girl,* believing she stole the show as an elevator operator seduced by the glamor of showbiz who died an alcoholic. The opportunity to see her in person and buy a monthly war bond at the same time was too good to pass up. She and Helen made a beeline to Union Square on their lunch hour.

The government's ad campaigns encouraged working people to invest 10 percent of their wages every payday in War Bonds, which seemed perfectly reasonable for Faye and other women who didn't have a family to support. With slogans like *You Serve by Saving* and *Bring Them Home Sooner* and *Back the Attack,* it seemed unpatriotic not to participate. Jimmy Stewart, Clark Gable, Barbara Stanwyck, Bing Crosby, and dozens of other screen stars all jumped on the bandwagon to promote the effort in commercials and appearances. Lana Turner was special, though—so beautiful and scandalous, just having divorced the famous band-leader Artie Shaw and swathed in rumors of torrid love affairs.

The sidewalk in front of the window was packed, spilling across Geary Street and well into the Union Square Plaza. Faye and Helen worked their way to the front and saw the platinum blonde beauty waving to the crowd from inside the massive picture window. Her little navy straw pillbox hat embellished with a crisp white silk gardenia sat on her hair, spun moonlight caught in a low chignon. She waved and blew kisses as the crowd clapped and cheered. She then stepped up to the mic, giving a brief speech about the importance of supporting the war effort.

"I want to thank you all for being here today…"

"She's so beautiful," Faye whispered. "Even prettier than she is on screen. And so petite!"

"I wonder how she keeps her skin so dewy, considering she's under bright lights so much."

"Well, however she does it, she should bottle and sell it," Faye replied.

"So remember—it's our war, too," Miss Turner continued. "We can all back the attack with Victory Bonds and Stamps! These wonderful cashiers are ready for business. For those who buy a $500 bond or more, I'll be signing my autograph—and any man investing in a $25,000 bond gets a big kiss from yours truly!"

The applause was deafening. The crowd quickly formed lines in front of the eight cashier tables. Music played as they made their way to the cashier and plunked down their $18.75 for a crisp new E Series Bond with a $25 face value.

With one last look at Lana, the girls pushed through the crowd and started back to the office when Faye heard a shout.

"Faye Baxter!"

"Is someone calling your name?" Helen asked.

They stopped and scanned the throngs of people. Faye was perpetually amazed by just how crowded the city was, even at a time when folks should be having lunch. Men in uniform, nurses in uniform, businesspeople, cops, trades- men, teenagers, moms pushing strollers, taxis, and cars in gridlock… Faye couldn't see anyone she recognized. About to give up, she heard her name being shouted again.

"Faye! Faye Baxter! Over here!"

Emerging from the clump of humanity on the opposite corner was none other than her next-door neighbor back in Evanston, Michael Pennington.

"Michael!" The familiar face filled her with nostalgia to the point where her eyes began to tingle.

Michael and Faye had been just one class apart all through school, often at the same parties, the same ball- games, the same movies on a Saturday night. The youngest in his family with three much older sisters, he frequently tagged along on Faye's nature outings with Pops. She thought of Michael as the younger brother she never had— and here he was walking toward her across Geary Street in San Francisco!

"Michael Pennington! I hardly recognize you in your uniform! Boy, oh boy, are you a sight for sore eyes."

She reached up to give him a hug as he lifted her off her feet in his embrace.

"Yeah, I got called up at the beginning of May. I'm out at Fort Ord for training, but I have a furlough this weekend. We ship out on Tuesday."

"I take it you know each other?" Helen asked with a smile. "Hi," she said to Michael, her famous Helen smile broadening. "I'm Helen."

"Goodness, where are my manners," Faye apologized. "Helen Beach, this is Michael Pennington, my next-door neighbor back home. I can't believe it's really you."

"I heard you were out here—and I also heard that you and Steve tied the knot."

"We sure did. I'm an old married lady now," she said with a wiggle of her ring finger. "But I'm not too old and married to know that you need some fun. If you don't have other plans, let us take you out for a big send-off tomorrow night."

"Can I bring some buddies?"

"Sure can!"

"Evie and I will join you and make it a real party," Helen offered.

"We live just on the other side of Union Square," Faye said. "Come to the apartment for drinks at six and we'll head out from there. It's the only front door on Fella Place. Just go up Powell to Fella, between Bush and Pine. Got that?"

"Yep. Fella off Powell between Bush and Pine," he confirmed. "I'm on my way to meet up with some buddies over in the Fillmore, so I better get going. Gosh almighty, I can't believe I ran into you."

"It must be destiny," Faye replied.

He held her gently by both arms and gazed at her, as if remembering when things were simple and life was easy.

"Faye Baxter." He sounded wistful as he said her name.

"Faye Connor," she corrected cheerfully.

"Oh, that's right," he said. "Steve Connor is one lucky son of a gun."

~

The following evening at three minutes to six sharp the doorbell rang. "Trick or treat," the three boys in uniform sang out as Faye opened the door.

"You clown," she said, giving Michael a quick hug, then turning to the other two. "Hi, I'm Faye. Come on in!"

"This is Greg from Baltimore and Percy from somewhere in Indiana."

"Have you heard of Nowhere?" Percy asked. "Well, I'm from the middle of it."

"That's a good one, soldier," Faye said, chuckling at Percy shaking hands all round. "Meet Helen and Evie."

Greetings were exchanged as beers were distributed and laughter began to dominate the conversation. The party soon decamped a few blocks away to one of San Francisco's most renowned and exotic nightspots: The Forbidden City.

"We'd never see a place like this back in Evanston…or even Chicago," Michael marveled as the sextet stepped through the door of the Forbidden City, located on Sutter Street near Chinatown's famed Dragon Gate.

Owned by the gregarious and smiling Charlie Low, who greeted guests in a snazzy red dinner jacket, the Forbidden City served up Chinese acts—and food—to American tastes. The interior was gaudy with gilt motifs and red drapery in what Faye imagined the Cantonese brothel style might be—kitsch so high it needed oxygen. Round tables with white linens and lamps shaded with what looked like little red paddy hats ringed the performance area that protruded out from the main stage, surrounded by an ornate gilt and red proscenium. It was exciting, slightly scandalous, and a lot of fun, perfect for a big "send-off," in Faye's opinion.

The boys couldn't have agreed more. They ordered one exotic cocktail after the next, chowed down on Crab Foo Yeong, Yum Yum Chicken, and good-old American steak—rare, if you please. The floor show started with Larry Ching, "The Chinese Frank Sinatra," and a dance review with scantily clad women in feathers and sequins—and very little else, then proceeded with Noel Toy, "The Chinese Sally Rand" and her mesmerizing fan dance. Between performances, the orchestra played, and everyone danced the night away.

"Look over there," Evie whispered to Faye and Michael as she and Greg from Baltimore swayed next to them. She nodded toward a banquette in the far corner of the main room. There, smoking a cigar and engaged in what looked like a discussion bordering on an argument, sat Jim Wallace, procurement manager for Gregor Corp and Evie's boss's boss.

A lifelong Gregor man, Wallace was in his early fifties with thinning hair and a sizable paunch. He ran a tight ship and had a reputation as a ladies' man, although Faye couldn't see the attraction.

"Wonder what he's doing here," Faye whispered back as the throng of dancing couples closed in and obscured her view.

"Well, everyone needs a good time once in a while," Evie said. "Even an old killjoy like Wallace."

When the crowd parted again, Wallace was standing, clearly steamed. He threw his napkin on the table and stormed toward the lobby. The man remaining at the table got to his feet and faced the dance floor. A tall, well-dressed Asian man, he wore round tortoise-shell glasses that gave him a scholarly look. The smile that appeared on his face as he watched Wallace's hasty exit revealed a gold front tooth.

"Guess Wallace wasn't having such a good time after all." Evie giggled as she steered Greg back toward the bar.

"Who was that?" Michael asked.

"Oh, just someone from work I didn't expect to see in a place like this."

"You mean, in the best nightclub of all time?" He smiled, pulling her closer as the music changed to "Always in My Heart." "This means the world to me and the guys, Faye. I can't thank you enough."

"Don't be silly, Mike. Think of all the hours we logged together, slogging through the nature preserves of Lake Michigan. What kind of friend would I be if I let you go without a send-off?"

"Boy, those days seem like forever ago. Life sure has changed."

"For better *and* worse, I guess," Faye agreed. "We all just need to get through this war and think of the future."

Michael drew her in close and put his cheek next to hers. After a long pause, he whispered, "I don't like to think of the future, or even next week. Mostly, I try to shake the feeling that I'm just not ready."

Faye's heart plunged.

Poor guy. What could I possibly say to comfort him? I'm sure every soldier there ever was has felt the same way, but how is that any consolation? Michael is so kindhearted—it's awful that he's even in this situation.

"Well, Michael Pennington, you remember that I'm here and will think of you every day until this war is over."

I hope that didn't sound too lamebrained.

"You're the best, Mrs. Connor."

It was well past midnight when the Fella Place trio put their sozzled soldiers into a cab and, with hugs and promises to write, sent them off.

"Lordy, that was fun," Helen said as they made their way home. "You've got a party boy in your past."

"Well, that's another thing the war has changed. Michael Pennington was never a party boy. He was just a brainy little kid, who would rather hang out at our house than get hounded to death by his older sisters."

Michael's confession that he didn't feel ready for what would happen next was still fresh in Faye's mind. As much as she tried to push it away, it seized her brain and held on tight.

"He was always a sweetheart, and still is. I'm still in shock that our paths crossed. But so glad they did."

As they walked the rest of the way up the hill in silence, Faye's thoughts gradually shifted to the mystery hanging over the evening—the brief sighting and sudden disappearance of the visibly agitated Jim Wallace.

What's your game, Wallace? A late-night meeting in Chinatown with a gold-toothed man where you clearly blew a fuse. Maybe it's on the square, but I've got a lot of questions.

12

In early June, news came of a stunning victory in the Pacific. The US Navy sank three Japanese aircraft carriers within the course of five minutes, thanks to the bravery of our dive bombers. Helen liked to think that her flyboy Rick was among them. Before the battle concluded, another carrier was sunk, a total of 322 Japanese fighter planes shot down and 3,500 Axis sailors killed in the mighty sea battle. As a result, Midway Island, with its vital US air base, remained under Allied control.

While morale around Gregor Corp offices received a much-needed lift, the victory renewed fears of retaliatory raids. Then, on June second at two thirty in the morning, the girls awakened to the air-raid siren blaring from the top of the Ferry Building and sprang into action. They made sure all black-out curtains were drawn, then huddled in the bathroom, the only windowless room in the house.

"If we get bombed tonight, I'm going to blow a fuse," Evie said. "Stan Cooper from Purchasing asked me to go to see Tommy Dorsey at the Rose Ballroom this weekend."

"Stan Cooper!" Helen exclaimed in disbelief. "He's at least forty-five years old and walks with a limp. You're really going dancing with him?"

"He's a nice, polite, shy guy," Evie said, defending her date. "Besides, it's Tommy Dorsey! I'd go with Tojo himself to see Tommy Dorsey. I just love a man with a big trombone," she mused.

With that she segued immediately into Tommy Dorsey's hit, "I'll Never Smile Again," to which Helen and Evie joined in on the second phrase. Then, calling on all those years as a second soprano in the church choir, Faye mustered her courage and belted out a harmony on the last stanza, much to the other girls' delight. Before the last note of the final verse died out, Helen chimed in with her Dorsey favorite.

"*The Dipsy Doodle's the thing to beware,*" she sang upbeat.

All three belted out the next lines with gusto.

"Hey! Keep it down up there!" Mr. Bailey's command from the alley cut them off and sent them into muffled giggles.

"Oops," Helen whispered. "I guess it would be pretty awful for the enemy aircraft to zero in on our caterwauling."

"I can see the headline now: *Nob Hill Destroyed. Poor harmony suspected,*" Evie chuckled.

Faye was more annoyed than amused. "But seriously, Bailey and that whole block monitor crew are supposed to be defending civilians, right? As in Civil Defense? So, is having a laugh with your pals endangering anyone?"

"I think he's drunk with power," Helen said, "or just drunk."

"Well, I don't trust him," Faye said, then after a pause added, "It's funny. I always trusted authority. My parents, my teachers, my employers, my government—it was just automatic. But these days, if you want my trust, by golly you've got to earn it."

Faye tallied up the receipts for a fourth time. Her reconciliation reports for gravel orders followed a pattern over the last three months. Deliveries were always short by just under the acceptable 2 percent, almost always right at 1.8 percent. It seemed like a minimal amount, but with the dozens of Gregor Corp construction projects in the region, it amounted to tens of thousands of dollars.

Faye also scrutinized shipping costs over the months. Gravel was purchased in bulk at discounted prices from suppliers that could handle the volume.

But the discounts seemed to be wiped out, and then some, by the costs of transporting the material to the job site—especially with the cost of gasoline and rail freight these days.

It makes me wonder if anyone higher up is really paying attention.

After she confirmed the accuracy of her accounting, she pondered her next step.

With a little close management, I'm sure we could reduce these overall costs.

Since shipping costs were a factor of time and distance, it only seemed reasonable that finding suppliers closer to the job site would benefit the bottom line. But she needed to have her ducks in a row. She'd continue to monitor the receipts and, at the same time, source multiple suppliers closer to each site and get some bids together. Remembering Pops's admonishment to "come with a solution if you're going to draw attention to a problem," she went to the library to use the phone books to start her research.

13

Summer in San Francisco was just plain odd to Faye. In Evanston, summer days never cooled off. Humidity and heat just continued to build all day until they burst into a thunderstorm at four p.m. every afternoon. Then, people would rush to sit out in their screened porches after supper to catch a breath of air before they retired to their stifling bedrooms and the all-night hum of the electric fan.

San Francisco's marine layer shattered Faye's Midwestern notions of summer. Every evening, fog snuck silently over the city, blanketing anything in its path with a muffled coolness that could be downright frigid. Most days, it pulled back through the Gate and hovered in an angry-looking bank, roiling just offshore until evening, when it slid in again. Some days it never retreated but clung to the buildings as if to taunt those shivering souls yearning to feel the summer sun on their faces.

So much for sunny California.

Faye held the collar of her spring coat tight around her chin as she walked home after work in July. The fog was so heavy that particular evening, she couldn't see but a block ahead, and the moisture that accumulated on the sidewalks made them treacherous. Her peep-toe pumps, so cute when she put them on that morning, were woefully unsuitable for the slick cobblestones of Nob Hill. As she stopped to extract her heel from a storm drain grate, she heard footsteps not too far behind her. But when she looked, she saw no one, only the cotton softness of the fog.

"Anyone there?" she called into the gloom. No answer, just the muffled blast of the foghorn every minute. If someone was following her, the fog kept it secret. She could only hope a thug wasn't lurking in the next alleyway. Or worse, an enemy agent with a luger.

Okay, this is officially spooky.

With her imagination in overdrive, she reclaimed her shoe and walked double time the remaining block to her flat.

"You're white as Jack cheese!" Helen greeted Faye from the dining table, pen in hand. With the tidy stack of letters on the table, Faye could only assume Helen was working her way through her list of soldier pen pals. Women on the home front were encouraged to write to soldiers, even those they barely knew, to boost morale. Helen took this request to heart. She had more than thirty servicemen on her list and wrote to all of them on a rotating basis.

"I'm just a little spooked. It's so foggy out, and I thought I heard footsteps behind me."

"That *is* creepy."

"I'm not even sure it was anyone. Could be Twee-

dledum and Tweedledee. Or it could just be my imagination."

"Well, there's something to cheer you up," she said as
she motioned to a packet of V-Mail envelopes on the
corner of the table.

Steve! Letters from Steve!

Faye grabbed the packet and dashed into her room,
shedding her shoes and coat along the way. Four letters! She
looked at the postmarks to make sure she read them in
order. This was the first time she felt she was getting some
real news. Using their code, she determined that he'd left
Australia, and was on his way to help repair a bombed
airbase on an island. No other specifics. Faye looked at the
map of the Pacific on her wall with push pins indicating the
latest battle locations.

That probably means Midway or New Guinea.

Looking at the islands in the far Pacific, her heart sank.
Both appeared too close to the active fighting.

*You'd better stay safe and come back to me in one piece, Steven
Connor.*

Faye's "errands" gave her an up-close introduction to San
Francisco and the surrounding cities. She got to know the
entire waterfront, from the Hunter's Point Shipyard in the
Bayview District to every building at Fort Mason, the Port
of Embarkation for troops and supplies. She knew how to
avoid the city's steepest hills and busiest intersections, as
well as how to navigate through the one-way grids of
downtown.

As the frequency of her assignments increased, Faye
began to look over her shoulder more and more. She

scanned her rearview mirror for suspicious cars. She started to avoid the lunchroom, lest she let something slip that would cause raised eyebrows among the gossip club. When she was out alone, especially on foggy nights, she stuck to routes where others were sure to be within easy earshot.

In late August, her errands got even trickier. Dimout regulations took effect for night driving to help avoid detection by any enemy subs or aircraft that might be lurking offshore. The speed limit was reduced to twenty-five miles per hour after dark, and cars were allowed only parking lights as illumination. Streetcars navigated by a trail of dim glow-in-the-dark stars embedded in the asphalt. She was relieved when Mr. Dalton told her they would try to schedule all future deliveries during daylight to avoid the dangerous night driving conditions.

Midway Island! Steve's on Midway.

His letter arrived in late August, confirming Faye's guess. "I've been having cinnamon toast for breakfast all week," his letter read. Cinnamon their code word for Midway.

Well, thought Faye as she looked at the wall map, *it's probably a whole lot better than the New Guinea jungle and poisonous snakes.* And although active fighting on Midway might be over, she knew danger still lurked. Snipers. Unexploded bombs. Land mines. Air raids. Dysentery. The litany of horrible possibilities flooded Faye's psyche, making themselves at home.

The anxiety Faye had felt all spring compounded with Steve's latest news. And it began to take its toll. Seldom hungry, Faye lost weight. She had to apply extra powder under her eyes to conceal the dark circles that began to appear. She spent many a sleepless midnight hour reading and re-reading the latest newspapers and studying a map of the Pacific, trying to determine how close Steve was to active fighting. When she did fall asleep, her slumber frequently morphed into nightmares so vivid, she would awaken with a start, shaking and sweating.

Though she seldom remembered details of her dreams, she experienced one recurring theme. She couldn't ever find Steve, despite searching for him in jungles, mazes, and forests where trees seemed to have eyes. One night her dream revealed a tall man in uniform at the end of a tunnel, but she could never reach the end. In another, she found him in an abandoned castle, but when he turned to look at her his face was blank. As the weeks passed, she came to dread nighttime and the prospect of even trying to sleep.

Faye had been in the tenth-floor conference room, taking notes all morning. As she rode the elevator back to her office, she pondered her priorities for the afternoon. She should really type up these minutes while they were fresh in her head, but there was also an important contract she needed to review. The fact that Simon Miller was waiting in her office, looking out the window, interrupted her train of thought.

"I didn't expect to see you here. Do you have a meeting with Mr. Dalton?"

Simon turned and smiled.

"No, just enjoying the view on this beautiful day," he

said in full schmooze mode. "It's too nice out to be inside. Let me take you to lunch."

Their paths crossed with some frequency these days, but this lunch invitation was a first.

"You look as you could use a nice fat burger and a good stiff drink," he added.

"Thanks heaps," Faye replied, kind of annoyed that, despite her best efforts, her pulse quickened every time she saw him.

Sure, she had men friends, but Simon's charm was too alluring for her to take a risk. In order to enjoy his wit and intelligence, she couldn't let her guard down for an instant. If she were single, it would be a different story, but she wasn't. After a time, it was exhausting.

"Come on," he prompted, turning back to the window. "It's a glorious day and, at the very least, you'll get some fresh air."

A walk in the sunshine with an attentive gentleman? The mere thought lifted the sorrow that had invaded Faye's outlook for months. Would she be betraying Steve?

Why would you even think that, sister? It's just lunch!

"All right, here's the deal. We'll go grab a quick sandwich at Franco's. I have a ton of work and some hard deadlines this afternoon, so we need to be back by one thirty. But," she said, softening her tone, "some fresh air sounds pretty swell right now."

Franco's, a little wood-frame shack near the western footings of the Bay Bridge, was a breakfast and lunch joint frequented by dockworkers, fishermen, and adventuresome office workers who wanted quick, filling, cheap food. Greeted by the aroma of sizzling beef and onions, Faye suddenly felt ravenous for a cheeseburger, her favorite. She and Simon ordered two with grilled onions, fries, and Cokes.

As Faye bit in, careful not to let the grease drip on her good blouse, she let out a sigh. "Umm. This tastes like pure comfort."

"Really," Simon replied, sounding slightly appalled. "It tastes more like I'm bidding farewell to my boyish physique to me."

"Well, you should put more ketchup on it then," she said before savoring her next bite. "All the bars back in Evanston served burgers just like this at lunchtime. Steve's Aunt Maureen worked at Smitty's near the high school. She used to sneak us into the kitchen on occasion for burgers and dirty fries. So, to me, this tastes like home, happier days, and doing something my mom wouldn't approve of, which is always sweet."

"Ah, well. That's worth any manner of risk to our youthful figures then."

They chatted about this and that—how some people prefer to call burgers "liberty steaks" these days, the city's scrap drives for metal and rubber, the recent crash of a blimp on patrol off the coast, and the seemingly endless conflict in North Africa.

"Hopefully, the Allies will be able to help out the poor Russians soon," Faye commented. "It sounds like the Brits are finally making progress against Rommel, and we should be able to really zero in on Europe."

"I can't imagine what it would be like as a civilian living through the wrath of the Allied forces as they try to over-take Germany."

Faye glanced at him while she sipped her Coke.

Have I misjudged him? Here's a hotsy totsy international man of mystery, showing concern for the common man. Perhaps he's less super-ficial than I thought.

"So, what's your story, Mrs. Connor? How did you come to San Francisco?"

By this time, the onions and burger grease worked their magic and, almost like liquor, lulled Faye into a happy haze.

"I followed my boyfriend out right after he enlisted. We got married in Salinas, he shipped out, I found a job, and here I am."

"But what of your family?"

"Pops is a math professor at Northwestern University. Mother is…mother."

"Do you have German heritage?"

The question seemed oddly specific and put Faye back on her guard.

Why is he asking that?

She answered with caution.

"I do, as do jillions of Americans. My grandmother's family was German, but they came to Ohio in the mid 1800's. She married a farmer whose family came from England and hardly ever spoke of the old country."

"So, no current ties?"

Connections with Nazi Germany?

"I must have distant relatives over there, but I don't know any of them. Why do you ask?"

"Just wondering where you got your beautiful blue eyes and blonde hair is all."

Oh, brother. There it is. Forget thinking he wasn't superficial. Time to change the subject.

"Let's blame the Celts who raided England in the Dark Ages. Hey, I'm still hungry. Let's split another burger!"

On their walk back to the office, Simon shared with her that he would be out of town for several weeks.

"I'm needed back in Ottawa, but I will probably return to the Bay Area later in the fall."

"Well, thanks so much for lunch. You were right. I needed a break." She smiled, although she was secretly cross with him. Here they were, having a perfectly friendly meal and he had to go and ruin it by making a pass.

"Keep those home fires burning, Mrs. Connor." He tipped his hat and strode off up Market Street.

Wise guy.

14

Just a few days later San Francisco got a humdinger of a reason to be jittery. A Japanese seaplane, launched from a sub, bombed two locations in southern Oregon, setting off public alarm all up and down the coast. Over the next few days as details emerged, it was reported that the attack was a reprisal for the raid on Tokyo a few months back. As it turned out, Tommy Doolittle, who was based at the Naval Air Station on Alameda, led the raid. Most thought the Oregon bombings should be considered as a precursor to potentially more damaging bombing raids. The Japanese hoped the bomb would start a forest fire. Luckily, the forests were damper than normal, and the fire didn't catch after the bomb dropped.

To San Franciscans, the event drove home just how vulnerable the West Coast still was to an attack or even an invasion. The public fear of bombings and enemy landings spiked, just like in the days immediately following Pearl Harbor. Each morning, as Faye stepped out of the Fella

Place flat, she looked warily skyward and wondered if this would be the day the bombs rained down.

As if in defiance to this attack on the homeland, San Francisco's military might was on full display the following week at the San Francisco War Show, organized as part of the dedication of the new underground garage built to double as a bomb shelter at Union Square. Faye wound her way through the crowds on her way home and, by chance, she ran into Aunt Liz.

They enjoyed catching up, despite the din of music coming from the "Victory Stage." The twins, who spent a large part of their summer with the Vacations for Victory in Agriculture program harvesting crops in Sonoma, recently returned to Los Angeles for their sophomore year. Ever the patriot, Liz took in soldiers, even setting up four extra cots in her dining room. Faye smiled to herself at the thought of high-spirited young men bunking down in the twin pink gingham bedroom, but she nonetheless admired Liz's energy and boundless hospitality.

Dancing lasted in the new plaza throughout the afternoon, the big band sounds interrupted by frequent pitches for war bond sales. Faye watched for a while, then headed up Powell toward her flat. The frivolity of the event seemed hollow to her, a façade of music and laughter masking the grim reality across the sea. Along with the general anxiety about an imminent invasion and concern about Steve's safety, a new emotion crept into Faye's head that afternoon: guilt. Everyone in San Francisco seemed to be having the time of their lives with all the drinking, dancing, and flirting going on, while thousands of boys were experiencing unimaginable horrors overseas.

~

A raging battle in the Solomon Islands took center stage in the news. The girls listened to every newscast and moved pins around to new active battlefields on what appeared to be specks in the South Pacific: Tulagi, Gavutu, Tenaru, and Guadalcanal. As news trickled in, anxiety at the Fella Place flat rose. Thousands of boys from the Army, Marines, and Navy were involved in the battle, and chances that they knew someone who'd been hurt or killed were pretty good. Just when they thought the Allied forces had triumphed, the Japanese mounted a new attack. For weeks they listened to the news and looked at the map every evening, hoping their friends and loved ones would survive the waves of attacks unscathed.

Just before Halloween, Faye was assigned a delivery up to Hamilton Field in Marin County, her first solo excursion so far north of the Golden Gate. As she passed the dairy farms of central Marin County, she marveled at how vastly the California countryside changed with the seasons. The golden—really dry brown—hills of summer were beginning once again to turn green with the autumn rains. The landscape today looked how Faye imagined Ireland and suddenly the lyrics of "When Irish Eyes are Smiling" invaded her mind. She hummed the tune, remembering the times Steve would sing it at Connor family gatherings.

Hamilton Field, about an hour north of the city, was an important fighter pilot training center, as well as home to squadrons of short-range fighter planes. As she pulled up to the white stucco entry gate, she stopped to show the guard her orders and ask directions to General Bennet's office.

The delays seemed to compound all afternoon. The general was in a meeting, so she waited in the reception room under the watchful eye of a uniformed secretary. Faye spent the next ninety minutes, satchel on her lap, listening to the sound of typewriters and watching the black hands of the military clock tick away the minutes, interspersed with the roar of airplane engines from the runways just outside.

General Bennet finally appeared just before five p.m.

"So sorry, and thanks for waiting," he said as Faye passed him the envelope. "We had a long-distance call to Washington, and I just couldn't break away."

"No problem, sir," she said, although she could see the light fading and clouds rolling in through the office window. She opened the satchel and handed him a messenger envelope. "I am to wait for your reply."

"Of course. I'll be right back."

Faye glanced at her watch, as if it would have better news than the wall clock. The president had declared year-round daylight savings last year to maximize productivity, so she had some time. She just wanted to be sure she could get back to the city before dark. Driving across the countryside during dimout was no treat.

Another twenty minutes and the general returned, the envelope closed and ready for its return delivery.

"Here you are, miss. Thank you again for your time this afternoon."

"Of course, sir," she replied, stuffing the envelope back into her satchel and grabbing her coat. "I know how busy you are, so I appreciate you giving this your attention."

She ran out to the car, jumped in, and tossed the satchel and her pocketbook on the passenger seat. She started the engine and quickly made her way south on 101, pushing her speed as much as she felt she could in the waning light. She was almost to San Rafael when the car jolted suddenly, then the wheel pulled to the right.

"Jeez Louise," she muttered as she pulled over to the side of the road.

Faye got out of the car and confirmed her suspicion: the passenger-side tire was as flat as a fritter.

Blast.

She inspected the dented rim. *Blast and damnation, I must have hit a pothole.*

She looked up the road and down. For all her self-reliance, Faye wasn't above playing damsel in distress and flagging down help. Sadly, this particular evening, there were no other cars in sight on Highway 101. Good thing Steve thought it was important for girls to know how to change a tire, because he'd taught her how and made her practice more than once. With a sigh of resolve, she opened the passenger side door, tossed her coat, gloves, and hat on the seat, and then rolled up her sleeves and set to work.

She was just tightening the lug nuts with the spare in place when a car pulled up behind her disabled vehicle and turned off its engine. She craned her neck toward the car. Was it a knight in shining armor or a rapist?

"Need some help, Mrs. Connor?" Simon Miller's voice came floating through the open window.

The wrench clunked in the gravel as she bolted upright. "What on earth are you doing here?"

"I'm following you." His dimples were on full display.

Faye rolled her eyes. "Yeah, right. No seriously. I thought you were in Canada."

"I was until last weekend," he said, emerging from his car. "I've been visiting some friends who own a winery in Sonoma. All of their grapes are going to raisins for the military this season, so they needed some cheering up."

"I still can't believe it. Of all the people to come driving by. But I'm glad to see you. Could you make sure these nuts are tight enough?"

"*Oui, mon capitan.*" He smirked as he threw his coat on the front seat and began to roll up his sleeves. "You changed this yourself? I am impressed."

"It's a secret skill," she giggled. "Don't let it get around."

As Simon checked the bolts, Faye took the flat and hoisted it into the trunk. She felt Simon release the jack, which he brought to her along with the lug wrench.

"That should hold."

Retrieving his suit jacket, he suggested, "Why don't you follow me back into the city, since we'll be in dimout soon. If the gas station on Lombard and Laguna is open, we can drop the flat off for repair."

Faye appreciated Simon's offer. As they crept southward toward the city, she felt relieved that she could use his taillights as a guide on the road. She also couldn't get over the coincidence that he showed up just when she needed an assist.

Better him than an ax murderer, she decided.

As they pulled into the gas station, Faye searched for any signs of activity.

"I think they're closed, but I'll go look around back," Simon offered, then strode off.

While she waited, Faye caught a glimpse of herself in the rear-view mirror. *Goodness! What a mess.*

Her cheek displayed a sooty streak and random curls had escaped the confines of her businesslike bun. She retrieved her hat and adjusted the angle to cover the stray curls, then got her handkerchief from her purse to scrub the grease off her face.

There. Not bad, considering…

As she placed her purse back on the seat, she noticed that the latch to the messenger satchel was undone.

Odd. I thought for sure I closed that.

She grabbed the case to lock it…and panicked.

The envelope. Where's the envelope with today's return communique? Did it fall out of the car while I was changing the flat?

She looked on the floor of the passenger side. No. Nothing. Panic, panic, panic.

She threw herself forward to look under the seat. Too dark to see anything, she thrust her hand under and felt around. *Blast.* Nothing. *How could I be so careless?*

Simon's knock on the driver's side window startled her.

"What are you doing?"

She flung open the door and jumped out of the car in obvious distress.

"I'm missing a very important envelope. Did you see it? It's an oversized messenger envelope with a red cord."

As Simon proceeded around the car to look from the passenger side, Faye yelled, "I'll get the flashlight from the trunk so we can look under the seat."

When she ran to join him on the passenger side of the car, he stood there smiling, envelope in hand.

"Here it is. It was way under the seat."

Yes! Thank goodness.

"Oh, thank you, thank you!" Faye grabbed the envelope and instinctively gave him a brief, hard hug. "My goose would have been cooked if I'd lost this."

For a split second, their eyes locked. In the twilight, his gray eyes had deepened to silken pools, hypnotic and so tempting. A prickly warmth raced down her torso and enfolded her very core. She could feel her resolve begin to crumble.

Move. Faye commanded herself. *Move now. Now!* She

looked away, a blush flooding her cheeks as she clutched the envelope to her chest like a shield.

Clearing her throat, she asked in her most business-like tone, "So they're closed, right?"

"Locked up tight as a drum. It says on the door they open at seven, so you'll have to drive with the spare tonight."

"Well, I really should get back to the office. I know Mr. Dalton is waiting for me. But thanks for all your help this afternoon."

"My pleasure, Mrs. Connor." He opened the driver-side door and doffed his hat as she slid behind the wheel. He gently shut the door and, with a "See you 'round," he sauntered back to his car.

Late that night, after Faye had returned the car and delivered the envelope, after Dalton had complimented her on her resourcefulness for dealing with a flat out in the middle of nowhere, she lay in her bed and replayed the afternoon in her head.

Simon Miller. How on earth did he happen to drive by?

She rolled over onto her side and cuddled up to her extra pillow, remembering how electrifying his body had felt during their split-second embrace. She frowned as she tried to reconcile her attraction. Steve was the only boyfriend she'd ever had, and her commitment to him was unquestioned. Yet, there was something exciting at play—the allure of adult passion, secret and illicit. She plumped up her pillow and gave a deep sigh.

Don't overthink it, girl. You had a flat, he turned up, end of story. Nothing to feel guilty about. Just be glad he saved your bacon.

And yet, she woke up with a start two times that night when her dreams crossed over into forbidden territory.

15

———

We have grown to be, not merely a united, but a devoted people. We accept our small privations as willing gifts, and we will face greater ones even with thankfulness. Our women are flocking to factory jobs such as women never undertook before, and walk the streets on their way home with visible pride in overalls and the marks of grimy work. The spirit to "give" and "serve" is everywhere… For the spirit of sacrifice (war) evokes, for the determination this time to win it for a lasting peace—give thanks!

San Francisco Chronicle

November 26, 1942

Thanksgiving was Faye's favorite holiday. No stress of gift buying. No endless social obligations. Just gathering to reflect on one's blessings and share a wonderful meal. It was always a big event in the Baxter household. Pops's brother and his family typically came down from Milwaukee, and there were always various strays—professors, grad students, and other friends—who filled the dining room to capacity. At the top of the guest list was Mrs.

Evans, a widowed neighbor and excellent cook, who took charge of the meal. As a result, Baxter Thanksgivings were known far and wide for a perfect bird, fragrant chestnut stuffing, and silken gravy.

Since 1940, there had been a certain amount of confusion regarding the beloved holiday. Traditionally celebrated on the fourth Thursday of the month in the US, Thanksgiving served a dual purpose as a national holiday of thanks and the beginning of the Christmas shopping season. To help stimulate retail business, President Roosevelt had moved the date in 1940 to the third Thursday in November, allowing a longer Christmas selling season. The change didn't really have any impact on sales and drew widespread public complaints, so this was the first year the holiday would return to its rightful place on the calendar: the last Thursday of November 1942.

"We could always go to Aunt Liz's," Midge offered. "That is if you can stand Uncle Henry's dad-blamed grumbling, which I doubt will pause even for Thanksgiving."

"Or," Faye countered, "we could host our own Thanksgiving with all our friends who have nowhere to go. I'm sure my flat mates would approve. We can set up a buffet on the kitchen counter and just cram as many people as will fit into the apartment."

Evie and Helen loved the idea and immediately began planning the meal and inviting their friends. In the end, they expected twenty-six people, more or less, and set about borrowing enough dishes and flatware to accommodate the crowd. They scoured the local groceries and managed to assemble the ingredients for a feast with only minor adjustments for rationing.

Evie, the only one with actual turkey-roasting experience, was appointed head chef. After prepping the stuffing, potatoes, sweet potatoes, cranberries, and vegetable casse-role on Wednesday evening, the girls woke up at six a.m. to start the cooking and arrange the tables. They pushed the sofa and chairs against the wall and positioned borrowed card tables end to end in the living room. By having two place settings at each end, they were able to create banquet seating for all twenty-six.

"Any overflow can stand at the kitchen counter," Faye announced as she and Helen covered the string of tables with white sheets to emulate tablecloths.

At four p.m., the guests began to arrive. Midge was first, accompanied by Winnie from her crew, Kevin, who was in the Coast Guard, and six pumpkin pies. To Faye's surprise, Simon Miller received an invitation from Helen, and he showed up with a case of very nice red wine, presumably from the secret stash of his Sonoma friends. She felt over-come by that double-whammy frisson of excitement and annoyance as he strolled into the apartment, a feeling she quickly dismissed.

You have too much else to think about right now, she lectured herself. *Now mash those potatoes, get that gravy in the boat, and stop staring at his biceps, Mrs. Connor.*

The meal was a beat-me-daddy-eight-to-the-bar success. Other than grace, a tear-jerker led by Faye, the evening was one of high frivolity. When every crumb of food and every splash of wine had been consumed, dishes were cleared, tables folded, and the little living room on Fella Place became a first-rate dance club.

"My compliments, Mrs. Connor," Simon remarked as

the crowd gathered their coats and finally departed. "I rather like your Thanksgiving traditions better than ours."

"I'm glad you could join us."

"I, for one, am thankful for your friendship, and for being included in your inner circle." He reached out and clasped her hand. "There aren't that many people I've met that I feel quite so at ease with. Maybe we could catch a movie sometime, just as friends." His thumb gently stroked her knuckles, which struck Faye as un-friend-like behavior. His touch ignited a yearning that bypassed her brain and went straight to her heart.

No way I'm going to sit in the dark for two hours next to this loaded pistol.

"Well…*friend*," she replied, "if you give me back my hand, I'll wrap up a piece of pie for you to take home."

After all their visitors departed, the girls set to washing the mountain of dishes that had been scraped and stacked, singing along to the tunes on the radio. Shortly before midnight, the doorbell rang.

"Oh, come on! Party's over," Helen said as she went to the door. She opened it, paused for a moment and shrieked. Evie and Faye came running out of the kitchen to see Helen with her legs wrapped around a boy in uniform, their faces locked in a kiss.

"She must know him," Evie said after several seconds.

The kiss continued uninterrupted.

"Let's assume this is Flyboy Rick, and he got a furlough," Faye replied.

They both watched as the boy walked Helen backward

down the hall, into her bedroom and slammed the door, still lip locked and without a word.

"Until I learn otherwise, I'm going to assume that Helen is not being held against her will," Evie said. "More pots for us, kiddo."

They returned to the kitchen and the last of the dishes. In a very few minutes, Evie turned the radio up to drown out the sounds coming from Helen's bedroom. It was abundantly clear that nothing was going on against anyone's will.

The next morning, Helen and Rick appeared just before eight, both fully dressed and packed for travel.

Introductions were made and Rick, with a sheepish but very satisfied grin, shook hands.

"Glad to meet you gals. Helen here talks a lot about you in her letters."

"Where are you assigned?" Evie asked.

"I flew raids during the Solomons push," Rick said. "Took a shot in the thigh and have been recovering in Honolulu. I'm pretty much 100 percent and have been reassigned to Fort Dix. I report next week, but I wanted to be sure to see Helen."

His gaze was pure adoration.

Helen, returning his gaze, broke the next bit of news. "We're catching the train this afternoon to sneak in a visit with his folks. I'll be gone at least a month but save my room for now. I don't know exactly what I'll decide to do, and I may want to come back."

"What about your job?" Faye asked. Although surprised by Helen's impulsiveness, she wanted to sound supportive.

"I'll send Mrs. Washburn a telegram before I leave town, and I'll be in touch when my plans firm up." She leaned into Rick's arm as she said, "If Rick is going to be stateside for a while, I want to be close to him."

Faye and Evie walked them down to the streetcar line, then waved furiously as the car set off toward Union Square.

"Take care, you lovebirds," Evie said wistfully when they were well out of earshot.

She linked arms with Faye as they turned back to the flat. "I don't know about you, kiddo, but I was awakened by the strangest noises all night long. I'm going back to bed."

16

———————

On the Sunday after Thanksgiving, Disaster Relief District #3 held a large-scale emergency drill for an incendiary bomb attack, with actors impersonating the displaced and wounded. As part of their Civilian Defense Corps obligation, Faye and Evie were assigned to the front door of Grace Cathedral, directing people to various departments within the basement for treatment or shelter. Their training had taught them to quickly assess injuries. The severely wounded went to triage, minor injuries to first aid, families with children were sent to the nursery, displaced—non-injured—adults, some with pets, went to the shelter rooms.

Several hours into the drill, a "broken arm" patient arrived, escorted by none other than Tweedledum and Tweedledee. Clearly annoyed that Faye and Evie held such high-profile positions, the two just glared at Faye as she assessed their patient.

"You gals must've had quite a Thanksgiving, didn't

you?" Mr. Bailey commented in an accusatory tone, a not-so-subtle attempt to reestablish his superiority.

"Excuse me?" Faye replied, noting again the *eau de gin.*

"Music until almost midnight. My word! It wouldn't surprise me if they could hear that commotion back in Tokyo."

"All good fun with no suspicious persons in attendance, Mr. Bailey," Faye replied cheerfully. "This patient should go to Clinic B—please follow the yellow line on the floor."

"We know where it is!"

With that, they shuffled their patient off to the assigned clinic.

Faye glanced at Evie, who had witnessed the exchange. "Oh, I feel safe," Evie said, rolling her eyes. "I wonder where one draws the line between defending the public and plain, boldfaced snooping?"

It seemed ironic to Faye that San Francisco's parades, which showcased military might, always seemed to occur during torrential rainstorms. The Win the War Committee planned a massive show of enthusiasm to mark the one-year anniversary of the attack on Pearl Harbor. Sure enough, the clouds gathered, and it rained steadily throughout the parade. Troops, nurses, and service organizations marched from the Ferry Building up Market Street to the Civic Center. Tanks, cannons, and floats, WACS, WAVES, nurses, British sailors, floats, and canine corps all sloshed through the downpour up Market Street. The rain pelted participants and spectators alike, but the undeterred thousands marched on, as if they could prove their resolve against the greater enemy by defying the weather.

For Faye, the show of national pride was insufficient to overcome her sense of foreboding. The afternoon stirred up layers of emotions she seldom allowed to surface. Worried for Steve, haunted by her last encounter with Michael Pennington, she ached to be held close by someone who could comfort her. Instead, she was crowded close to Evie and several other work friends, watching the festivities from beneath her umbrella with a sense of despair. All this effort, all this show of force and patriotism. Did it really do any good? Battles still raged in Tunisia, New Guinea, and Russia, hundreds of thousands of boys remained far from home, spread all over the globe and in harm's way.

"Evie, I'm going to head home," she whispered as she tied her rain scarf a little tighter.

"But the parade's not over. You okay?"

"All this hoopla seems kind of detached from the reality our boys are facing. Maybe it's the rain, but I'm in a gloom. I'm going to tuck in with some hot chocolate and my book and hope for a sunnier day tomorrow."

Faye's emotions did a complete about face a few days later with the news that Midge's crew completed construction of a Liberty ship in record time: fourteen days, one hour and nine minutes! The evening after the launching ceremony, she joined Midge and a few of other Kaiser Shipyard #2 women welders for a celebratory bar hop.

"You dames are nothing short of dynamite!" Faye toasted as they settled into a table at the Top of the Mark. "If you're not careful, you're going to give men a bum rap."

"I'll get soused to that," Midge responded, igniting a

new peal of laughter. "I hope this shows those he-men supervisors that we can hold our own on the line."

They all raised their glasses and chanted their own version of the Shipyard motto in unison, "Down the ways in fourteen days and down the hatch!"

The bar at the top of the Mark Hopkins Hotel was the highest point in San Francisco, known for its 360-degree views of the city and the Golden Gate. It represented a favorite "last drink" spot for departing soldiers, and there were plenty of men in uniform there on this particular evening with a "night to remember" on their minds. Before long, Midge's party attracted several admirers more than happy to keep the alcohol coming. Round after round of whiskey highballs appeared that everyone gleefully imbibed.

Faye, the only person who had to work in the morning, gave her excuses just before eleven.

"You and the other girls are welcome to crash at our place," Faye offered.

"Thanks for coming out, but hopefully, we'll have better offers for accommodation." Midge winked and giggled as she jitterbugged off with a dark-haired captain.

In the wee small hours of the following morning, Faye woke up with a headache and went to get some aspirin and water. The living room sofas were vacant, and she could only conclude that the shipyard crew was otherwise occupied.

Well, good for them. They worked hard and deserve some fun.

As she lay in the dark waiting for the aspirin to take effect, it struck her how much the war had changed just about every aspect of life for the women of America.

Shoot, eighteen months ago, we wouldn't even be allowed to work in a shipyard. Back then, girls feared doing anything that would ruin their reputation. I hate to say it, but maybe something good will come out of this war.

~

"You certainly have done some fine research, here," Mr. Dalton commented after reviewing the charts on the table before him. "I have to say, I am impressed."

Faye had been in his office for twenty minutes, presenting her findings of the gravel purchase reconciliation over the last year. She'd prepared graphs documenting the monthly shortfalls, as well as comparison charts of shipping costs versus using more local suppliers. Material waste and potential cost saving were clearly illustrated. Faye had practiced her talking points, dressed in her black suit for extra confidence, and stated her findings clearly.

"It's really a matter of tracking the trends. Because I reviewed the reports over the last several months, I was in a good position to notice a few issues and suggest solutions."

"Are you sure these suppliers are able to handle the volume?"

"I spoke with the ops guy with every one of them, and they're all comfortable with the quantities, based on what we've ordered over the last year. It'll take a little more coordination on our end, but the savings would more than justify hiring someone to monitor the orders and liaise with the suppliers. I've included the salary for a Gregor coordinator in my comparison."

Dalton studied the charts in silence, then peered at Faye over his reading glasses.

"Very impressive, Mrs. Connor."

"I realize there are contractual agreements with current

suppliers that need to be honored. But now you have the information, should you need it."

"And I will be sure to bring this up at the next executive meeting."

Faye fought to keep her annoyance in check, shifting her weight from one foot to the other, pondering what to say next.

So that's how this works. I put in months of research to come up with a strategy, and now I have to wait while a milquetoast mid-level manager presents it to the real decision makers. I suppose it's the best I can hope for.

"Thank you, sir."

17

———————

The girls almost walked right past him: a sailor, crumpled in the back vestibule of the florist shop near the entrance to Fella Place. They were on their way back from work via the fish market on Bush Street. It was crab season, and the girls intended to try their hands at making cioppino, the iconic fisherman's stew believed to have originated in North Beach. After Evie's recent experiment with Victory Loaf, a bland concoction of potatoes, breadcrumbs, peas, and carrots that supposedly resembled meat loaf—it didn't, they eagerly embraced the prospect of a steamy stew full of fresh sea bass, sweet shrimp, and crab.

"We still have some sourdough left from last night. It's probably a little stale, but we can toast it up, and it'll taste good as new," Evie commented as she planned out the accompaniments.

Her voice apparently disturbed the young man, because he flinched. Both Evie and Faye spotted him at the same time—drunk and in a stupor among the bins of cuttings and wilted blooms waiting for trash pickup. The girls exchanged glances, not quite sure how to proceed.

"Should we call the cops?" Faye whispered.

"Let's just play this one by ear," Evie replied. "He's probably on liberty and had too much of a good thing."

With that, Faye cautiously approached him. "Hey, sailor, you okay?"

"Of course, I'm okay," he slurred, clutching a bottle of tequila. "I'm a hero. A great big fuckin' hero with a great big fuckin' medal to show for it."

The girls exchanged glances again. "Let's get him inside and sober him up," Faye whispered and Evie nodded in agreement. "I'm sure he's just struggling through a rough patch."

"Well, you look like you could do with some hot coffee and supper," Faye said with her perkiest attitude to the young man. "We live right over there, so come with us. Even a hero needs to eat."

As Faye helped him up, he slumped heavily on her shoulder, his rancid breath like a blast of toxic gas in her face. Although her reflex was to cover her nose and pull away, she held firm, resolved to give this "hero" an appropriate welcome.

"Hey, you're pretty cute. Too bad I'm married," he slurred as Faye guided him across the alley and up the stars to their flat.

"Well, I'm married, too, but we can still be friends. Whatta ya say?"

"Yeah, sure. I'm short on friends these days."

Half an hour later, after a shower and three cups of coffee, Gunner's Mate First Class Jeff Blake regained his thought processes and his ability to speak coherently.

"We got here in the middle of the night. Today was filled with hoo-haw-haw and blah, blah, blah, and I've been blotto ever since."

"Are you on the *'Frisco?*" Evie cautiously asked.

The *USS San Francisco* had returned to its namesake city heavily damaged from the Pacific sea battles. The girls had read how its original captain and an admiral had been killed in action, and a junior commander had taken charge to rout the enemy and bring the damaged ship home. After a pomp-filled welcome ceremony on the Embarcadero that morning, the ship headed right over to the drydocks at Mare Island for repairs.

"Yes, ma'am. The *Fighting 'Frisco.*" He momentarily glowed with pride, then dropped back into a facial expression of melancholy. "Supposedly a 'lucky ship.' She survived Pearl Harbor, ya know. Even had a torpedo glance right off her hull without so much as a scratch. And then we got to Guadalcanal."

"I know you guys had a rough time out there," Faye comforted.

Jeff dropped his head and paused a full minute. "Rough? Shitballs! It was hell, plain and simple, pardon my French."

He rubbed his hand across his forehead and massaged his temple, as if to quell a headache, before he continued. "We took forty-five direct hits, including a plane that deliberately crashed into us and started a massive gas fire. More than a hundred were killed, including most of my unit." He lifted his head and made direct eye contact with Faye. "And you know what the worst thing is? I had nothing to say about being there, watched dozens of my buddies get blown to smithereens, can't understand why I survived, and they're calling me a hero."

Faye gently put her hand on his arm, small comfort for someone so distressed, but she really didn't know what else to do.

"I can tell you that I was terrified for weeks on end, just scrambling to stay alive and take out as many Zeros as I could," he continued. "There was nothing noble or heroic about it. I was following orders and wishing with all my soul that I was somewhere else."

Evie set a steaming bowl of cioppino in front of him, giant crab legs protruding from a pool of savory deliciousness—a fragrant broth of white wine, tomatoes, garlic, thyme, and parsley. The aroma seemed to lift Jeff out of his quagmire.

"Thank you, ma'am. Dang, that smells great." He took a spoonful of the broth, then several more.

"Well, I know the *Frisco* was key to us keeping Henderson Airbase on Guadalcanal," Evie offered in consolation. "They're saying that battle turned the tide in the Pacific."

Jeff speared a prawn and chewed thoughtfully. "Tell that to Mookie Morris or Rick Manetta or Buck Stephens, or any of my other pals, who are now cold and dead at the bottom of the ocean," he said. Then, after a swig of Coke, he recalled, as if visualizing it all again, "I watched that torpedo go right under our bow then bee line for the *Juneau* like a bolt to a lightning rod. The only thing we could do was crap our pants and watch the sharks start to gather." Then, remembering he was at the dinner table, he added, "Pardon my language, ladies. I keep forgetting I'm back in civilization."

"No need to apologize," Faye replied. "Truly. After what you've been through, just tell your story however you like."

After a few more bites, his spoon clanked against his dish. "Why am I here? What makes me special? At one point, a *kamakazi* crashed right into us. One minute we were in control, the next minute we were broiling in an inferno. Fire everywhere, people screaming... Stan Lewis, the gunner next to me, was burnt to a crisp before my eyes. Right next to me. It could just as likely have been me."

"Look, I'm sure nobody plans to be a hero," suggested Faye, not quite sure what to say that would be comforting. "My guess is that ten years from now, you'll look back and see the significance of this experience to our ultimate victory in this war."

"Maybe you're right." He cracked open another claw with a nutcracker. "Maybe I'm just tired and miss my family, but I also know I'm being honored for something I want to wash from my memory forever."

When the last claw had been cracked, and the last drip of broth sopped up by the last chunk of sourdough, the girls walked a sober and sated Jeff Blake back to the streetcar.

"Ladies, I feel like a new man. I can't thank you enough. I have to say, some good grub and sympathetic ears have worked magic. I feel like I can get through tomorrow, then beginning Wednesday I'm on furlough for Christmas. I'm headed to Denver for two weeks to see my wife and meet my little baby son."

He opened his wallet and pulled out a tattered snapshot of a smiling woman holding an infant.

"Aww," Faye cooed. "He looks just like you."

"Yeah." Jeff smiled at the photo again and placed it

tenderly back in his wallet. "I'm so proud of him, and I've never even laid eyes on him." His voice thickened with emotion.

"Well, good luck to you, sailor," Faye said. "I have a feeling that once you're home, a lot of the chaos you've been through will make more sense."

He gave them a casual salute as he boarded the crowded car.

"Bye! Good luck!" They waved and watched the streetcar disappear down the hill.

"Poor guy," Evie said as they walked back to the flat. "He's physically unharmed yet mentally a mess. And dollars to donuts, there are many more like him."

Faye just nodded, petrified by the thought that Steve could be among the damaged.

18

I cannot say 'Merry Christmas'—for I think constantly of those thousands of soldiers and sailors who are in actual combat throughout the world—but I can express to you my thought that this is a happier Christmas than last year in the sense that the forces of darkness stand against us with less confidence in the success of their evil ways.

—President Franklin D. Roosevelt

Christmas Address to the Nation, December 1942

With Helen gone, her vacant room became a hot commodity for guests from the East Bay and out in the Avenues. Midge claimed a space, sharing the bed with Hannah Goldman, who worked in Faye's department and lived in the Outer Richmond. The sofa was staked out by Evie's cousin, Betty Brice, who visited from Los Angeles where she worked on the aircraft assembly line down in Hawthorne.

The holiday guests brought a new liveliness to the talk around the breakfast table. With coffee and sugar scarce, the conversation became a welcome diversion from their toast and weak tea. News of Europe's Jews being sent to camps had just begun to creep into the US news, and Hannah was frantic for her relatives in Rotterdam.

"We haven't heard from them in months, which is really unusual. They always send letters and gifts for the holidays, and there hasn't been a peep."

"Not to frighten you, but I read just last week that the Nazis are planning to build the world's largest prison for Jews and other people they deem undesirable," Midge said as she leaned over a bowl of steaming water at the counter. The Shipyard had its own hairdresser, but in between her weekly shampoos, Midge used a quick steam and towel dry to freshen up.

"I saw that, too, and I'm just sick about it," Hannah noted. "Tante Elsa and Oom Max are so well respected. They've had a jewelry shop for years. Tante Elsa is a former opera singer and a prominent patron of the symphony. Both of their children are studying in Heidelberg, or at least they were until '39."

"Can the Red Cross help you locate them?" Faye asked. She had just plunked a brick of oleo into a bowl and was attempting to mix in the tablet of food coloring, so it looked uniformly yellow. This late in the month the butter ration had been used up, so they were left with margarine and honey for their toast—and there were few things less appetizing than a streaky spread on your morning toast.

Hannah slowly shook her head. "My dad is working with the American Jewish Committee and the State Department to try and get them visas, but so far no luck. Restrictions on immigration are tighter than ever. There are hundreds of thousands of families in the same situation. It's like the whole world—not just the Nazis—has it in for the Jews."

"Don't you want to go back to Washington and take matters into your own hands?" Midge barked, rubbing her steamed hair vigorously with a towel. "We women have shown ourselves capable of doing men's work, maybe we should be allowed to fight, too. Mrs. Roosevelt said just last week that women might have to register for the draft if the war continues. Goddamn it. I say, the sooner the better. Those Nazis won't stand a chance against a riled-up Illinois farm girl."

~

On Christmas Eve, the Gregor Corp offices closed at two p.m. with a toast of non-alcoholic eggnog in the main conference room, after which bonus checks were distributed.

An extra $150!

Faye felt positively flush as she stopped by to make a deposit at the Crocker Anglo Bank on her way home. She'd never received such a windfall. Back in Evanston, the law firm had given out hams at Christmas, which were always welcomed but now seemed downright provincial. She deposited the bonus check into her savings, then rushed home to change for church. She, Hannah, who, though Jewish, was not one to miss a party, Midge, Cousin Bettie, and Evie planned to go for drinks at The Top of the Mark with a larger group of friends, then to Grace Cathedral for the midnight service.

Even though she'd spent many hours in the basement of the cathedral for her Civil Defense responsibilities, Faye had never been inside the sanctuary. She was hit by a wave of emotion when the group entered the neo-Gothic cathedral doors and made their way up the stone aisle. The nave, with its stained-glass windows, glowed with candlelight. The congregation joined the choir for a carol-sing, and all the girls fought back tears. Peace on earth, goodwill to men. It seemed an impossible wish.

The holiday traditions of Faye's childhood were long gone this year. Instead, she and her flat mates all slept in, then exchanged small gifts—the limit was $2.50—over French toast with homemade jam, a gift from Aunt Liz. A little before noon, they made their way to the USO on O'Farrell, where they had signed up to serve turkey dinner to men in uniform. Faye found herself on the gravy detail, and she spent the afternoon flirting with an endless line of lonely soldiers.

That evening, with the aroma of turkey and onions still clinging to them like scum on a pond, the girls went to see *Holiday Inn* at The Embassy. Despite her normal aversion to schmaltz, Faye found herself weeping during Bing Crosby's "White Christmas" number. She couldn't help it. Her brain was flooded with nostalgic thoughts of past Christmases. As the girls walked back up Nob Hill, they recounted their best Christmases ever. For Faye it was no contest: Christmas 1940, when Steve proposed. She twirled the rings on her left hand as she recounted the evening to the girls—the large, wrapped package that contained another wrapped box, then another, then another, until the last held a black velvet box from Marshall Field Fine Jewelry.

"Aww…that's so sweet."

"It's so Steve! For a big, tall guy, he can really be a sap."

The memory played over and over in Faye's head that night as she tossed and turned. She didn't tell the girls about how the make-out session that followed Steve's proposal lasted long into the night. It was the first time Faye could fully imagine the thrill of sex. The thought of that evening, of the warm wetness and Steve's firm fingers invaded her consciousness. Finally, at about three a.m., she gave up, switched on her lamp, and began to re-read Steve's most recent letters.

For being in a war zone, where just a few weeks ago thousands of young men had fought and died, his tone seemed nonchalant.

> *The ocean is so blue and clear, we can see the reefs from the cliffs…hope all is well with you… We're all fine here, played touch football in the sand after our Thanksgiving … We didn't have turkey, but some of the boys caught a huge halibut and we feasted like kings… I love you, my Faye.*

19

New Year's Eve loomed large on the horizon. Faye dreaded its arrival. With Steve gone, the thought of drinking too much and partying until the wee hours sounded unbearable. She'd rather stay home with a pot of tea and the latest Agatha Christie. But Midge would have none of that.

"Are you bananas? It's a brand new year and you want to skip the fun part? No dice, sister." The sentiment was seconded by Evie and amplified by nearly everyone at the office, single or married. As the girls dressed and primped for the evening, Faye tried to find some enthusiasm for the night ahead.

Their group merged with another gaggle of acquaintances in North Beach and took in the early glamor-boy review at Finocchios. Faye had never seen a female impersonator before and was sure the folks back home would be absolutely scandalized. It was hilarious. The bespangled performers were spectacular, the humor ribald, and the talent undeniable.

When the show let out, the group worked its way back down Stockton, stopping at the bars approved to serve men in uniform. A whisky sour here, a dance there, gin fizz here, another dance there, Faye soon allowed the buzz of the liquor to lift her spirits.

Then, there he was. As midnight drew close, Simon Miller was somehow by her side.

"Where'd you come from?"

"Not sure where I've been, but I must be in heaven now."

Oh, puh-lease.

The smoky tones of the Dukes of Rhythm filled the club as Faye began to sway. When Simon asked her to dance, she knew she should decline, but what was the harm of one dance? When his arm went around her waist and pulled her tight, she knew she should object, but his body felt so strong. When the band began to play "Auld Lang Syne," his eyes locked with hers.

Will he kiss me? Should I let him?

Simon slowly leaned in closer, closer…and at the last split second swerved and placed a gentle smooch on her right cheek.

"Happy New Year, Mrs. Connor."

She stared back at him as a smile gradually teased her lips.

You just passed the test, Simon Miller, leading me not into temptation. Maybe we can be friends after all.

"And a Happy New Year to you, Mr. Miller."

As the music played on, she struggled to recall her last kiss from Steve at Fort Mason—almost a whole year ago. Her thumb instinctively stroked the ring on her left hand, as if the momentary contact would bring the fading memory back into focus. Try as she might, she couldn't quite conjure the feeling clearly. It was only when the girls piled into a cab for the ride home that she acknowledged to herself her disappointment that Simon had decided to be a gentleman. A good kiss, deep and wet, from a handsome someone—anyone—seemed mighty appealing right now.

20

I do not prophesy when this war will end. But I do believe that this year of 1943 will give to the United Nations a very substantial advance along the roads that lead to Berlin and Rome and Tokyo.

—Franklin D. Roosevelt, President of the United States

State of the Union Address, January 7, 1943

War news was grim that January. US troops had invaded French North Africa the previous November and were getting trounced by Rommel's well-disciplined, well-supplied German forces. Although Henderson Field on Guadalcanal finally seemed secure, there was a battle raging in New Guinea, where the Japanese had just invaded. That's where Arnie was last stationed, and Midge was beside herself with worry. The only good news: The Red Army had stopped the German advance at Leningrad and the tide seemed to be turning in the Allies' favor.

A letter from Helen containing a check for her January

rent informed them that she was going to stay in New York. Flyboy Rick had been assigned stateside, and they had married at City Hall in Manhattan last week. Faye and Evie spent an entire Saturday packing her trunk, carefully folding all her cocktail gowns in tissue and placing her shoes in paper bags.

"I'm going to miss Helen, but I'm really going to miss her wardrobe," Faye lamented as she bid her favorite blue satin farewell. "I guess my black dress will be seeing more action now."

"Chin up, sister. There's a war on."

After a pause, Faye conceded. "You're right. At least we have events to dress up for. A lot of the world is just rubble and ruin."

Hannah Goldman claimed squatter's rights to the extra room and moved in the day after the shipping company picked up Helen's New York-bound trunk. A 5-percent victory tax, which Pops said was really an income tax, was imposed on all wages beginning that January, so the girls' paychecks were smaller. They both appreciated having Hannah move in right away so she could cover a third of the rent.

Hannah had moved up to the Bay Area from Los Angeles in early '42. Her father was a wealthy Hollywood lawyer and her mother an activist for numerous social causes, a background that added spice to the breakfast conversation. She had strong opinions and didn't mind sharing them, as long as it didn't ruin her manicure. She grew up in Bel Air where her parents hosted dinner parties for the likes of Eddie Cantor and Hedy Lamarr. In addition to bringing a new moral compass to the flat, she proved to be an endless source of reliable and very juicy gossip on the Hollywood scene.

The big domestic challenge that winter was the shortage of certain food items. The population of San Francisco had increased by 95,000 since Pearl Harbor, and supplies were stretched to the limit. No one was going hungry, but there was national rationing on several food and sundry supplies: sugar, coffee, butter, whiskey, ketchup, bobby pins, tin foil… even chewing gum. Prime cuts of beef, lamb, and pork were in short supply and consumers were encouraged to try sausages and organ meats. Many of the city's neighborhood butcher shops closed for lack of meat to sell, and the black market for rationed and rare goods gained momentum.

To help offset shortages, the girls installed galvanized metal planters on the roof deck for their version of a Victory Garden. They planted neat rows of leaf lettuce and spinach and, thanks to the netting that kept off the pigeons, had a good crop of winter greens within a month. To supplement their crop, they made a weekly visit to the new Farmers Market at Duboce and Market Streets, where Victory Gardeners from all over the Bay Area could sell or trade their surplus.

Ice cream and coffee were sorely missed, as was beef. Hannah put her considerable flirtation skills to good use and sometimes charmed the butcher into slipping an extra packet of stew meat into the bag along with the Sunday chicken. All three girls considered flirting far less subversive than buying goods on the black market. They often cooked up a big pot of beans on a Monday that would last them all week, supplemented by macaroni and cheese or creamed tuna on toast. Evie and Hannah liked liver and onions, but Faye just ate onions on toast when that was on the menu.

Dinner dates provided a welcome break from the culinary monotony for Evie and Hannah. A constant stream of young men fetched the girls on Friday and Saturday evenings, and even on an occasional weekday.

Since New Year's Eve, Faye had declined to socialize. She replayed that evening over and over in her head, scrutinizing her bothersome attraction to Simon. She couldn't blame it all on the music or the booze. She decided to blame it on loneliness. She knew there was a big difference between sexual desire—what she perhaps fleetingly felt for Simon—and love—what she was sure she had with Steve, and there was no question that her priority was to protect what she had with her husband. Besides, Simon made it clear that they were friends and only friends. She embraced that status.

But temptation seemed to be everywhere. In her resolve to stay true to Steve, she found herself alone with the dregs of the bean pot on many a weekend.

Penance.

The frequency of Faye's courier runs picked up in mid-January, and she found herself out of the office several times a week. She made deliveries as far away as Camp Roberts and the newly commissioned Travis Air Base in Vacaville. Hamilton and Alameda runs were now routine, as were trips to defense bases around San Francisco Bay. She hoped the increased activity foretold a military breakthrough of some sort.

One winter afternoon she was asked to make a delivery to Fort McDowell, an army installation on Angel Island. Accessible by a ferry from Tiburon in Marin County, Angel Island once functioned as a processing center for Chinese immigrants, and it currently served as an internment station for enemy aliens and prisoners of war. As the ferry glided past the dozen barracks surrounded by high razor wire fencing on the island's northeast shore, Faye reflected on an article she'd just read last week: Italian American families, many of whom had been subjected to curfews and had their fishing boats confiscated, had been asked to host Italian prisoners of war for dinner!

Sometimes, I wonder if the muckety mucks in charge of this war have any common sense at all!

~

On the first day of February, Irving Berlin's musical *This is the Army* came to the War Memorial Opera House, the last stop on its national tour. Gregor Corp distributed a large block of tickets. The morale-boosting program of rousing songs and show-stopping production numbers had drawn huge crowds since it opened on Broadway last year. It also received the enthusiastic endorsement of Mrs. Roosevelt. At first Faye was not wild about going, but she changed her mind when she found it would benefit the Army Emergency Relief Fund for families and children of war veterans.

The Opera House was packed to its gilded rafters that evening, mostly with men in uniform. Faye sat in the Dress Circle with a group of work friends, including Simon— their first meeting since New Year's. He sat three seats down, next to Hannah, who filled him in on news of Bing

Crosby's house fire, the fact that President Roosevelt was secretly in Casablanca when the film *Casablanca* was released, and how the actor Ronald Reagan was going to make a movie of the play they were about to see. Simon seemed thoroughly engrossed in Hannah's inside scoop on the Hollywood set.

What an extravaganza! The production included more than 300 soldiers, singing their hearts out to tunes like "This is the Army, Mr. Jones" and "God Bless America." It seemed like the authors threw in everything but the kitchen sink—minus any mention of bombing, combat or death.

If this is really the Army, then Steve's letters are accurate. It is like summer camp.

Despite the thin plot and the bold-faced propaganda, the power of the music proved impressive. "This is the Army, Mr. Jones" stayed in her head as the group made their way over to John's Grill for a nightcap.

"That was quite a spectacle," Simon commented as he caught up with her.

"But so removed from what our boys are really going through, it's almost laughable."

"How astute you are, Mrs. Connor. Not drawn in by all the patriotic clamor?"

"Oh, it was certainly engaging. I just contrast the messaging with what I'm seeing at the newsreels."

"You are a shrewd one." He smiled. "By the way, have you read Beryl Markham's new book—*West With the Night?*"

"Not yet. Is it good?"

"It's excellent. Markham was a pilot in Africa in the '30s and she reminds me of you. Sensible, capable, smart."

"Married?" she asked, knowing full well she was being impish.

"Oh, several times." As he held the bar door open for her.

"Well, sounds fascinating. I trust she likes martinis, too, 'cause that's exactly what I'm craving now."

There. Just friends sharing a laugh and book recommendations. I can do this.

21

———————

A bouquet delivered to Faye at her desk, reminding her that it was her first wedding anniversary. White roses—her favorite, a whole dozen of them, accompanied a note from Steve in his own handwriting.

> My Faye,
> Thinking of you and our future together.
> I love you more than words can say. S

She sucked in her breath as tears silently slid down her cheeks, remorseful for ever doubting her love for Steve and feeling overpowered with longing.

How on earth did he manage this bouquet? she wondered.

Faye's answer came later that night when she joined Midge for drinks. Over champagne cocktails made with Sonoma's cheapest sparkling wine, she learned that Midge was in cahoots with Steve on this.

"I confess. I was his accomplice," Midge admitted as she sipped her glass of bubbly. "After all, I was witness to the happy event a year ago, so I was glad to help. Steve wrote to me last month, asking if I'd arrange for the flowers. He even sent a note to accompany the bouquet. I'm telling ya, kiddo, he had all his bases covered."

"That's so like Steve. Thanks for your service, Midge. You are a gentlewoman and true friend."

"Who can weld a flawless seam and still attract the cutest boy in the room," she said with discernible pride.

They giggled as they clicked their glasses and then drank deeply.

"Gosh, it's hard to believe we've been out here a whole year," Midge said after a long sigh. "I say it's been a good year, even with our husband and boyfriend gone. We've both grown as people and as working women, and we've had experiences I for one will never forget. It even seems as if our troops are finally figuring out how to fight and win."

Faye held her glass up for another toast. "Here's to winning, and to the boys coming home."

With Midge headed back to the East Bay, Faye decided to stop off at the neighborhood market on Sutter on her way up Nob Hill. Ever since the war started, many grocery stores, restaurants, and service businesses were open twenty-four hours a day to accommodate the round-the-clock work schedule. This came in handy for some late-night provisioning, especially when she remembered—as she did that evening—she'd used the last of the milk that morning.

Fifteen minutes later, she emerged from Della's Market,

her net tote bag heavy with canned milk, peanut butter, margarine, and some apples, and headed home on Bush Street. She was about to turn up Kearney when she heard some breaking glass and a muffled cry for help from Belden Alley. She made her way quickly and silently to the intersection and carefully peered into the alley, assaulted by the aggressive stench of garbage and urine. It took a second for what she was witnessing to register.

One sailor lounged against the wall, holding a bottle of whiskey, smoking a cigar, and rubbing his crotch. Another had a young woman pinned against the wall, his hand covering her mouth. The girl was dressed in expensive silk, her lip split and bruised, her fine Chinese features contorted with fear. As she looked over the sailor's shoulder, her eyes made contact with Faye in a silent plea for help.

"Hey!" Faye shouted, not considering for a split second that she might also be in danger. "Leave her alone!"

Startled, both sailors jerked around and looked at Faye, then traded glances and sniggered.

"Well, lookie here, Howie," Sailor Cigar said. "This party is one girlie short and here's a babe just when we needed one. You're an answer to our wishes, blondie."

Faye didn't know whether to run for help or take them on. She looked at the girl again and knew she couldn't leave her even for a few minutes. Who knows how long it would take to find a cop or an MP? As the sailor circled around Faye and backed her into the alley, her memory flashed back to something her mother told her when she started working at the law firm—and knew instantly what she would do.

Plan in mind, she slowly backed further into the alley as she gave Sailor Cigar her most alluring smile. Her goal was to position herself as close as possible to Sailor Howie and his captive.

"Well, this could be your lucky night, sailor," she said in a voice as low and sexy as she could manage. "How do you like it? Nice and rough? Slow and deep?"

Mesmerized by the suggestion, Sailor Cigar threw the smoldering end of his stogie away, took a deep swig of whiskey, and leered at Faye's breasts as he followed her deeper into the alley. "Howie, you take the chink, and I'll do this hot blondie here." He set his bottle on the pavement and closed in on Faye.

Wham, bam!

In an instant, Faye jammed her knee as hard as she could into Sailor Cigar's groin. As he crumpled at her feet, she swung her tote bag with all her might, thankful for Della's two-for-the-price-of-one sale on canned milk as it made contact with the side of Sailor Howie's face, knocking him out cold on the pavement.

With that, she grabbed the girl's hand, ran with her back out onto Bush Street and didn't stop until they were plumb out of breath. They were just a block from Fella Place when they paused, panting.

"Dang, you should take up martial arts, sister," the Chinese girl said, her voice pure California without a trace of an accent.

"Are you all right?" Faye asked through her panting.

"Yeah, I think so. A little bruised."

"Would you recognize those guys again? Do you want to make a police report?"

"No way," she said with certainty. "The cops would just say I was asking for it. I know how white cops treat my people."

"Listen, I live really close by. Let's get you some coffee and some ice for that lip."

"Yeah, that would be great. I'm Madeline Chu, by the way."

"Faye Connor," Faye responded.

"If you don't mind, I'm going to call you Fearless Faye, Warrior Goddess."

As soon as her heart stopped racing and they both resumed normal breathing, Faye led the way to the Fella Place flat, relieved that they'd come through the assault mostly unscathed. Rape—or "a man forcing himself on you"—was something her mother had warned her about.

"Just remember, if you kick a man right in the crotch, it will put him out of commission for several minutes," Mrs. Baxter had instructed without much elaboration. At the time, Faye felt it was an odd suggestion for her prim-and-proper mother to make and wondered if it was even true. Now, she would be eternally grateful for the tip.

Madeline Chu sat at the kitchen table, a tea towel of ice against her lip. Her bias silk dress was well cut and her updo made her look older than her actual age—twenty at most, Faye guessed. Faye fried up some egg sandwiches while Hannah and Evie got the scoop.

"Do you live in Chinatown?"

"Good heavens, no," Madeline said, her nose wrinkling with distaste. "We moved out to Richmond two generations ago. We can't own property out there, but Grandfather called in some kind of political favor to lease a few lots for a family compound."

"Two generations!" Evie exclaimed. "How long has your family been here?"

"My great-great-great-grandfather Chu Ming came here

in 1849 during the Gold Rush," Madeline relayed with pride. "He was one of the first Chinese to arrive in California. Like so many others, he thought he could make his fortune on 'Gold Mountain'—that's what my people called California."

"Did he?" Hannah asked.

"Not hardly," Madeline giggled. "Gold was harder to find than advertised and, shortly after he arrived, most of the Chinese were being hired to construct the railroad, which didn't appeal to old Ming. Instead, he stayed in San Francisco and took in laundry. He eventually earned enough to buy the building he was in. That, as it turns out, secured our family legacy."

Her story was cut short as Faye put a plate of sandwiches on the table and poured the coffee.

"Oh, yum! I'm starving."

"How did you get hooked up with those sailors?" Faye asked.

"Yeah, that was really stupid. I know better, believe me. I was out with my friend, Christie, and things got out of hand," Madeline said, caught between her hunger and her sore lip. She carefully bit into the soft white bread and chewed for a few seconds before she continued. "We were all dancing and had way too much to drink. I'm not sure when Christie decided to vamoose, but I wasn't thinking straight, and I remember the sailors saying they would show me their ship."

"Ship, indeed!" Hannah said as her cup clattered in its saucer. "They really wanted to show you their 'torpedoes,' if you get my drift."

"Yeah, I guess. I'm such a lamebrain. The irony is, two blocks farther west or north, and the Cantonese Commandos would have been all over them. I'm just lucky

Fearless Faye here happened to walk by and had the guts to give it to 'em good."

"Look, you're young, but you learned a valuable lesson for the price of a split lip," Faye said. "Just remember that some men are creeps, and it's not your fault."

Evie immediately picked up on that train of thought. "There are lots of lessons here," she said. "Don't get drunk. Don't go with someone you don't know. Always have a friend with you…"

"And if all else fails, kick them in the nuts," Madeline added. "I got it, ladies."

Faye glanced at her watch and saw that it was half past midnight on a work night. "Holy cow, it's late. Do you have to work tomorrow?"

"No. I just got a new job—a neighborhood reporter at the *Chronicle*," she said with pride, "but it doesn't start until next week. We were celebrating."

"Well, we all have to work, so as soon as you finish your coffee I'm going to call you a cab. But first, let me give you an extra toothbrush and let you freshen up. I'm sure your family will sympathize more if you don't come home smelling like booze."

As the taxi pulled away, Faye turned to see Mr. Bailey in full block warden regalia lurking at the corner.

"Socializing with enemy aliens?"

"No, Mr. Bailey," she responded with certainty. "Definitely not. You know as well as I do that all enemy aliens have been evacuated."

"So, she's not Japanese?"

Faye narrowed her eyes and stared straight at him.

"Since her family has been in this country longer than yours or mine, I'd say she's American."

Bailey leaned close and squinted at her from under his helmet.

"I've got my eye on you."

"So you've said."

Faye stood to her full height and held his gaze. With an exasperated sigh, Mr. Bailey turned on his heel, headed back across Powell Street and into the night.

22

<hr>

The breakthrough in the fighting that Faye and the rest of America hoped for came in late January and February on two fronts. The Japanese finally suffered defeat at Guadalcanal, and German troops surrendered to the Red Army in Stalingrad.

Weather had been especially bitter on the Eastern Front, and the Nazis proved to be no match for the full force of the Russian winter. Faye listened to the reports on the *CBS World News Roundup* on the car radio as she drove back from an early document drop-off at Fort Funston. Stalingrad, surrounded and under siege for months, suffered untold brutality and starvation, and Faye shivered at the thought of eating rats and burning furniture for warmth. She felt fortunate to have a warm bed and food in her belly. Creamed tuna seemed downright luxurious compared to boiled rat.

~

The full horror of what was happening overseas came into better focus a few weeks later, when Faye received a rare call from home. Long distance calls were expensive, and Pops was frugal by nature, so Faye knew even before the operator clicked off that this wasn't good news.

"Pops? Is everything okay?"

"Not good, Faye."

Uh, oh.

"It's Michael Pennington. He was killed in Tunisia."

"Oh, Pops, no."

The tears began to flow. Not Michael. Not that kind, frightened, insightful boy she'd danced with just a few months ago.

"I thought he was in the Pacific."

"Evidently his unit was reassigned for this push to secure the Kasserine Pass."

"Is Mrs. Pennington all right?"

"Not really. She and the girls are pretty shook up, as you might imagine. Mom is taking them casseroles. It's terrible business, dealing with grief."

"I can't believe he's gone. It's heartbreaking—especially because all the coverage I've seen calls that battle an Allied victory."

"It shows just how inexperienced our military is," Pops commented bitterly. "Fredendall and Anderson are idiots who should be sacked, and Patton's a blowhard. The truth of the matter is the foot soldiers are paying the price for our incompetent leadership."

"Well, give the Pennington family my condolences. I'll write to them this afternoon."

"What do you hear from Steve?" Pops seemed to need reassurance that this tragedy was limited to Michael for the moment.

"I'm pretty sure he's on Midway. They sent him in to rebuild the airfield and supply station. As far as I know, he's still there."

"Well, let him know we think about him often. Work going okay?"

Like everyone else in her life, Pops knew only about her office job, and not anything about her extracurricular assignments. If only she could share her pride in doing important national security work.

"It's going great, Pops. There are so many projects in the works all over the US and Canada. It's really good experience for me. It's just so sad that, while I'm getting all this great experience, boys like Michael are losing their lives."

"I know, Faye. Well, I'm going to hang up. I'm sure these long-distance charges are adding up. Just wanted you to find out about Michael from a friendly voice."

"Thanks for calling, Pops. I love you."

"Love you, too."

Professor Baxter, one of the least demonstrative people in the world, rarely said, "I love you." Faye knew then that he really must be shaken.

After replacing the handset gently in its cradle, Faye just stared at the phone for several minutes while snippets of her many experiences with Michael flashed through her head. Building summer forts in the backyard. Catching tadpoles in drainage puddles. Crossing paths at the Homecoming Game. Helping Pops plant vegetables every spring. Dancing with him at the Forbidden City so recently. A few minutes later, she went to her room and wept silently until the wee hours of the morning.

Pops's thoughts on military leadership were evidently shared by the top brass. The US command in Tunisia was relieved of its duties, and General Dwight Eisenhower was brought in to reorganize and re-energize the Allied troops in anticipation of an invasion of Sicily. "Ike" proved himself a capable leader during the final days of the campaign in Tunisia, and he rallied both the respect of his men in the field and the hearts of those at home. The whole of the free world, it seemed, loved Ike.

With the change in command, the Allies commenced a program of round-the-clock bombing of Germany. Both the RAF and the US Army Air Corps targeted cities and key sites deep within the Third Reich. The campaign not only disrupted transportation and manufacturing capabilities, it damaged the morale of the German people. Like most Americans, Faye wanted to believe this was the beginning of the end, a push to finally crush Hitler on his home turf.

On Valentine's Day, which fell on a Sunday, a group of girls from work decided to treat themselves to tea at the Fairmont Hotel. While restaurants were subject to rationing, it was not as severe as public allotments, and the girls looked forward to some sweets on what promised to be a fun diversion.

Faye dressed in her new crystal-studded snood—just like Ginger Rogers wore in *The Major and the Minor*, her basic black suit and her stalwart black peep toe shoes. She penciled her brows, coated her fair lashes with mascara and, after applying two coats of her new Elizabeth Arden Victory Red lipstick, set off up the hill to the Fairmont.

The landmark hotel atop Nob Hill was dressed to the nines for war, its windows sandbagged, its marble-columned lobby festooned with American flags and packed with men in uniform. As Faye made her way to the Cirque Bar, she passed rows of cots in the lobby, dining rooms and ball-rooms. At the request and encouragement of Mayor Rossi, hotels used any available space to accommodate soldiers, and the Fairmont quickly pitched in.

Faye's group of eight or so gal friends took up a bay in the far corner of the Cirque, with its whimsical murals of dancing horses and acrobats. The tea menu was well worth the $1.25 tab: delicate smoked salmon sandwiches, crumpets with jam, petit fours, strawberry tarts, boysenberry ice, and pot after pot of fragrant Darjeeling tea. The group nibbled the afternoon away, sipping tea, smoking cigarettes, and reminiscing about their beaux across the seas. They told each other stories, chatted and laughed for the best part of the afternoon.

As they departed shortly before six, Faye passed the lobby and stopped dead in her tracks. There in front of the reception desk stood Mr. Herman Smith of Gregor Corp deep in conversation with Simon Miller's so-called cousin in all her red-lipped glory.

What on earth are they doing here together? Are they checking in?

Faye giggled to herself at the thought of a scandalous tryst between the wattle-necked octogenarian and the sleek ice maiden. The thought amused her all the way back home.

War does indeed make strange bedfellows.

A few weeks later, Faye received a letter at work, delivered to her desk. The oversized envelope was bright red with her name in care of Gregor Corp embossed in gold foil. The scent of sandalwood emerged as she broke the wax seal and withdrew a heavy linen invitation.

The pleasure of your company is requested at a
Dinner Given in Honor of
Madame Chiang Kai-Shek
by the
City of San Francisco
and the
San Francisco Chamber of Commerce
Palace Hotel Garden Court
Table 2
March 26, 1943

Across the bottom corner of the invitation, handwritten in perfect Catholic-school script, was a note:

Fearless Faye,
Please join me and my family for this celebration.
With eternal gratitude,
Madeline Chu

Faye was flabbergasted. This banquet was all the buzz. San Francisco had anticipated a visit from Madame Chiang for years. Born Soong Mei-Ling in Shanghai, Madame Chiang was married to Generalissimo Chiang Kai-Shek, head of China's nationalist government. Her father traveled in America as a boy and ultimately attended Vanderbilt

University. Mei-Ling was raised a Christian and educated in America beginning at age nine, graduating from Wellesley College when she was just nineteen. Beautiful and articulate, she was the perfect luminary to tap into big-time American bucks to support her husband's cause. Among the residents of Chinatown, she was widely adored.

Madame Chiang's visit, originally planned for the previous fall, needed to be rescheduled due to illness. This dinner promised to be the event of the season in San Francisco, and here she was, a Midwestern WASP, invited to witness history from Table 2. Many of the tickets were being auctioned off to benefit the Chinese Relief Committee and bids went as high as $200 each!

Just who are these Chus? More importantly, how do they rate Table 2?

Faye had just finished composing an acceptance note to Madeline when a small parcel dropped on her desk with a whap. Startled, she looked up to see Simon Miller smiling down at her. She hadn't heard boo from him since the night at the theater, and she felt caught off guard.

"What's that?" she asked warily.

"Let's call it a gift for a friend."

Then it hit her. Coffee. The dark, roasty aroma that permeated the bag was intoxicating. Faye could hardly keep her eyes from rolling back in her head. Coffee rationing started last November, and the Fella Place trio normally ran out of real coffee about halfway through the month. Postum, which tasted more like burnt toast than coffee, proved to be a poor substitute they never really embraced.

She missed her morning cup-a-joe laced with cream every single day.

"And why are you giving this to me?" Faye inquired coolly as she stared lustfully at the bag.

"Because I'm working with Dalton on a project for the next few months, which means we're going to be seeing each other a lot. I'm just trying to be friendly. Besides, I need a favor."

"Oh, it's a bribe then."

"Hardly a bribe. I just need to know your approved suppliers for ammonium nitrate. It's for a presentation I'm doing next week."

"You can get that from purchasing."

"But I can also get it from my friend who loves a good cup of coffee."

"Well, only because the future of an important project is at stake." She grabbed the coffee, tucked it into her desk drawer, and then started thumbing through her ledger and making notes. "Ordinarily, I wouldn't accept your so-called gift, but my flat mates would kill me if I didn't bring this home. I hope to high heaven it's not from the black market, so don't you dare tell me if it is."

"My lips are sealed."

Yeah, right.

She snapped the ledger closed and tore the page out of the steno pad.

"Here's what I have," she said, offering him the list with a smile. "There may be more, but these are the ones this division has paid recently."

"You're a brick." He slipped the list into his briefcase and withdrew a book. "One more thing… I thought you'd enjoy this."

He handed her a copy of *West With the Night*, an illustration of Beryl Markham in her aviatrix gear on the cover.

"We can discuss it over a drink sometime. Just remember, it's mine and I want it back."

With that he tipped his hat and walked down the hall to the elevator.

Still a mystery but turning out to be a pretty good friend.

Over the next few weeks, Faye attended meetings at which Simon was present, taking minutes and distributing follow-up lists of action items. The topic was strategies to maximize energy output in the St. Lawrence and Great Lakes regions. Simon contributed impressively and often, with a smooth delivery and detailed knowledge of the technologies and capacity.

For such a smooth operator, he's got some major brainpower going on. But I still have to wonder what his cousin is up to and if he's at all clued in.

23

____

On the evening of the banquet, Faye stood before her closet and pondered her choices, sorely missing Helen's extensive wardrobe of formal gowns. This was the event of the decade, the finale of three days of hyperactivity throughout the city. Madame Chiang's arrival on March twenty-fifth was followed by a motorcade through the financial district and Chinatown, then a parade. An enormous banner with her likeness hung on the YMCA building on the Embarcadero.

Thousands upon thousands of people—mostly Chinese Americans dressed in rich brocades and furs—lined the route from Market Street, along Grant to Stockton to Post and then to The Palace Hotel. Even at seven thirty in the morning when the girls set off for work, the streets were already packed with revelers yearning for a glimpse of their heroine.

Faye's choice of evening attire was meager at best: her black fitted suit or her three-year-old black dressy dress with the sweetheart neckline.

Well, whichever I wear, I'm sure I'll be underdressed. My best hope is that I don't offend anyone.

She selected the dress, hoping she could trick it out with some accessories. Hannah came through: her red velvet evening pillbox with a black face veil and red shoes with bows would add an auspicious flair without being inauthentic.

"There," Hannah said, adjusting the veil. "You look just like Barbara Stanwyck in *Remember the Night.* Except your bangs are better."

"And I don't have Fred MacMurray mooning over me," Faye added as she turned and checked the seams of her stockings—her last pair from before the war. She turned back full front to the mirror and sighed.

"Well, thanks for your help. This will have to do. I'll just stand proud and hold my head high."

"You'll knock 'em dead, Mrs. Connor. Here, let's add some spice."

Hannah pinned a rhinestone brooch to her shoulder, then Faye pulled on black elbow-length dinner gloves, draped her fox stole casually over her shoulders and hoped for the best.

"Let's get you a taxi, Cinderella," Hannah said, dialing the cab company. "You can't arrive at the ball *shvitzing* from a hike across town."

The cab crawled down Kearney, then turned onto Market and joined the line of taxis and limousines waiting to approach the hotel entrance on New Montgomery Street. Crowds stood behind the roped-off red carpet, straining to see the dignitaries arrive. When an attendant opened the cab door, Faye made her way into the marble-columned lobby, bedecked for the occasion in a riot of spring flowers and flags, both Chinese Nationalist and American. She stood in the check-in line, hoping to spot Madeline among the throngs of Chinese celebrants: men in formal black tuxedos and most of the women in form fitting silk dresses of every color in the rainbow.

"Mrs. Steven Connor," she announced to the host. "I'm with the Chu party."

"Of course, Mrs. Connor," the host said, crossing her name off the list. "The Chu Family cordially invites you to join them for cocktails in the Tapestry Room. This way, please."

The host guided her through the throngs waiting to be allowed into the three banquet rooms and up an elegant staircase to an intimate reception room, adorned with gilt and crystal and filled with some fifty or so people she didn't recognize.

"Faye!" Madeline's voice came floating through the crowd.

Thank goodness she's here.

Madeline was hardly recognizable. Her lip was fully healed and cloaked in deep red lipstick. Her sleek, dark hair was caught in an elaborate chignon, revealing the most exquisite jade earrings. Her dress, a traditional *cheongsam* in an arresting peacock blue, embraced her petite figure like a gentle hug.

"I'm so glad you could come!" Madeline grabbed her hand. "My parents want so to meet you. And so does my Auntie Mei-Ling."

"Mei-Ling?" Faye questioned, then her brain made the connection. "As in Soong Mei-Ling? Are you related to Madame Chiang?"

"Well," Madeline giggled, "she's not my real aunt, but mummy knows her from college and she's my godmother. When I was little, we would meet up with the Chiangs in Hawaii for holidays. She thinks I'm terribly uncouth and far too American these days."

Welcome to the Table 2 crowd.

"Anyway, she should drop by soon. In the meantime, come meet my *real* relatives."

Madeline grabbed Faye by the hand and pulled her through the room filled with silk, cocktails, and polite chatter. Here was her brother Howard, handsome in his formal wear. Next a clutch of young women—the cousin squadron, according to Madeline. Finally, Madeline introduced her parents, Douglas and Anna Chu, to the spellbound Faye.

Mr. Chu looked down at Faye from behind his tortoise glasses and broke into a smile.

"Ahh, Mrs. Connor. We meet at last. I want to thank you for the assistance you gave my daughter."

Faye had to struggle to keep her train of thought and control her breathing.

Little do you know that I've seen you before, Mr. Chu. That gold tooth is a dead giveaway.

The next day was Saturday. Faye lay in bed as the sun streamed through her window, recalling the events of the previous evening. After she recovered from the shock of meeting the man who had argued with Mr. Wallace at the Forbidden City, she relaxed into a conversation with Mr. Chu. It turned out that his company owned the vast majority of real estate in Chinatown—and he didn't bat an eye when Faye told him she worked at Gregor. Mrs. Chu was petite, elegant, and so interested in Faye's work.

"Auntie Mei-Ling" joined the cocktail party long enough to greet her former classmate, chat with the senior Chus, kiss Madeline on both cheeks, then scold her for the high slit on her dress. She warmly pressed Faye's hand when they were introduced and thanked her for coming to Madeline's rescue.

Criminently! Does every Chinese person in the vicinity know about the episode in the alley?

Governor Warren, in office for just a few months, joined the Chu party before the dinner gong sounded. He was accompanied by Mayor Rossi, his bald pate glistening with sweat, who rushed around pumping hands, as if the fact that Chinese Americans had just been granted voting rights was top of mind. Mrs. William Baldwin, evidently the matriarch of a long-time San Francisco family, gravitated to Faye as one of the few other Occidentals in the room, and she confided that she didn't think much of the wartime newcomers to San Francisco.

"They're simply ruining the atmosphere," she commented with a lilting Norwegian accent. "You can hardly move anymore, there are such crowds everywhere."

Faye just nodded and smiled, not revealing that she was one of the offending group.

When the dinner gong sounded at eight thirty, the doors to the Garden Court opened and Table 2 took their position at the front of the hall near a giant illuminated peach-colored pagoda on the dais. Lanterns, streamers, and dozens of flags festooned the hall; tables sported gold-rimmed china, elegant crystal, and towering centerpieces of spring flowers.

Then there was the banquet, sumptuous even by prewar standards: four courses plus coffee and three wines were served by an army of waiters in red jackets and white gloves. Crab in aspic with tender celery hearts, artfully decorated consommé, guinea fowl with a wild rice croquette—crunchy outside, creamy inside—and roasted tomatoes were a mere preamble to the show-stopping dessert: miniature pagodas carved of peach sherbet—almost too exquisite to eat.

The toasts and speeches were brief and moving. A full orchestra provided a mix of Chinese and big band music, which Faye and the younger Chus enjoyed to its full advantage. It was an enchanted, exotic dream of an evening from the minute she walked up that red carpet and entered the Palace until well after midnight when Howard Chu walked her home.

It occurred to Faye, as she enjoyed her memories in the soothing warmth of the morning sun, that she'd been included for one reason: she'd trusted her instinct to help someone in trouble.

Take a memo, Mrs. Connor: Your gut will always lead you to do the right thing.

With a smile on her face, Faye rolled away from the window and drifted back to sleep. She was still foggy on the connection between Jim Wallace and Mr. Chu, but that could wait.

24

Arnie Platt was dead.

Midge had seen his name in the paper, called his sister back in Springfield to confirm, and tracked Faye down at work to share the news. He died in Buna, New Guinea, just after the first of the year. Details were sketchy, but Faye knew there was a push at that time to retake a vital airfield.

"He was a courageous, honorable, and kind man, and funny, too," Faye said, her voice quivering as she raised her glass. The girls were well into their second martinis in Arnie's honor.

"I'm glad I saw his name in the paper, or I'd never know," Midge commented through her tears. "Arnie and I were still in the early stages of romance, and I'd never met his parents. I only knew his sister, because she came up to Evanston for the Northwestern-Illinois game in '41."

The upbeat strains of "Paper Doll" coming from the jukebox hid the sounds of the girls weeping. It was just after three in the afternoon and the bar was already crowded with pre-dinner imbibers.

"So much potential…gone. His parents must be beside themselves with grief." The tears flowed freely down Midge's cheeks. "I hope he knew how much I cared for him. We never even said 'I love you' to each other, but we sure had some fun. And here I was, all these weeks, having sweet dreams of him, and he was lying dead in the jungle."

"I saw how he looked at you, Midge, and how happy you made him. He clearly adored every second he spent with you." Faye's tears flowed, as well.

Midge drained her glass and popped the pimento olive in her mouth, chewing it with determination for several seconds. "Although I'll never see it, I know the telegram from the government says that he died honorably in service to his country. I say who cares about honor. He's still dead."

Faye signaled to the bartender for another round. For once she saw the wisdom of drowning one's sorrow.

The sadness of Arnie's death intensified courtesy of the grim news from both sides of the world: A group of escaped POWs from the Philippines relayed details of the Bataan Death March, and the unspeakable horrors thousands of American military and civilians still endured in camps. At the same time, the embattled Jewish Ghetto in Warsaw was under siege, escapees being captured in droves and shipped to camps.

This has got to be a mistake.

Faye was reviewing receipts from raw materials deliveries for the last month. Since her proposal to Mr. Dalton on the gravel purchases was denied—"So sorry, Mrs. Connor, we have too many existing contracts in place to make a change in suppliers."—her role had expanded to include reconciliation for all Western Division Infrastructure purchases. Unlike gravel, which was shipped in bulk, ammonium nitrate was shipped in fifty-pound bags, so the receipts should match perfectly with the purchase order. But she was six bags short.

One of the projects must have made an inventory error when the shipment arrived.

Ordinarily, she'd ask Mr. Dalton about the shortfall, but he was traveling until Thursday. She didn't even know who to call in the various divisions. After checking all the receipts one more time, she decided this was too much of a discrepancy to let slide.

She thought for a minute. This was a corporate procurement issue, which was managed by none other than Jim Wallace.

Well, he *doesn't know I saw him flip his lid at The Forbidden City. I need to suck it up, be professional, and do the right thing.*

Folder in hand, she walked down the hall to Procurement. Sylvia Giametti sat at the reception desk.

"Hi, Syl, is Mr. Wallace available? I just need five minutes."

"Hey, girlie girl. Let me check." She picked up the phone and, after a brief exchange, ushered Faye into Wallace's office.

Jim Wallace was perhaps in his late forties, but up close, looked twenty years older. His hair was thinning, his belly protruded far beyond his belt, straining the buttons of his white dress shirt that displayed a few stains from whatever he'd eaten for lunch. Flecks of what Faye could only imagine was dandruff contrasted with the dark rayon of his business suit. His gray eyes lit up when he saw Faye, as if she was bearing a big chocolate cake instead of a problematic report.

"Well, little lady, come on in and let's see what I can do for you." He motioned to close the door of his office.

Uh-oh. Creep alert.

Faye had never directly interacted with Mr. Wallace before, so, despite the repulsion that was beginning to grow in the pit of her stomach, she decided to give him the benefit of the doubt.

"I'm compiling last month's reconciliation, and need to ask about a discrepancy," she said in her most all-business tone, taking a seat at his little conference table and opening a folder.

"Discrepancy. That's a strong word to come out of such a pretty little mouth," he said, sitting next to her.

Determined to remain professional, she cleared her throat and continued.

"I was reviewing this audit this morning, and I can't quite reconcile the receipts. I'm showing that the deliveries of ammonium nitrate to our operations were six bags short last month. Because it's a potentially explosive material, I thought I'd call it to your attention."

Without looking at the papers on the table before him, he leaned closer and asked, "Why do you have this?"

He must have had onions for lunch.

Trying not to wince as his breath hit her nose, Faye leaned back. "Excuse me?"

"Gals like you don't normally do audits, so why do you even have this information?"

"Mr. Dalton asked me to start the reconciliation while he was gone. Is there a problem with that?"

"This is considered confidential."

"I have a security clearance."

Without breaking eye contact, he picked up his phone and asked the switchboard for Personnel.

"Wallace here. Could you please confirm a security clearance for Miss Connor in Dalton's office?"

After a lengthy pause he said, "Right," and slammed the receiver back on its cradle.

Wallace paused for a moment, then looked at the file. "So, what's the issue, then?"

"It's right here. The purchase order is for 1,667 bags shipped from Benicia. The foreman at the Army Airfield out in Merced signed for 1,661."

"Well, there's your problem, doll. His handwriting. That one is actually a seven."

Faye scrutinized the receipt closely.

Dang! I guess it could be a one. It's bad enough to raise the alarm for nothing, but worse yet to have this scum-bucket lord it over me. That'll teach you to flap your yap, Faye Connor. Just apologize and hightail it out of here ASAP.

"I am so sorry to trouble you, Mr. Wallace."

"Well, it's an honest mistake. Listen, I'm sure you have other things to occupy that pretty little head of yours, so just leave this file with me. I'll take care of it. Don't give it another thought. I'll close the loop with Dalton as soon as he's back."

His onion breath once again hit her full force. Faye felt the revulsion gathering at the back of her throat, like a putrid furball. She could feel her face flush in anger and humiliation. In a flash, two things were crystal clear: she wasn't going to make any headway, and she wanted out of there as quickly as possible.

"Of course. And thanks so much, Mr. Wallace," she said in her syrupiest tone. "You've been such a big help. I so appreciate your time."

Wallace rose when she did and followed her to the door.

"If you ever need anything, Miss Connor…anything."

"It's actually *Mrs.* Connor."

"Even better," he said with a wink as he opened the door.

In your dreams, you seething bag of dirt.

Faye beat it back down the hall and remained agitated for the rest of the day.

How can he be so condescending? I had every right to review that report and ask those questions. Well, he said he'd take care of it, so I'm done.

Jerk.

That evening, she discussed the incident with Evie.

"Oh, yeah, Wallace." Evie nodded knowingly. "Wallace-the-Willie, as he's known in our department. He has quite a reputation. The sad thing is, I know at least three people who have fallen for it."

"You mean he seduced them? That middle-aged poor excuse of a man? Yuck!"

"He lured them in with the promise of a big promotion," Evie said as she nodded.

"Can't we report him?"

"Who to? His boss? Herman Smith is an even bigger philanderer, I might point out. Personnel, which is run by another old man? I've seen women who've been fired for pointing fingers."

"It's not fair."

"Sure, it's not, kiddo, but if you're looking for justice, you won't find it in the business world," Evie said, shaking her head. "Some powerful men think secretaries are their own private playthings. The higher ups on the org chart seem to be the worst offenders."

"Mr. Dalton's not like that."

"No, and you're lucky. My advice is just zip it and steer clear."

"This makes me so mad I could spit," Hannah Goldman declared one morning at breakfast as she read the latest news out of Poland. She still didn't know the fate of her relatives in Rotterdam, but based on news reports, she could only assume the worst. "Jews are being gassed by the trainload and no one seems to care." She folded the paper and sipped her tea.

"Surely, after all the effort the US has put into defeating the Nazis, we will not turn our backs on the Jews," Faye responded as she dipped her dry toast into the yolk of her single soft-boiled egg. With butter and jam in short supply, yolky toast was becoming the girls' new breakfast favorite.

"I wouldn't be so sure, *meine goyische* innocent. Even in Hollywood, well-known stars are running as fast as they can from their Jewishness. They know it's the kiss of death at the box office. Edward G. Robinson's real name is Emanuel Goldberg. George Burns is Nathan Birnbaum. Even Eddie Cantor, who at least takes a public stand against anti-Semitism, knew that Isidore Itzkowitz was a door to nowhere in showbiz. Aversion to the Jewish people is kind of baked into Western Civilization."

"Come on, Hannah. Surely you're exaggerating. It

could be they just wanted a name that was easier to pronounce. Besides, a name change is not a matter of life and death. The whole point of fighting this war is to defeat fascism and give people around the world their basic freedoms, including freedom of religion."

"That's what they want us to believe, but actions speak louder than words, sister. Remember when the *SS St. Louis* was turned away in 1939?" Hannah asked, referring to the refugee ship that was not allowed to dock in the US after being turned away by Cuba. "The hundreds of Jewish families on board were sent back to Europe, and who knows what happened to them. Nothing good, I can assure you."

"But, to be fair, how could the State Department have foreseen the fate of those passengers?" Evie countered. "It was 1939, and no one really knew about the camps at that point."

"I call that a lot of hooey. The State Department knew, but the US had strict limits on immigration—even those seeking political asylum. You can thank the Nationalists in charge of the State Department for that. No one, not even the great FDR himself, saw a need for exceptions. It was a very dangerous precedent that the rest of the Allies were happy to follow. You wait," she warned as she poured her second cup of tea. "Next month, when the US and Great Britain meet in Bermuda to discuss the Jewish issue, you watch how much is accomplished."

Faye recalled Hannah's warning at the end about April when she saw the coverage in the papers. At the conclusion of the Bermuda Conference, plans for post-war Jewry remained unclear; the conference frittered away the days trying to defer responsibility. US immigration quotas were not revised and the British prohibition of Jews seeking refuge in Palestine remained firmly in place. The conference floated the idea of relocating Jewish refugees to Africa until the end of the war, because of transportation difficulties in Europe.

Africa? Ridiculous! Faye envisioned the logistics nightmares that would entail. *Hannah was right. Jews aren't welcome anywhere. And most Americans don't seem to give a fig.*

A few weeks later, seated next to Hannah at a benefit dinner for Jewish relief at Temple Emanu-El, Faye proudly wrote out a big fat check.

The war in Africa was over! Mussolini's African Empire and Hitler's strategy both fizzled in the deserts of Tunisia. The entire continent was cleansed and purged of Fascist and Nazi tyranny.

Finally, some progress.

Faye felt certain that Sicily would be liberated next. Then, the Allies would march right up the boot of Italy and into the heart of Europe. She looked at the map above the dining table and imagined US forces getting closer and closer to Berlin.

The rainy winter of 1943 gave way to a foggy spring. More than once, Faye found herself on courier duty in the wilds of the San Mateo Coastline or the Marin Headlands when the fog rolled in and made driving difficult. She crept her way along the narrow roads, hoping to high heaven she wouldn't meet a military transport or supply truck coming from the opposite direction.

Meetings on the Canadian hydroelectric projects concluded in mid-June, rather abruptly in Faye's opinion. One day she was full speed ahead on agendas and planning, the next day the plug was pulled. She was to prepare a summary to date for the files but cancel all meetings for the foreseeable future on order from the corner office. Her experience running errands for Dalton had taught her what *not* to do in situations like this: ask why. She was fully aware of her need-to-know status. Canceling meetings, as it turned out, was almost as much work as setting them up, and Faye found herself at the office until well after eight p.m. for the rest of the week.

Around the same time, Faye felt with some regularity that she was being followed. Signs were subtle, so subtle she was able to rationalize them. The dark-suited men loitering in alleyways as she walked home, careful to avoid eye contact, could be guys having a smoke. An unfamiliar, unmarked delivery truck waiting opposite the garage where Mr. Dalton parked his car could be a new supplier.

Nonetheless, a growing sinister feeling began to invade her psyche, mostly at night or when she was alone. She wondered if she should share her suspicions with anyone, and then decided to wait until she discovered more concrete evidence. The last thing she wanted was the top brass to think she was being a scaredy-cat girl, unfit for the assignment.

As much as she wanted to believe her head was playing tricks on her, the feeling persisted. She took extra care to go out only in groups, keep to well-lit places, and stay ahead of her imagination.

A rare Saturday of summer sun prompted the Fella Place trio to pack up a picnic and head to Lands End for an outing at the beach. With temperatures in the nineties predicted for the weekend, the girls wore their bathing suits under their sun dresses. The rationing of leather shoes— three pairs per person per year—contributed to the popularity of canvas shoes, and all three friends sported espadrilles in vivid fabrics with rope soles and ribbon laces. Spirits were almost as bright as the sunshine as they walked down the hill and caught the Geary streetcar to the Outer Richmond.

On such a warm day, the girls knew that Ocean Beach, with its popular Playland-at-the-Beach amusement park, would be swamped, so they opted instead for the more secluded Baker Beach, closer to the Golden Gate. They exited the streetcar at Thirty-Second Street and walked a few blocks north through Lincoln Park. Trails through the cypress and eucalyptus trees led down to the beach, its soft gray sand dotted with bright umbrellas. The girls spread their blanket and spent the afternoon sunning and gossiping.

"Just think. There could be enemy subs right out there," Evie said, gazing out at the horizon.

"What a thought! It looks so postcard perfect," Faye replied as she slathered her legs with suntan oil. Now that she so often went without stockings, she took this opportunity to get some color on her all-too-pale limbs.

"It's true," Hannah chimed in. "They're probably just biding their time until they get the order to storm this very beach."

"They'll have a doozy of a challenge." Evie gestured to

the cliffs behind them, swathed in camouflage netting, the olive-colored cloth ties fluttering in the breeze. "Do you see the fortifications up on the hill? Not only do they have big cannons up there, they have sub nets and mine fields all over the entrance to the bay."

"It's hard to believe all those explosives are lurking right under the surface." Hannah squinted at the bridge and the calm waters that, today, reflected the clear blue sky.

Faye listened to the other girls' chatter, withholding the first-hand information she had of the lay of the land in the Presidio and the many fortifications around the entrance to the bay. She'd been many times to the posts on both sides of the bay and seen the massive harbor-defense guns up close. She held her tongue rather than project anything other than an ordinary citizen's knowledge.

"I, for one, want to forget about what's under the surface and drink in this glorious sunshine," Faye said, hoping to change the subject. Despite her efforts, the steady stream of warships, troop carriers, and supply ships under the bridge was an impressive reminder of the conflict across the sea, so Faye tried another avenue.

"A day like today makes me want to think about life without war," she said, stretching out on the blanket. "Let's imagine that war is over. What will our lives be like? Hannah, you go first."

Hannah didn't miss a beat. "I'm going to marry a nice Jewish boy, who will approve of my going back to school to get my law degree. Maybe Melvin Steinberger. He always liked me in college, and I'm sure he will go to work for his dad's production company down south when he gets home."

"Ooh-ooh. Hollywood," Evie teased.

"The crossroads of glamor and power, yes, that's where

I want to spend my life. Besides, UCLA has a great law school, and they may accept more women after the war. We'll have a little Spanish colonial in Westwood where I will host the most brilliant dinner parties. Our house will be a salon for people from the arts and politics, always engaged in the most fascinating exchange of ideas." She sipped her Coke, then continued, "I might work, just part time, of course, for the cause of a Jewish homeland in Palestine. Of course, I will have several precocious children, all excellent students, musicians, and athletes." After a brief pause, she added wistfully, "I really should write to Melvin."

"Would you ever move to Palestine to help build a Jewish homeland?" Faye had heard vague whispers of such a plan for after the war.

Thinking for a few seconds, Hannah replied, "Doubtful. I'm glad to send money and talk up the cause, but *kibbutz* living just isn't for me. The desert just can't be good for the skin, and mine tends to be dry as it is. How about you, *meine goyische* Faye?"

"Oh, gosh. My after-the-war dream changes on an hourly basis these days. Steve and I always thought we would head to Texas where he would work in the oil industry, but I don't know any more. I like working, but I know the boys will all need our jobs when they get back. Besides, I always imagined myself with four or so kids, and I do want to be a great mom and role model for them."

"Watch out, suburbs, here comes Faye," Evie chortled.

"We'll probably end up back in the Chicago area," Faye continued. "This experience has taught me that family is important, no matter how much they annoy you at times."

"So, all of your work experience will go for nothing when the war's over?" Evie sounded incredulous.

"It's not for nothing. I've learned organization, budgeting, and negotiation, all valuable housewife skills, right? I may be good at my job, but it's temporary—just for the duration. How about you, Eves?"

After a thoughtful pause, Evie said with conviction, "I want to be the CEO of Gregor Corp."

After a very weighty pause, all three girls broke into peals of laughter.

Dream on, sister.

By the end of the summer, the tide of war in Europe had shifted considerably. Newsreels documented the invasion of Sicily in July, and the girls spent several evenings a week in the Telenews Theater to keep up on events. In late July, Mussolini lost the support and confidence of the Italian people and was arrested. By early September, Italy was out of the war.

As the girls discussed frequently at the breakfast table, Italy's surrender didn't mean there weren't some hard days ahead on the Italian Peninsula. The German occupation force viewed Italy as a last stand, and they appeared ready to fight to the death to maintain their grip on The Boot. Excitement that the US was about to gain a foothold on the European mainland mingled with apprehension about major battles to come.

Closer to home, the defense efforts only seemed to intensify. Fire watches for Japanese air raids were commonplace these days. Stations set up throughout the city could distribute gas masks and provide aid in case of an attack with chemical bombs. And a village of barracks sprang up practically overnight in Civic Center Plaza, part of the seemingly unending effort to house the continual stream of service men shipping out or shipping in on a daily basis.

The September twentieth issue of *Life* magazine arrived at the Fella Place flat with a shocking exposé that included the first images of dead Americans ever published. The girls shared the issue, which fueled an animated discussion over their boiled eggs and toast with margarine.

"Where these boys fell, a part of freedom fell," Evie read, the magazine open to the image of three dead soldiers on the beach at Buna. "Why would they show this?" she asked.

"To sell magazines," Faye suggested, glancing over her shoulder. You couldn't see faces, just twisted bodies washed up on the shore, the bombed hulk of a landing craft in the background.

How sad. Arnie died on Buna. One of these bodies could be Arnie Pratt.

"People are so gung-ho to see dead soldiers sprawled out on the beach?" Evie looked upset by the images.

Ever the conspiracy theorist, Hannah surmised, "I think it's a ploy by the government to start renewed energy for the war effort."

Faye and Evie raised their eyebrows in unison and exchanged a glance of skepticism.

"Think about it," Hannah continued, her typical tone of determination apparent. "This war has been dragging on for months—much longer than anyone imagined. The US got involved late in the game and had a rough few months in the beginning. People are exhausted by the fear of invasion and just want this to end. These images show John Q. Public, very graphically, why we still need to stay involved."

"You could be right," Faye conceded, studying the page, "but just think of how the families of these boys must feel."

"You think the US government is going to care about the feelings of a few families versus the sentiment of the entire American public?"

The silence was broken only by the crunch of toast.

After a long pause, Evie added, "Well, maybe a final rally of support will make the difference. We've taken Sicily and are working our way toward Rome. That's some real progress. A little rah, rah, rah from the home front may just move the ball into the endzone."

"'End' being key," Faye added. "It may be the fourth quarter, but I still don't see an end."

26

———

One evening at the end of September, Faye and Mr. Dalton worked late on a quarterly report. Dalton left just after seven thirty, and Faye stayed on to finish collating. As much as she hated to admit it, the empty building gave her the heebie-jeebies. Creaks and groans and phantom footsteps seemed to emanate from the darkened hallways.

Stop it! There's a security guard in the lobby and one at sixth floor reception. You're making yourself cuckoo.

She gave her head a vigorous shake, as if trying to dislodge the panic growing in her imagination, and focused hard on the report.

Faye finished up just after nine and, as a reward for slogging through a tedious project, treated herself to a plate of pancakes at Sears Fine Foods, which was right on the way home. When she emerged, tummy full and anxiety level severely reduced, the fog was on the deck and visibility was less than a block. As she made her way slowly up the hill, a crowded cable car emerged from the mist on Sutter and was again enveloped before it got to Pine, leaving Faye alone on the slick sidewalk.

Her footsteps echoed off the buildings on the opposite side of the street, only adding to that creepy feeling of being followed. Her pulse, elevated from the climb, started to race and her imagination took off. It was just that kind of night when trees took on a spooky halo and every sound was amplified. The uphill path home seemed to grow longer, rather than shorter, as if her trepidation had immersed these familiar streets in a viscous stupor.

Halfway up the hill, Faye stopped quickly and glanced over her shoulder, trying to see through the fog.

Now you knock it off, Faye Connor. You are really bonkers tonight.

The feeling of being stalked had gotten the better of her more than once, and she was determined to keep her wits together. Her pace quickened as she glanced back down the hill, looking for signs of someone else on the street.

Finally on the home stretch, she turned the corner into Fella Place. A hand shot out from the shadows and grabbed her arm. She shrieked and jumped back, flailing as the arm crept up to her neck. She screamed again, her sense of reality muffled by the thundering of her heart.

"Faye, it's me."

Mist swirled around a lone streetlight, obscuring the face behind her. But the voice, as familiar to her as her own nose, finally registered. *Steve.*

"Steve?"

His arms were around her, hugging her close. His scent was different—tobacco, booze, armpits in need of a shower, and damp wool—but he felt so right. *Steve. Is he real? Is he here?*

Tears began to flow silently, and her answer came as his mouth made its way across her cheek and found hers.

Faye's flat mates were both out that evening, so she and Steve had the place to themselves. She was glad to find some pork chops in the fridge. She sent Steve to the shower while she cooked him some supper. Adding some greens and beets from the roof garden, she put together a decent meal for him.

As she watched him scarf down his supper, Faye still couldn't believe it.

He's here. All in one piece and evidently starving.

Three eggs and a nice fat chop disappeared, then he tackled his salad, answering Faye's questions between bites.

"I'm so sorry I had to work late. Were you waiting long?"

"Only about an hour or so. Gave me time for it to sink in that I was back stateside. I would've wired you, but one day I was hacking through the jungle clearing supply roads and the next I was yanked out of my unit and on a transport home."

He'd volunteered for a new assignment. Details were sparse: he just knew he would be sent to the "European Theatre of War." The US forces that had landed in Salerno earlier in September were slowly making their way north, so Italy was a good bet.

"But I'm yours until the fifth, sweet pea." He reached across the table for her hand. He looked tired. His face, tan from the tropical sun, sported new fine lines at the corners of his green eyes. And there was something different about those eyes.

Was it sadness?

"I can't believe you're really here." Tears slipped down Faye's cheeks as she clutched his hand. "I think of you every waking moment and dream about you all night long."

Steve pulled her from her chair and into his lap. He snuggled his freshly shaved face into the curve of her neck. His gentle kisses kindled a feeling that made the desolation of the last year and a half evaporate. As his hands found the hooks on her bra, Faye pulled away slightly and looked him straight in the eyes. The joyous spark she had known for all those years was gone, but, right now, the lust she saw would do just fine. She left the dishes unwashed in the sink and led him to her bedroom.

It took Faye less than a day to begin to wonder who this man really was. He looked like Steve but he behaved like someone she'd never met. Her Steve was supportive and chatty, always cracking jokes and ready for fun. Now he acted subdued and distracted. He rarely initiated a conversation, answering Faye's barrage of questions with terse, incomplete responses.

It became clear early in his visit that the "everything's fine here" line he repeated in his letters bore no resemblance to the truth. He didn't want to talk about his time in the Pacific, so Faye stopped asking after the first day. As exhausted as he seemed, he rarely slept. Rather, he smoked endless cigarettes and stared into the darkness for hours.

He knew about Arnie's death and seemed to sink into grief for his good friend when he was around Midge. Sensing this, Midge made herself scarce and Faye missed her moral support. The hours clicked by filled with a fretful uncertainty for Faye. *Should I keep trying to get him to open up? Will I say something that sets him off? Will he ever confide in me again?*

For ten days, Mr. and Mrs. Steven Connor strolled aimlessly around the city. They used to communicate without saying a word, but that kind of connection seemed long gone. Golden Gate Park was glorious this time of year, and they spent hours in the botanical garden—meandering in silence along its pathways. Many of the park's vast lawns had been turned into victory gardens, and they wordlessly watched men and women tend to neat plots of vegetables marked off by low picket fences. They held hands, fingers entwined, as they mutely traversed the hills from the Sutro Forest to the Marin Headlands. In the evenings, they met up with Faye's friends or took in a movie. Even in social settings, Steve seemed disengaged and distracted, and at times impatient for the evening to end.

She flashed back to last year when they found Jeff Blake drunk in the alley and witnessed the aftershocks of his experience on the *USS San Francisco*. The one big difference: Jeff had opened up and talked freely to them about his feelings. Steve was locked down, utterly silent.

One night as they joined a group of Faye's friends at a bar, Simon Miller appeared out of the crowd and gave Faye a hello hug. Steve was immediately on guard, like the alpha male of a pack of wild dogs. As the two men shook hands, Faye watched Steve stiffen, his eyes darting suspiciously from her to Simon, a look of hurt with a healthy dose of resentment creeping across his face.

"Simon and I have worked on some projects together," Faye explained after her initial introductions. "He's an expert on hydroelectric systems."

"Oh, really. And what branch are you in?"

"I'm a Canadian civilian assigned to the office of the Minister of Mines and Resources."

Steve's eyes narrowed. "Sounds pretty cushy." He took a deep swig of his whiskey and soda.

Faye stared at him in shock. In all the years she'd known Steve, he was rarely sarcastic and never rude.

Simon, *bless him*, made the first move to break the very awkward silence that ensued among the three of them.

"Well, I'm on my way. Faye, we'll see you soon. Steve"—he offered his hand—"it was a pleasure."

"Right." Steve reluctantly shook Simon's hand.

Simon simply disappeared back into the crowd.

"So, tell me about this Simon guy," Steve demanded as soon as Simon was out of ear shot.

"He's a colleague and a friend. We met through work. We cross paths outside the office now and again. He's interesting to talk to."

"Friend, eh? Does he know that?"

"He certainly does, and I am really disappointed that you even ask."

"Well, he looks at you like he'd like to be more than friends."

"Steven Sean Connor! I am surprised at you. I've had lots of guy friends over the last six years we've known each other, and you never once acted jealous. Not once. This is *me. Faye.*"

Steve had no response. He just drained his glass and sat there, obviously seething.

"I'm going home." She walked purposefully toward the door.

By the time Steve caught up with her, his suspicion had

turned to remorse. "Sorry," he whispered as he caught her arm. "I don't know what's got into me."

Hand-in-hand, they walked the remaining blocks back to Fella Place—again in silence.

The full extent of Steve's unseen wounds became clearer to Faye on a visit to Playland at the Beach. Steve was excited at the prospect of a visit to the amusement park, and Faye hoped the day would help him finally relax. They whooped and laughed on the Big Dipper roller coaster and Shoot the Chutes, then snuggled close on the Ferris wheel as they enjoyed the views clear across San Francisco and far out to sea. Each time they approached the crest of the wheel, Faye anticipated the weightless sensation that came at the beginning of each descent—a floating feeling that buoyed her spirits. Steve pulled her close, Faye gave in to a wave of relief.

Good. He's here in the present.

The mood held while they shared an IT'S-IT ice cream sandwich but crashed into sheer terror in the Fun House.

Faye saw his eyes flood with anxiety as soon as they walked past Laughing Sal, a giant automated puppet that cackled loudly and incessantly at the entrance to the hall.

"We don't have to do this one," Faye suggested, offering him an easy out.

Steve pushed forward with uncharacteristic bravado. "Why not? I'm fine. It's just a fucking doll," he barked.

Faye sensed his anxiety intensify with every passing second.

They were halfway through the mirror maze when Steve's apprehension morphed into full-blown panic. He broke into a flop sweat and began to breathe rapidly. He jerked to-and-fro, confused and clearly terrified. Faye grabbed his hand and pulled him back through the front door to a park bench across from the entrance.

"Steve, are you all right?" Faye asked gently, rubbing his shoulders.

Steve just sat there, silent and shaking, his head in his hands.

"Steve, talk to me. What's going on? Please let me help."

No response. No eye contact.

After a good ten minutes, his shaking began to subside. Without a word, he pulled Faye into a hug and held her close for several minutes. Then he released her and stood. "Let's go. I'm really tired."

They wordlessly rode the streetcar back downtown, and Steve napped for the rest of the afternoon.

After that incident, Faye, wracked with worry, didn't know what to do. She was perplexed, not so much by Steve's volatility as his refusal to engage. His silence fueled her mounting concerns, and she grew more and more frustrated because she didn't know how to help him. She began to make excuses, to her friends and to herself.

He's seen things he'd rather forget. I'll be patient. He's leaving again in a few days, and I don't want to spend our precious time together bickering. I'll just be patient. He just needs rest. I'm sure he'll be back to his own self soon. I'll be patient.

While Faye managed to get most days off during Steve's furlough, there were a few days she had to work, and Steve was on his own. Bad idea. Both times she found him sloppy drunk on her bed, reeking of cheap whiskey and struggling silently with his own demons.

As for the sex, it was a disaster. More than once, Steve couldn't perform, which only made him more sullen. The few times they were successful, he was brusque and demanding, so unlike her Steve. Neither of them could relax. It was fast, forgettable, and frankly embarrassing.

The last night of his leave, Faye lay awake beside Steve, who was fretfully drifting in and out of sleep. She realized now that love was rare and, since her high school days, she had taken it for granted. She turned on her side away from Steve as tears spilled silently down her cheeks.

I want him back.

On October fifth, as she watched the troop train pull out of Martinez station, Faye wondered if the Steve she knew would ever return. The sadness she felt was not so much for his departure, but for the realization that he was never really home and the growing fear that he might already be gone for good.

"You've got to give him a break," Midge counseled. "Who knows what he's been through. I've read some accounts of the Pacific campaigns that give me absolute nightmares."

"I understand that, really, I do. But he can't keep it bottled up," Faye replied after a long pull on her highball. "It's like he's lost his trust in me. It'll drive both of us nuts."

"Look, there's more of this war to come," Midge continued. "Who knows how long it will go on, but I'm sure retaking Europe isn't going to be any kind of cakewalk. If Steve's headed that way, he'll be in the thick of it. There's bound to be even more emotional damage. You're lucky. At least he's still alive with all limbs attached."

Faye could tell Midge was thinking of Arnie and caught the tremor in her normally strong voice.

Midge took a long drag on her cigarette, then continued. "Listen. You can work on the emotional stuff when he's back home for good. If time heals all wounds, I'm thinking that includes those of the mind. You and Steve have something too special to let it slip away."

"Hey, sugar, you rationed?" A young soldier interrupted, gazing hopefully at Midge.

She immediately took the bait. "Well, private, I see you're on active duty."

"You bet I am. Wanna dance?"

Midge stubbed her cig into the ashtray as she said to Faye, "Hold that thought and order another round while I dance with the private here. What's your name, soldier?"

"Private First-Class Arnold Harris from Baltimore, Maryland. You can call me Arnie."

The girls both froze and looked at each other. Then a slow smile spread over Midge's face.

"Well, Arnie from Baltimore, I hope your stompers are good and greased, 'cause I feel like knocking one out."

Faye sipped her drink and puffed shallowly on her cigarette, admiring Midge's ability to find joy every day, despite her loss. She and the private cut quite a rug among the other couples on the dance floor. Arnie Platt would be proud.

Steve's letters started to arrive the week after his furlough, faster than she was used to due to his stateside posting. His tone sounded upbeat and confident, a total departure from the Steve she had just seen.

I'm at Camp Abbot in Oregon for specialized training. The program is really interesting. It's comforting to know I'm not that far away from you and will try to visit again before we ship out. I'll keep you posted.

Faye read his letter with decidedly unsettled feelings, wondering what she should believe. As she folded it and returned it to the envelope, she scolded herself. *He is your husband, for better or worse. Maybe this is the 'worse' part. Don't wig out. Let's look forward, not back.*

Steve returned to her in mid-November, about ten days before Thanksgiving. It was a quick visit, just overnight, as he needed to catch a train to meet up with his new unit, the 19th Engineering Regiment, in New York the following week.

One night. About twenty hours. Faye decided to make every minute count.

Wearing a new wide-brimmed velvet hat with an elegant peacock feather, Faye met him at the Ferry Building and took him to the Saint Francis Hotel on Union Square. If they were going to have any meaningful repair of their relationship during this layover, she wanted to do it out of earshot of her roommates. The way she figured it, an opportunity to mend their marriage was well worth a splurge. She reserved a deluxe room in the opulent hotel, and she felt Steve begin to relax as soon as they stepped into the marble and gilt lobby.

It worked.

At Faye's suggestion, they ordered in a room service supper and dined near the picture window, the city twinkling in the background. The dimout order had just been lifted, so the city's lights shone brightly once again. The glorious view from the twelfth floor gently fanned the embers of romance that had for so long been dormant. They sat admiring the lights of Union Square and nursing a very expensive bottle of bourbon for several hours. Steve talked about his recent training and news from his family. Faye told him a string of funny stories about her San Francisco experience. They chatted and cuddled and, as Steve continued to relax, he very slowly opened up.

"Nothing prepared me for war. It's terrible, sweet pea."

"I can't imagine."

"How could anybody who hasn't been there?" he whispered, remembering. "Before I shipped out, my only experience with death was when Grandpa Mike died. He was eighty-seven years old, laughing right up until he dropped dead on the golf course. Remember his wake?"

Faye nodded. "He was laid out in his Sunday suit, surrounded by his friends and family, all telling stories and drinking up a storm."

"Well, in combat people are dying left and right. No one even pauses. One minute you're schlepping through the jungle with your buddies, the next minute the guy next to you is blown to smithereens."

"Oh, Steve." Faye snuggled in tighter.

"One time, I was sent in for the third wave. So grisly. I was knee deep in mud, rain so thick I couldn't see the end of my own nose and dead soldiers lining the trail. I probably knew some of them…most of them…but when you're under fire, you just need to keep moving. There's no time to honor them or their sacrifice. We all knew it was only blind luck that we weren't lying there, too."

Another pause. Faye stayed silent, her breath in sync with his.

"So many of my friends are gone," Steve continued. "Arnie, Ron Beckham, and George Foster from my class."

"I didn't know about Ron and George. We only found out about Arnie because Midge saw his name in the paper."

"Ma just told me that my cousin Frank is MIA in Italy." Tears began to slide down his cheeks. "They're all dead or captured, and I'm here with you."

"Steve, you can't feel guilty because you survived."

"But I do." He suddenly grabbed her into an embrace. "I know it's important to defeat Fascism, but I'm afraid to die, Faye. And I'm ashamed to say it."

For several minutes, he just clung to her and wept. Faye held him tight. When he finally calmed, he rose and looked out the window. "You deserve better, Faye. I shouldn't bring this sadness home."

Faye spun him around and looked him straight in the eye. "Now you listen to me, Steven Connor. We are married. For better or worse. What impacts you, impacts me. Your pain is my pain." She lifted her hand to his cheek. "And your joy is my joy."

"I love you so much."

She kissed him gently. He gathered her into his arms, kissing her back, his hand finding its way under her skirt, teasing her thighs. She stood up and stepped away from him, stripped off all her clothes, and guided him over to the bed.

This time the sex was astonishing. For a few hours, there was no war, no fear, no guilt, just their bodies eager, wanting, pleading for more. They broke free of sadness and soared in the pure bliss of each other. Spent and comforted, they fell asleep, cuddled together, Steve's smoky, bourbon-laced breath deep and even on her cheek.

The next morning broke clear and crisp, not a wisp of fog in sight. As they rode the streetcar back down to the ferry, Faye felt as if a huge weight had been lifted from her heart. Steve's arm around her shoulders sparked memories of all those years together back in Evanston, carefree and in love. While Faye knew full well that all was not right with the world, she at least once again had hope.

27

F or Thanksgiving 1943, the girls hosted another knock-out dinner. The cast of guests included some returnees, but several new faces. Midge and her friends from the Kaiser Shipyard returned, Midge bringing a sergeant from Minnesota who was stationed at Fort Point. Hannah had just started seeing a nice Jewish lieutenant, who was accompanied by two more buddies from his unit. Madeline and Howard Chu stopped by for dessert and drinks. Notably absent were Helen and Simon Miller.

Hmm. Simon Miller.

It occurred to Faye that, ever since the Niagara talks broke off, she'd barely seen Simon. The one time their paths crossed was that night in the bar with Steve—an encounter she'd rather forget.

Then, as if the mere thought of Simon made him materialize, the doorbell rang—and there he was. Dapper as ever and bearing a bottle of French cognac—she wasn't about to ask where that came from, he was greeted by a cheer from the crowd.

"Sorry I'm so late," he said. "My superiors should really recognize your American holidays."

"Well, let's get you a plate. There's plenty of food left," Evie said, scooting over to make room beside her. "What have you been up to lately? We haven't seen you around the Gregor Corp offices much."

"I've actually started on a new assignment," he said, clearly enjoying his place as the center of attention. "I've been tapped to work on refugee resettlement."

The buzz of conversation around the room stopped to hear Simon's story.

"This refugee situation in Europe is far worse than anyone imagined. With displaced Eastern Europeans, liberated Jews, and war brides, we're anticipating a massive migration wave over the next several years, both in the US and Canada. I'm on loan to a multinational group to try and figure out how to process and house folks until they can be resettled."

"Gosh, how interesting," Hannah gushed, leaning in closer to Simon while she noticeably batted her eyelashes. This project was right up her alley. "I should think even locating missing relatives will be a monumental task, much less providing shelter, food, and hospital services until they can find permanent homes."

"Very true," Simon said solemnly. "There are thousands of displaced people all over Europe whose homes have been destroyed. Besides, national boundaries will surely change. Poor Poland is certain to be redrawn yet again."

"Have you thought of getting the Hollywood crowd involved? I'm sure I can put you in touch with some people who can help…"

"This is the best Thanksgiving ever!" Madeline plunked

herself down next to Faye and pulled a sleek Art Nouveau cigarette case out of her evening bag. "Have a cig?"

Faye accepted a Camel, lit up, and settled back in her chair. She'd met up with Madeline now and again for drinks or tea over the last several months and always enjoyed their conversations. It impressed Faye that a young woman from a wealthy family was so willing to roll up her sleeves and do the grunt work. "So, Miss Chu, how's life as a reporter treating you?"

"Well, my editor sends me out to any event in China-town. Period. He's got it in for me because, I'm a girl, I'm not white, and I have a college education, something no one else in the newsroom has," she lamented. "My dream is having a big fat front-page byline instead of being the Chinese girl reporter. Send me to cover City Hall, the dock-workers union, I'll even take the Tenderloin police beat—anything where there's hard news. If I have to cover one more Cherry Blossom Parade or Tai Chi tournament, I'm going to gag."

"Knowing you and how persistent you are, you'll get there," Faye replied. "I've been meaning to ask: how does your father know Jim Wallace?"

"Baba knows everyone. Who is Jim Wallace?"

"Just one of our execs. I saw him arguing with your dad months ago at the Forbidden City."

"Arguing! How exciting. Well, there's only one way to find out. Let's ask him."

"*Oh*, that won't be necessary. I'm just curious and thought you might know."

"Listen, Douglas Chu is not only well connected, but a straight shooter. If he knows this Wallace guy, he'll tell you. If he doesn't, he'll tell you. If it's none of your beeswax, he'll tell you." She took another drag. "I know! Baba and I have *dim sum* every Saturday. Come join us this week," she suggested. "He'd love to see you again, and we can ask about Wallace in casual conversation."

"I accept! Even if the Wallace topic goes nowhere, I'd love to get to know your father better."

As the evening wore on, dishes were stacked, people departed, new faces arrived, tables were pushed back, the radio was turned up, and the dancing began. Faye circulated among the crowd, collecting glasses and replenishing drinks.

"Another?" she asked Simon, offering a tray of whiskey highballs.

"Don't mind if I do!" He took a glass, then patted the chair next to him. "Come sit." Faye helped herself to the last highball, plopped down next to Simon, and held up her glass.

"To peace," she toasted.

"To peace," he replied.

They both drank deeply.

"And how have you been, Mrs. Connor?"

"Frankly...embarrassed."

"For Pete's sake, why?"

"For the way Steve treated you in the bar."

A smile teased Simon's mouth. He lit a cigarette and exhaled the smoke in a steady stream.

"He was just protecting his woman."

"Don't make excuses for him. He's known me for years and is well aware of friendships I have with men, which in no way lessens my commitment to him. His behavior to you was inexcusable."

He gently took her hand across the table.

"Maybe he sensed my true feelings."

Not sure she heard him right, Faye leaned toward him and lowered her voice, not wanting to be overheard.

"What are you talking about?"

"I've been stuck on you since you doused me in coffee, Faye. But I knew it would be a mistake to get involved."

Are you kidding me?

"And why is that?" she whispered, her voice smooth and low.

"Lovers are a dime a dozen. Friends are something rare. Besides, you were obviously in love with someone else and I have a hard time with rejection."

Little do you know, Simon Miller, that there have been many times over the past year when I would have been your lover. All that smoldering manliness is hard to resist when loneliness sets in. But you are right—it would have been a mistake.

"Thanks for being so wise," she replied after a long sip of her drink. "Steve was in bad shape during that visit, but we've sorted through a lot of issues. This blasted war is tough on marriage."

"I suppose he's headed to Italy, then?"

"That seems to be where the action is these days. He really didn't share very much information at all."

"These coming months are going to be especially tough in Europe, I fear."

"I'm terrified to think about it too much."

"Well, if you ever need a friend…" He held up his glass.

"Deal."

They clinked on it.

～

A bit later, when the dancing was in full swing, Midge cornered Faye in the kitchen. "Pistol Packin' Mama" with Bing Crosby and the Andrews Sisters blared from the other room, and Faye glanced in surprise at Midge, the Dance Queen of the Bay Area, when she picked up a towel and started drying dishes.

"I thought you'd be leading the conga line."

"I will be, but I wanted to ask you something. Is it all right with you if I put the moves on Simon?"

That's out of the blue. But as the seconds passed, it made more and more sense. *Midge and Simon. Brilliant.*

"Why wouldn't it be?" Faye purposefully tried to sound nonchalant.

"I don't know. You seem to see him a lot at work, and I just want to make sure you don't have any objection. And it could have been my imagination, but I thought you two might have a thing going."

"A thing! Midge, you know me better than that. I'd never betray Steve."

"Just checking. You know me: the more gentlemen admirers, the better! I've kinda had the hots for Simon from the first moment we saw him on the ferry, but I was with Arnie then."

Midge set the plate she was drying down with a clatter and picked up another.

"Before you give your final answer, think about this carefully," Midge continued. "There's no way this flirtation will be permanent. So, when we break up, which we probably will in a month or so, I want to be sure it won't cause any uneasiness for you at work."

"Don't worry. Our project got put on hold, and he seems to be involved in this refugee thing. I doubt our paths will even cross. Thanks for asking, but you get a thumbs up from me. Have fun but be careful. He's quite the ladies' man."

She leaned toward Faye and in her sultriest voice said, "Perfect for a man's lady, don't you think?"

With that, she tossed the towel aside, kissed Faye on the cheek, and made a beeline back to the dancing, a look of pure resolve on her face. The tune had changed to Lena Horne's smoldering rendition of "Stormy Weather," and Midge was not one to let a slow dance go to waste.

Faye shook her head as she scrubbed the roasting pan. She'd long both admired and been horrified by Midge's free and easy view of sex. On the one hand, having lots of practice in the bedroom had its appeal, but Faye wondered how Midge rationalized the dangers—like the potential for pregnancy or some awful disease. There had been so many articles in the papers about how cases of syphilis and VD were at all-time highs, not to mention the decided possibilities of a broken heart or a ruined reputation or all of the above. As she set the roaster on a towel to air-dry, she argued silently that Midge was a strong girl who knew how to weld a Liberty ship together from bow to stern. Surely, she could take care of herself in the romance department.

After all the guests departed and Faye climbed into bed, she reviewed Simon's confession in her head. All those months when she thought they were just friends.

I guess I'm not the only one with secrets to keep. I wonder how many more are floating around.

The following Saturday, Faye walked over Nob Hill and descended into the heart of Chinatown for her brunch with Madeline and Douglas Chu.

"Just meet me at the corner of Sacramento and Stockton. Trust me—you'll never find the tea house on your own," Madeline had instructed.

She was right. Hang Ah Tea Room was tucked away in a narrow alley across from one of the few green spaces in Chinatown. Its unmarked doorway in a weathered brick building held no clue of the delights inside. Madeline exchanged pleasantries with the host and then led Faye to the far corner of a small dining room. Mr. Chu stood smiling at what seemed to be their regular table.

"Welcome to our *yum cha*, Mrs. Connor. It's a pleasure to see you again!" As always, Mr. Chu was impeccably dressed and groomed.

"We always start with tea, which is the cornerstone of *dim sum*," he explained, pouring Faye a cup of fragrant brew from the pot on the table. "It is said that this tradition began as little snacks in the tea houses of Guangzhou and made its way to San Francisco in the 1920s."

"We've been coming here every Saturday for my entire life," Madeline added. "When I was about ten, it turned into a regular date for just Baba and me."

"One neither of us dares to miss."

"Well, I am so honored to be invited to join you," Faye said as a waiter appeared with a heavily laden steam cart. The aroma was delicious. The three tiers of the cart were stacked to overflowing with bamboo baskets and covered serving dishes. After an extended exchange between both Chus and the server, the cart disappeared, and five dishes remained on the table.

"This is just a start," Mr. Chu explained and gestured to the dishes with his chopsticks. "Here we have shrimp *shumai*, bean curd, taro dumplings. These are pork meatballs, and here we have a special treat—phoenix claw."

"Which are chicken feet, but don't be scared. They're delicious," Madeline reassured her.

After a brief chopsticks tutorial, Faye tasted every dish. The conversation centered around the war, of course, some new real estate projects Mr. Chu was planning, and Madeline's strategy for becoming a Pulitzer Prize winning reporter. With the second round of food—soup-filled dumplings or *xiaolongbao*, barbecue pork buns, and sesame balls, Mr. Chu asked about Faye's work.

"Gregor Corp is involved in just about every major construction project on the West Coast," he commented, pouring another round of tea. "It must be an exciting place to work."

"Oh, it is," Faye said, who noticed that Madeline raised her eyebrows twice in a row, a silent signal that this might be a good time to steer the conversation toward the question at hand.

"In fact, I was wondering if you ever had any business with Gregor Corp?"

"Why do you ask?"

"Well…" She paused to formulate the best way to ask. "I was with a group of friends at the Forbidden City nightclub several months ago, really before I even knew Madeline, but I remember seeing you there. You were meeting with one of our executives, a Mr. Jim Wallace. I was just wondering if there are any projects we might be collaborating on."

Madeline's smile and subtle nod reassured her that the way she had posed the question was acceptable, and Faye began to relax.

"Ha!" Mr. Chu said abruptly and speared another sesame ball. Faye and Madeline just looked at each other, wondering if he was angry or amused.

After a few seconds he said, "I hope I don't offend you when I say this, but I am surprised Mr. Wallace is employed by a company as esteemed as Gregor Corp. He seems to be interested only in enriching his personal estate, and willing to do just about anything to achieve that goal."

Faye stayed silent, processing what she'd just heard.

"But"—Mr. Chu looked up with a smile—"I have the utmost respect for many of your colleagues. Which department do you work for?"

"I work with Mr. Dalton, Raymond Dalton. He's head of ops for the West Coast."

"Oh yes, I am aware of Mr. Dalton. I've heard him present to City Council many times on expansion of the airport runways."

"He's been a really good mentor to me," Faye said. "He's so knowledgeable and generous about sharing his experience. The airport project is important, as it will help with a transition to a civilian economy after the war."

"I agree. I can envision commercial air travel to Asia someday. With the technological advances we've made for the war effort, the world is bound to get smaller and more accessible in the coming decades."

"Baba, could we have mango pudding for dessert?" Madeline asked, grabbing an opportunity to steer the conversation into less contentious waters.

"Of course, but I think your friend should also try the egg puffs."

With the meal finished, Mr. Chu strode off to his office and the girls headed to Union Square to do some shopping.

"Well, we really didn't learn anything, except your dad

doesn't have much respect for Jim Wallace," Faye commented. "But thanks, anyway. I really enjoyed the food and getting to know your dad better."

"Oh, this is not over." Madeline smiled.

"Why, Madeline Chu, what *are* you up to?"

"Even at the neighborhood news desk, I can do some snooping. Let me poke around and see what I can learn about Mr. Jim Wallace and why he ticked off my dad. Who knows," she added, linking arms with Faye, "it could lead to a scoop!"

28

In January of 1944, a second front opened in Italy between the towns of Nettuno and Anzio, some forty miles south of Rome. After a successful amphibious landing with no opposition, the Allied command made a serious error in judgment. They paused to consolidate their position. During that pause, the Germans repositioned eight divisions of artillery forces from other areas in Italy to the Alban Hills above the Anzio beachhead. The results proved to be disastrous. Thousands of American and British troops were killed, and the Allied advance stalled for what turned out to be four months on the Anzio Plain.

Blast. Just when we thought our boys had a leg up, this happens.

Faye stayed glued to the papers and news broadcasts that week, following the conflict on her wall map. As the casualty numbers started to come in, her fretfulness grew. The engineering corps, while not first into battle, often had to clear roads, repair bridges, and clear mines in advance of the troops. In many ways, their work could be more dangerous than actual combat.

Was Steve in Anzio, easy pickings for the German gunners? Was he in Montecassino, trudging his way through the snow toward the monastery-turned-German-outpost that held the Allied advance in check? Or was he already wrapped in mattress ticking and waiting to be identified among thousands of other fallen comrades. Her old companion, Mr. Anxiety, returned to Faye's life, and she, once again, began to look worse for wear. Lack of sleep, lack of appetite, and a general sick feeling began to sap her energy and take its toll.

Finally, in early February, a few V-Mails from Steve arrived. He was in England. His unit was preparing for what Faye guessed would be an invasion of Central Europe—the invasion Churchill had been asking for and the Germans had been fearing for more than a year. They'd worked out a new code during his furlough based on national foods: brie was for France, tea for England, spaghetti for Italy, chocolate for Belgium, gouda for Holland and so forth.

"I'm feeling fine, and I hope you are well, too."

Well, some things never change.

Faye continued to read, "Thought I'd take a few minutes to write to you during my break. It's a rainy day and a hot cup of tea sure hits the spot."

There it was, clear as day on the tissue-thin page! England! She remembered the trip Pops and Mother had taken her on when she was sixteen. First to London, where Pops had given a paper to the Royal Society of Mathematics—quite an honor—and then to Paris, where she tried out her schoolgirl French and spent hours in the Louvre. It seemed impossible that these enchanting cities were now at the forefront of this terrible war.

England was the land of Shakespeare and Chaucer and

wonderful clotted cream treats. She wondered if Steve might sneak in a visit to Stonehenge if he was anywhere nearby. As an engineer, she knew he'd appreciate the ancient stone circle, standing proud like a coronet on the Salisbury Plain. She sat down to suggest just that in a return V-Mail.

The other bit of news Faye received that week was not so encouraging.

"I'm running into brick walls everywhere," Madeline Chu reported over highballs at the M&M Tavern, a favorite watering hole for *Chronicle* reporters. "I asked two of my uncles if they knew anything about my dad's rift with Wallace, and I am striking out everywhere. I know they know something but aren't talking. Whatever Wallace did seems to have miffed just about every elder in Chinatown."

"Well, thanks anyway. I appreciate you asking around."

"Oh, I'm only just beginning," Madeline said as she smiled. "The more people don't want to talk, the more the reporter in me is intrigued! Because whatever he did was really bad."

She took a cigarette from her silver case and offered one to Faye.

"They have me covering the Lunar New Year festivities coming up, so I'll be really immersed in community stuff for the next several months." She lit up, exhaled, and took another sip of her drink. "It may take me a while to get to the bottom of this, but I'm good at the long game."

Faye lit her cigarette and marveled at Madeline. She was, as always, impeccably dressed, today in a gray suit and green velvet hat angled low over her left eye. But in the months since Faye first found her in that Tenderloin alley, she'd gained a confidence that was remarkable. The innocent girl she'd helped out had blossomed into a capable and very determined young woman.

"Well, cheers to you, Miss Chu." Faye held out her glass for a clink. "I'm so glad we're on the same team."

Midge had gone radio silent since the New Year. Faye figured she must be caught up in the euphoria of Simon Miller's seduction in her off-work hours, so she really didn't give Midge's quietness a second thought. Then came a cry for help.

It was a Sunday during the second week of February. Hannah and Evie went to donate blood at the Red Cross headquarters and then were going to the movies to see *Two Girls and a Sailor*. Faye begged off, saying she felt tired and wanted to have a quiet day before the work week started again. In reality, after what she'd just been through with Steve, she couldn't sit through another frothy musical about the war.

All that day, Faye luxuriated in the solace of the empty flat. Now that she knew Steve was in England, she slept better, but she still had this general feeling of exhaustion. This was her day to rejuvenate. After reading the papers, she mended her gray cardigan, took a nap, and made herself a nice plate of creamed tuna on toast with peas on the side. She was just washing up when the phone rang. It was Midge.

"I need your help." She sounded stressed, downright desperate, so unlike Midge. "I wouldn't ask, but Uncle Henry and Aunt Liz aren't home, and I'm really in a bind."

"Of course. What's up, pup?"

"They needed volunteers for the scrap drive. I've been down here South of Market sorting scrap metal all afternoon—and my purse got snatched!"

"Oh, no, are you all right?"

"Sure, but I'm stranded without so much as bus fare. Everyone else has gone. I had to bum a nickel from the security guard to make this call. Can you bring some dough and come get me? It's getting dark, and I'm afraid to walk in this neighborhood. I'm at Pier 30, and the guard said he'd wait with me until you get here."

"Of course," Faye said without a second thought. "Pier 30. Be there in twenty minutes."

Like most San Franciscans, Faye felt wary about venturing South of Market after dark. It was a district of docks, warehouses, factories, rail yards, sweatshops, and flophouses, where the down-and-out mingled with the up-to-no-good. But Midge was her dearest friend in all the world, and she needed her help. There was no question that Faye would bail her out.

Fearless Faye to the rescue!

San Francisco's piers fanned out from its bay front on both sides of the Ferry Building. The piers going toward the Golden Gate had odd numbers; those going south toward Hunters Point had even numbers. Pier 30, normally a bustling shipping facility during working hours, was not too far south of the Bay Bridge anchorage. Faye reviewed the bus routes in her head and frowned: the closest she could get to Pier 30 on the streetcar was Rincon Park, which may have been fine during daylight hours, but left many scary blocks to walk after dark. The bus was on a Sunday schedule, which left her with a potential twenty-minute wait at the terminal.

Fudge it. Midge is worth cab fare.

She grabbed her beret and her jacket and headed up the block to the taxi stand at the Mark Hopkins Hotel.

"Are you sure this is where you want to go?"

The cabbie looked incredulously at the darkened warehouse on Pier 30. The parking lot was empty save a half dozen or so vagrants loitering around a bonfire they had built in a discarded oil barrel.

"This is it," Faye assured. "The guard is supposed to be waiting for me. Can you wait for about five minutes while I go find my friend?"

"You got it, girlie. Be careful out there."

Faye opened the cab door warily as she gathered her courage. It was dark. Really dark. What's more, the fog was beginning to roll in from the water. A single light glowed above the warehouse door on the other side of the large loading area. Faye walked to the entry gate and looked for the guard, wishing she'd brought a flashlight with her. The guard wasn't there, but the big sliding door into the warehouse was wide open.

"Hello? Midge?"

Her voice echoed off the concrete floor and the cavernous warehouse, piled with palettes of crates arranged in tidy rows.

Out of the darkness came Midge's voice, which sounded pretty far away and a bit off. "Faye, I'm here."

"Where?"

"Back here, on the right."

As Faye rounded the stack of crates, she saw a light coming from the back of the warehouse.

"Well, toots, are you ready to go or not? This place is

creepy so let's skedaddle." Faye yelled as she walked toward Midge's voice.

In the far-right corner of the warehouse, where the storage crates were stacked at least twelve-feet high, she found Midge—*not* ready to go. Her hands were bound behind her, and she was seated on a work stool. The body of a uniformed man was face down on the floor, limbs splayed and blood oozing out onto the concrete from under his torso. Holding a gun to Midge's temple was Simon Miller's red-lipped so-called cousin.

"Good evening, Mrs. Connor." The Ice Maiden's voice was just as frigid as ever. "We meet again."

In contrast, Midge was absolute mush, soggy and defeated. "I'm so sorry, Faye. They made me call you."

"Wait, what? What the bejeezus is going on?"

At that moment, Simon Miller himself stepped out of the shadows.

"Simon! Thank goodness you're here! What's going on?

In the dim light, Faye watched Simon's face morph from his normal, engaging countenance into something sinister.

"Simon? Are you okay?"

"You little fool, don't you get it?" he sneered, grabbing her wrist.

"*Ow!* You're hurting me!" She struggled to free her wrist, but Simon held tight.

"You've been duped. Do you understand? *Duped!* I lured you into my trap like the willing chump that you are."

It took Faye several beats to process his words. She looked straight into his eyes, searching for the person she had come to trust. No dice. The sophisticated humor, the empathy, the familiar camaraderie had disappeared, leaving them vacant and callous.

Am I really such a sap?

She yanked her wrist free and headed over to Midge, only to be caught from behind, swung around and slammed cheek first against a stack of crates. Pain shot through the back of her head as he jerked her to face him. Then his lips crushed hers as his tongue violated her mouth, her shocked body slack and unbelieving.

As his hand crept under her blouse and he grabbed her breast, Simon's voice rasped in her ear. "I am not your friend, Faye. If you fight me, it will only make things worse. We have the upper hand here. I played my cards well, and now it's time for the big payout."

"Get off me, you creep! I don't know what you're up to, but you won't get away with it."

Red Lips turned and spoke to Simon in what surely sounded like German. Then he answered. In German. Her mind flashed back to the evening of Mr. Smith's house party. The same voices.

So that's the deal. You're agents of the Reich.

Faye's knowledge of German was limited to food items and a few Christmas carols, but she knew from the very tone of voices that the near future would be challenging. Red Lips yanked Midge to her feet and both girls were marched through a door at the back of the warehouse. They found themselves in what must have been a break room of some kind, now barren except for lockers, one table, a few rusty chairs, and the aroma of low tide.

As both girls were forced to sit in chairs and their hands and feet bound, it occurred to Faye that Simon had purposely used them as pawns. He was lying all this time about being a Canadian engineer. Did anyone suspect, or was everyone as clueless as she? He evidently had done a great job of hoodwinking some very smart people and putting himself in a position to intercept some high-level tactical plans.

Surely someone must have suspected.

She cleared her throat and used her most commanding Fearless Faye tone: "Would you please tell me what this is about. Midge? Do you know?"

Red Lips took the lead. "She knows nothing. Now, Mrs. Connor, we have it on good authority that you have been serving as a courier for the OSS."

"Well, I would say your authority is not really that good, because I don't know what you're talking about."

"Do you deny your involvement?"

"Why should I tell you anything?"

With that, Red Lips took a revolver out of her coat pocket and let off a shot in Faye's direction, missing her head by inches. Both girls screamed and cringed, the sound of the gunshot ringing in their ears.

"Because we have guns, and you are tied to these hideous chairs."

Simon stepped into the light, his face twisted and cold. "Sweet little Faye, so wide eyed and midwestern. You didn't really think I cared about you, did you? I only care about who and what you know, and I'm willing to cause much distress in order to secure your help."

"Who are you?" Faye's eyes narrowed as if hoping to see inside his brain. "The Nazis will be defeated, you know." There she said it.

His response was cold and rote. "Our cause is noble and will triumph. Your naiveté is tiresome. Your all-American brand of democracy is as doomed as your Jewish friends. You've never had to scrounge for food or watch your family's fortune become worthless before your eyes at the hands of the western industrial complex."

She met his intensity with an emotionless calm, looking him straight in the eye. "How do you think this will end, Simon? What do you really want?"

"Access, Faye. We want you to get us into Fort Cronkhite and Fort Funston. We've been following you for the last year and know you are a familiar face at both places."

So, there *had* been someone following her. All these months. All those foggy nights walking home alone, imagining she heard footsteps. And that explained how he miraculously appeared up in Marin when she had that flat tire.

Gosh. I need to learn to listen to my gut.

Fort Funston was near Lands End in San Francisco and Fort Cronkhite was located on the Marin Headlands. Simon was correct. She had visited both many times and was well known to the guards. They were miles apart on opposite sides of the Golden Gate, but they shared an important attribute. Both had massive sixteen-inch guns, key to the coastal artillery defense network. She knew good and well that these were both prime espionage targets.

"You overestimate me, Simon, if that's really your name. I'm only permitted on those bases occasionally when I'm running errands. I'd never get past security without a specific appointment."

"That has been arranged," Red Lips said, holding up a familiar looking briefcase, the one Dalton kept in his bottom desk drawer under lock and key.

"How did you get that?"

Simon just glared in response.

"Now, ladies, here's how this will go," Simon instructed.

"We will all walk calmly to the car we have parked outside and take you to the staging point for our base visits, which will occur tomorrow. Mrs. Connor, you will do exactly as we say, or Miss Swanson will pay the price."

The girls exchanged glances. Queasy and sweating, Faye wanted to take a deep breath and think for a few minutes before concocting a life-or-death plan.

Too bad I'm not carrying a shopping bag full of canned goods today.

Then she remembered the keys in her jacket pocket, a classic self-defense tool she'd learned to use in her Red Cross training.

Think, Faye, think. If I can just figure out how to distract Simon so he drops my wrist, I can grab keys and gouge him in the face.

It could work, but then she saw Midge.

Oh yeah. What about Midge? Red-Lips is holding a freaking gun to her head!

Simon holstered his weapon and began working on the knots that bound Faye to the chair. As the rope loosened, he grabbed her wrists and held her firmly to him, one arm across her chest. Just as he reached for his gun with his free arm, there was a crash from the front of the warehouse.

Red Lips said something in German and Simon replied. Holding her gun in front of her, Red Lips left Midge tied to her chair and noiselessly made her way out the door, presumably to investigate. While this was happening Faye just stared at their feet—her sturdy oxfords with the block heel, his lightweight boat shoes and no socks. She knew she had to act before Red Lips returned.

This could work, or it could be curtains. But it's our only chance.

Taking a deep breath, she mustered every ounce of strength she could and *wham*, slammed her heel down on the shapely arch of Simon's right foot.

Simon shrieked and dropped his gun. Faye broke away, kicked the gun across the room, and rushed for Midge. The door to the room banged open and a half-dozen men, some in suits, some in uniform, poured in, guns drawn.

"Freeze! FBI! Drop your weapons!"

Shots rang out. Faye couldn't tell who started it, but she knew Simon had recovered his gun because there was a definite exchange of fire. That's when she felt a sharp pain rip through her shoulder, and she sank into darkness.

29

———————

The smell of antiseptic. A dull pain in her shoulder. A raging thirst.

Come on, sister, open your eyes.

After a concerted effort, Faye managed to pry her eyes open to a slit position. The morning sun streamed through the window behind an easy chair, which held a sleeping Midge, making her blonde updo glow like a halo.

Did we die? Are we in heaven?

Faye closed her eyes again and breathed the stale medicinal air deep into her lungs.

Surely that smell wouldn't exist in heaven, so I must be in the hospital. But I'm alive. Thank you, God.

She tried for a few minutes to reconstruct the events that brought her from Pier 30 to this hospital bed. No luck. She remembered the FBI arriving and shots ringing out, but that was it.

She opened her eyes again and tried to sit up. Her head ached like a son of a gun. As she lifted her chest, her shoulder hurt more, and she noticed the bandage.

Hmm. Was I shot? Never mind. I'm going to plumb dry up and turn to dust if I don't get some water.

She reached for the call button just as Midge awakened with a start.

"Oh, good, you're awake," Midge said, leaning in close. "Hey there, cookie. How do you feel? I was so worried about you. Was last night a gas or what?"

Typical Midge, trying to diffuse a tense moment with humor.

"Is there some water?" Faye croaked.

"Here ya go but take it easy." Midge held a metal cup and straw as Faye sipped, slowly at first, then with more purpose.

"What happened? Did I get shot?"

"How much do you remember?"

"I remember the FBI coming in and all the shots that were fired. Did they shoot me by mistake?

"It was actually Simon. I think it was payback for breaking his foot. You really slammed the tarnation out of it. The good news is, he was so incapacitated that the Feds were able to nab him and pin him down easy as pie. Way to go, baby doll."

"It's kind of his own fault. Who wears boat shoes to a kidnapping? That'll teach him to double-cross me!"

"I'll say. Anyway, he's in custody and the dame is dead."

Faye was surprised. Surely Red Lips was worth much more to the Feds alive. "Did the cops take her out?"

Midge shook her head. "She offed herself. Poison pill. Must've seen the writing on the wall. They were holding her in a paddy wagon in the parking lot and found her dead when they took Simon out to lock him up."

"How awful. I'm kinda glad I blacked out."

Midge bent closer, gently pushed Faye's hair back from her face and said somberly, "Listen, Faye. I can't tell you how sorry I am. I was such a patsy and fell right into their trap. I was sure they were going to kill me, especially after they took out the guard. But I want you to know: You've been a true friend to me, and I would never knowingly do anything to hurt you."

"I know, Midge, but thanks for saying it." She paused and took another sip of water, then settled back on her pillow. "It's really not your fault. He had me fooled, too. We all thought he was just a smooth-talking hunka heartbreak who knew his way around the dance floor."

"He turned out to be quite the snake, all right. Really dreamy and fun to date, but a snake nonetheless," Midge confirmed, sounding defeated. "I'm going to start doing background checks before I put the moves on anyone from here on out."

The little ambiguities that had surfaced during her relationship with Simon over the last few years crystalized into the stark realization that she'd been conned. They'd *all* been conned. He had hoodwinked them all, even Mr. Dalton, and he had almost gotten away with it.

"Anyway," Midge continued, glancing at her watch, "the G-Men are coming to debrief us in about a half hour, and I'm going to need some strong coffee. Want some?"

"No, I'm going to stick with water for right now."

Footsteps approached and a man with white hair and clad in a white coat entered the room.

"Mrs. Connor. I'm Dr. Blackthorn. How are you feeling this morning?"

"Okay, I think, doctor."

As he held Faye's wrist to check her pulse, Midge moved

toward the door. "I'm just going to pop down to the cafeteria, so you two can talk."

"You had quite an evening," Dr. Blackthorn noted, "but you're in pretty good shape. Your face is bruised, but no concussion. The gunshot wound to your shoulder was superficial. We've cleaned it well, but you didn't need any stitches. You'll have to keep it dry with a clean dressing for another two weeks or so. Do you have someone who can help you do that?"

"Yes. I have plenty of friends who can help out."

"Now, just a few routine questions. Do you have any history of diabetes?

"No."

"High blood pressure?"

"No."

"Cancer?"

"No."

"Pneumonia or rheumatic fever?"

"No."

"Female problems?"

"No."

"When was the first day of your last menstrual cycle?"

Faye paused. Never one to closely track her periods, she did some quick calculations in her head. She'd finished her period about a week before Steve's visit. Did she have a period in December?

"I think it was November seventeenth."

Dr. Blackthorn looked at her over his reading glasses. "Could you be pregnant?"

Again, Faye paused. "I suppose I could be."

"Just to be safe, I'm going to order a test." Dr. Blackstone made some notes. "So…blood pressure's good, pulse is good… We should be able to release you tomorrow. I'll want you to rest for the next two weeks."

Faye was barely listening, wrapped in her own euphoria. *A baby. Steve will be thrilled beyond belief. The timing is not ideal, with Steve gone and all, but we'll manage.*

Even though she knew she was jumping the gun, she slid her good arm over her belly, cradling what she hoped was snug inside.

That afternoon, Faye's steady stream of visitors—Midge, Mr. Dalton, the police, agents from the OSS and the FBI—clarified all her nagging questions. As soon as Simon was in custody, he started to sing, hoping for leniency. His real name was Simon Peters. He was neither Canadian nor German, but Belgian. His family were industrialists from Antwerp whose factories in Germany had been hit hard by assessments to fund the reparations imposed after the Great War.

Wanting to get their son out of the chaos of Europe in the 1920's, his parents sent young Simon to prep school in Toronto, where he perfected his English and his knowledge of all things Canadian. He returned to Europe for university in the early 1930's when the economy and social unrest seemed to stabilize. His knowledge of hydroelectric engineering was genuine, having studied the subject at The Technical University of Munich.

While in Munich, the birthplace of the Nazi party, he became enamored with Hitler and his cause. When time came to serve the Reich, his natural charm, mastery of English and ability at impersonation made him a perfect foreign agent in this country. He became a valuable resource for reporting key infrastructure and military targets, as well as the movement of ships, troops and goods.

That explains why he was always turning up unannounced and staring out my office window. It wasn't me he was there to see, but the ship activity on the bay.

As for Red Lips, she was an Axis operative who entered the country from Montreal, just before Faye and Midge first met her. Her name was Greta Kruger, and she was part of the espionage network tasked with neutralizing the Bay Area coastal defenses to help facilitate the Japanese invasion of California.

"This is why they tried to kidnap you," the head G-Man explained. "Just by trailing you over the last year or so, they determined that you were a trusted presence at most all the bases involved in coastal defense. Their most recent assignment was to take out the big guns protecting the Golden Gate. They figured that you were their ticket past the guard."

"But how did you know we were at Pier 30?" Midge asked.

"We'd had our suspicions about Miller for a few months," the man from the OSS volunteered, "but could never quite catch him with the goods."

"That's why the Niagara project was suspended," Dalton explained. "We knew it was compromised, but we didn't have the evidence to connect it back to Miller."

"We had a tail on him yesterday and just lucked out. And *you* lucked out," the G-man added, nodding to Faye. "Our men were already in the parking lot when you arrived, undercover as vagrants."

Faye recalled the group of men gathered around the trash-can fire.

"Plus, your cab driver was worried about you when you

didn't come back. He radioed the police when he heard a gunshot. We were surprised when the cops showed up, but I'm glad they did," the G-Man said. "You can never have too much backup when you're dealing with Nazi filth."

When the men from law enforcement departed and Midge went to get a sandwich, Dalton stayed behind.

"My dear, I know you've had quite an ordeal. For whatever my part may have been in causing you any danger, I want to apologize. But this case isn't closed, and we need you to stay involved.

"What do you mean?"

"There's still someone high up at Gregor who's working for the Germans."

"Who?"

"That's the thing. We don't know for sure. Miller claims he's in the dark and he only took orders from Kruger and his contact in Montreal. But you are well placed to help us find out."

"What do you want me to do?"

"Stay alert. Keep your ears open. Look for anything that doesn't make sense."

She opened her mouth to reply as Dalton put up his hand to silence her.

"Not now. We'll talk later. Right now, you rest. We'll have an intensive briefing and training when you're back at work."

As he rose to leave, he said again, "Thank you, Mrs. Connor. Your company and your nation owe you a big debt of gratitude. This war will be won through the efforts of people like you."

30

———————

While at home recovering, Faye thought about her next steps. With both of her housemates at work all day, she appreciated the opportunity for quiet reflection, especially since she had just received a call from Dr. Blackthorne's office to confirm her pregnancy. Lots to think about.

She felt so excited to be carrying Steve's child, but she recognized one huge downside. Women "in the family way" normally stopped working. She didn't feel inclined to stop right now, especially with almost seven long months ahead of her before she gave birth. She truly loved her job. Besides, as Dalton pointed out, Faye was uniquely positioned to help identify the enemy agent still at Gregor. She decided then and there to keep her condition under wraps from everyone—except Steve—for a few more months. Then, she hoped the "huge debt of gratitude" owed to her by her company and her nation could be cashed in for the right to work up until her due date—and then potentially after she gave birth.

A working mother? They'd never in a million years go for it, but it's worth a try.

As her wounds healed over that two-week period, Faye struggled with the realization that she'd lost a friend: someone she was always glad to see and who had become a valued confidante, especially when she needed a male point of view. The bruise on her face, which was quickly fading from eggplant-purple to yellow, brought back the humiliation of his deceit. Again and again, she cycled through guilt, anger, and finally a sense of loss for the camaraderie that vanished right along with Simon Miller.

"Look, cookie, you've got to stop blaming yourself," Midge consoled as she stopped by on her way to her afternoon shift to help change Faye's dressing.

"I know I'm not entirely to blame, but my naiveté certainly contributed."

"To what? To making Simon a Nazi? To his twisted plot? To his Jekyll and Hyde personality? I was conned as much as anyone, but I'm pretty sure the bad guy got caught in the end. And don't forget, you helped the cops capture him by smashing his instep. I wouldn't have had the moxie to do that. I was just shivering in my boots while you kept your cool and took decisive action. That was an ace move, pure and simple."

Faye leaned forward and held a wad of gauze over her wound while Midge wrapped fresh bandage around her chest and shoulder.

"I suppose you're right."

Midge tied off the bandage and snipped the ends of her neat knot.

"There," she said. "Now, I'm going to make you the best grilled cheese you've ever tasted, then tuck you in for a nap."

Later that afternoon, Faye wrote the letter to Steve she'd been composing for days in her head.

> *Our baby is due to arrive in mid-August. I know it's early in our marriage, but I hope you're as excited as I am. I'll always remember that we created this child on that wonderful night at the St. Francis. For now, I'd like to keep this just between you and me. It's still very early, and even though I'm feeling great, I want to be sure all is well before we share this joyous news with anyone.*

As much as she wanted to tell the future grandparents, she knew it would be asking for trouble. They all would want her to come home immediately, and she just wasn't ready to deal with that kind of argument.

She decided against telling Steve—or anyone for that matter—about the incident at Pier 30. What good would it do? She and the baby were both all right in the end, and everyone had enough to worry about without her adding to their anxiety. Besides, she was sworn to secrecy.

Two weeks later, Faye received the doctor's clearance to return to work. Her wound had scabbed over nicely and only the slightest tinge of yellow remained on her cheekbone, nothing a few pats of Max Factor foundation wouldn't conceal.

On her first day back, she learned she'd been promoted—out of the secretarial pool and into project management with the title of Assistant Manager. She would be working with Mr. Fred Nugent, an experienced and kindly gentleman who had come back from retirement for the duration. He reminded Faye of the professors that had filled her childhood home and the two clicked right away. Besides the perk of "more responsibility," Faye was thrilled with a $2.50 a week pay increase.

Gosh, there's nothing like cold hard cash to make someone really feel useful and appreciated.

Faye's new job meant a new office—an actual office— next to Mr. Nugent's spacious executive suite. Its single small window framed Coit Tower perfectly, and if she leaned out and looked to the right, she could see a sliver of the bay. There was only room for a desk, a few file cabinets, and one guest chair, but she didn't care about size.

Her new responsibilities challenged her. Her duties included contract reconciliation and negotiation with suppliers and subcontractors—kind of like shopping for bargains on an industrial scale, as she explained in a letter to her parents.

During her second week back at work, she received a summons to a meeting at the Federal Building, presumably to review sourcing for some upgrades at Hunters Point Naval Shipyard. As she entered the small conference room, she knew this was, instead, the briefing on her surveillance assignment. Dalton introduced an Agent Paige from the FBI and a woman from the OSS, code name Balboa.

Wearing a nondescript brown suit and no makeup, Balboa looked more like a junior high school librarian than a government intelligence officer. She opened a file on the table in front of her and started to speak.

"Because you have access to contracts and files throughout Gregor operations, you are in a good position to observe anything unusual. We suspect materials are being diverted, either to be redirected to enemy operations or to support a suspected scheme to sabotage Gregor's new construction projects. We need your help in identifying these diversions."

"But I don't understand," Faye asked. "How does diverting material lead to sabotage?"

Dalton took the opportunity to explain. "Let's say a delivery of rebar never arrives, which disrupts the construction schedule. In fact, the delivery has been diverted and has been duplicated exactly by sub-grade product. So, the site receives a late delivery that they are thrilled to finally get and installs sub-grade rebar in an airport taxiway. At the first bout of cold weather, kablooey, the concrete crumbles, which puts a runway out of commission. In the meantime, the original rebar is resold and the mastermind profits."

"Is that why the project with Canada was curtailed?"

"Well, that project was still conceptual. We knew something was amiss when we did a background check on the Simon Miller person. His education was legit, but his studies in Munich were a red flag and the government in Ottawa hadn't heard of him. We also found he had several identities, so we pulled the plug as soon as he became a suspect."

"So, you still think there's someone at Gregor Corp involved?"

"We're certain," Agent Paige said.

"It's hard to believe Simon doesn't know who it is," Faye considered.

"That's the way these fifth column operations work," Agent Paige explained. "Miller was the inside man who took his orders from Miss Kruger and a contact in Canada. He knew Kruger directed one other person inside Gregor, but he swears he doesn't know who it is."

"Well, it will be easy to look for irregularities in deliveries."

"That sounds like a good start," Balboa commented. "And I don't think I need to remind you to be discreet, trust no one, and report only to the three of us. We will have off-site progress meetings every week, right here at this time."

"Does Mr. Nugent know about any of this?" Faye asked Dalton.

"No, and he won't need to," Dalton replied. "You are kind of an autonomous operation now, above the administrative status and with great access to every department at the company. You report to Nugent, but he doesn't rely on you to get his work done. Everyone likes you, so use it."

"Keep your eyes and ears open for anything—and we mean *anything*—out of the ordinary," Balboa instructed.

"I can certainly do that."

All the way back to the Gregor Corp headquarters, Faye wracked her brain for suspects and came up empty. While she didn't approve of the business practices of several executives, she couldn't imagine any of them as traitors.

Who could it be?

31

As Faye combed the ledgers over the next few weeks, signs that the war might be winding down seemed to be everywhere. A tall, vigorous general named Charles de Gaulle was in the news as the leader of the Free French and the Allies were within spitting distance of Rome. Training in England continued for "something big, something soon." At home, the block wardens were disbanded—*good riddance!*—and the air raid center in the basement of Grace Cathedral was closed, along with coastal watch stations. Rationing of food, gasoline, and certain consumer goods remained in effect, but these had become routine.

It took a good month before Faye heard back from Steve. Safe, still in England, and "practicing hard for a big concert," he sounded thrilled with her news. Faye's letter was delayed in reaching him because they had been on maneuvers. He wanted her to return to Evanston immediately.

If you don't want to live with your parents, stay with mine,
he wrote. *Or rent a little apartment in town. It's important
that you don't take any chances and that you are close to
family should you need them.*

Hmm. Faye folded the V-Mail and put it in the cigar box
where she kept Steve's letters. *I really don't feel I need to go back
to Evanston. I've got plenty of help here, with all my girlfriends. I'm
sure, once they know about the baby, they'll be lining up to help in any
way they can. I'll just pretend I didn't read that part.*

Faye's little office proved to be the perfect setting for her
surveillance assignment. It was just down the hall from the
archive, which held dozens of years of ledgers and files. She
came in a half hour earlier than the secretaries, so she
could gather the materials she needed for the day undetected. When she met with Mr. Nugent, it was always in *his*
office, so this assignment remained entirely off his radar.

Working around her normal duties, it took her a few
weeks to confirm a potential pattern of short deliveries, one
she had suspected years ago.

*This may be all within company guidelines, but the pattern is
clear. I knew I should have trusted my gut when I first started reconciling the gravel receipts for Mr. Dalton's monthly report. This is
perfect—within what's accepted, hard to trace.*

She sipped her tepid tea and pondered her next move.
*It could be nothing, after all. Before I stick my neck out, I want to be
sure I have my facts straight.*

She grabbed her hat and headed to the bus stop. Mid-
Peninsula Gravel, the supplier in question, was just down in
Belmont. She could get there in about forty minutes on the

express bus, just in time to talk to the drivers at the end of their shift.

"Gravel deliveries had consistently remained 1.6 to 1.8 percent under the contracted amount," she explained at the next FBI/OSS briefing.

"But that's within the acceptable waste allowance," Dalton said.

"I know that's company policy, Mr. Dalton, but I went down to Mid-Peninsula gravel and talked to three drivers. They are a major supplier for our current project at the Port of Stockton. In fact, they seem to have been the preferred contractor for all of our Northern California projects."

"And?"

"They all thought that was high. These guys take pride in being able to deliver per the contract and claim that waste is never more than .05 percent."

"So, I did some calculation. On the Stockton project, we ordered nearly 250 truckloads of gravel over a one-month period. The acceptable "waste" rate on that order was seventy-three cubic yards, which works out to almost four and a half truck loads. Multiply that by all of Gregor Corps projects requiring gravel since 1942, and the amount is significant."

"Interesting," Balboa said.

"I think this is worth investigating further," Dalton commented. "It could be the truck is offloading some product prior to coming to our site, and the culprit is counting on the overall waste allocation to cover it up."

"Thanks, Mrs. Connor. We'll take your notes and copies of those receipts and put our team on it."

Faye handed the file to Balboa.

"Our investigation could take some time," Agent Paige added. "You may not hear any report for quite some months if ever."

"I understand."

"Good work. But remember, this could be something or nothing, so stay vigilant."

Secluded in her office, Faye enjoyed the early months of her pregnancy undetected. Several times a day, she'd run a hand over her stomach as she felt life begin to grow, delighting in the feeling of bubbles and butterflies. She'd lay awake late at night, thinking of names and planning how to rearrange her room to accommodate a crib. She didn't care if it was a boy or a girl but knew in her heart-of-hearts that Steve would like a boy.

What will you be like, little one? I hope you have green eyes like your father.

She felt good, both physically and mentally, and was well into her third trimester before she began to show. Then one morning in May, she couldn't button her skirt over her expanding waistline. She knew the gig was up, and she was going to have to start telling people. She started with the Connor and Baxter households back in Evanston, jotting off letters to both families and hoping for the best. Then, she invited Midge to dinner on an evening when all three of her roommates were home and spilled the beans over a lovely salmon loaf.

After everyone was served, she tapped her fork against

her glass and said, "I have some news. In the middle of August, a new baby Connor will be joining us."

A shriek went up all around the table, all the girls rushing to hug her and—this was weird—look at her tummy. Everyone spoke at once.

"A baby. How fun... Does Steve know?... Are you feeling okay... What about work?... Old Man Nugent will flip his lid... How does it feel?"

"Wait a sec. Everybody calm down." Faye raised her hands. "I've known about this for a few months. Steve was last home in November, right? I'm feeling great and, yes, Steve knows. As for work, I'm hoping you'll help me decide what to do."

The girls talked for a good few hours as the dinner dishes were cleared and a loaf of banana bread was served.

"If you want to stay, stay," Evie said. "I for one will be excited to see you through the pregnancy and help out after you deliver."

"Me, too," Hannah said. "I'm good with babies. I had to take care of my baby sister when I was twelve for two whole months when my mom was in the hospital with pneumonia."

"Have you told your boss?" Midge asked. "I know a few girls from the shipyard who were fired when they got knocked up. Another was forced to take a long leave without pay. Will they even let you work while you're pregnant, much less as a new mom?"

"Well, while we're still at war, I figure they're desperate," Faye said, sipping her tea. "Just look at Mr. Nugent. He had to move back from his retirement cottage in the foothills. And I know two of the boys in my department who are really smart, but they dropped out of high school to get some work experience before they turn eighteen and are eligible for the draft. If they're hiring high school dropouts, I'll bet you they'll let me stay on."

Faye was correct. After quelling their initial fear that she was going to resign, both Dalton and Nugent were more than happy to work out a secret arrangement. She could tell that both men were embarrassed by the topic and would rather just ignore it entirely. Business as usual for as long as possible.

Dalton sounded as if he was trying to convince himself it was okay for Faye to continue. "A few years ago, we had so few women working here. Those who were had to resign when they got married. Now, I can't imagine keeping our doors open without you married women." He took a long, thoughtful pause before he continued. "Let's just play this by ear, but I have no objection to you continuing to work as long as you are able, and as long as you are discreet. We will, of course, require a note from your doctor that it's all right for you to continue to work. We wouldn't want to put your health or that of your baby in any kind of jeopardy."

"And," Nugent added, "we would ask that you just keep it under your hat as much as possible. We'll keep you in your office with desk work and assign one of the secretaries to take notes for you in meetings. Kind of behind the scenes, so to speak. We don't want every married woman on the payroll to think it's okay to get in the family way."

That really didn't make sense to Faye. It was beginning to be obvious that she was pregnant; was she not supposed to acknowledge it? Then again, maybe she should just accept their vagueness of policy as a positive for now. The fewer clearly defined rules, the less chance she could get in trouble for breaking one.

"That's fine with me, gentlemen. I promise to be discreet. But please remember: I am pregnant, not sick, so there's no need to adjust my workload."

"That's a request that's music to my ears," Nugent said.

Both Steve's and Faye's parents were not quite so eager for Faye to assume a "business as usual" routine during her pregnancy.

"Are you sure you don't just want to come home?" Mother asked in a rare long-distance call. "We can turn the guest room into a nursery, and we'll be able to help you out."

"Oh, thanks so much, Mother, but I'm feeling good and have lots of friends out here to help. I'll come home if things become too much for me to manage. I promise. In the meantime, why don't you and Pops plan on joining me out here around my due date? That would be mid-August."

"We'll talk about it, but it will be difficult. The Navy's running training programs on campus and your father's teaching extra classes, so a trip west probably won't be possible until later in the year. I'll check his schedule."

Faye was secretly thrilled with the timing. She knew full well that Alice Baxter would never venture to make such a trip on her own. And as much as she loved her mother, Alice's anxious presence could suck the energy out of the room. She much preferred the thought of her brigade of friends seeing her through, even though none of them had first-hand knowledge of childbirth.

Blind leading the blind. Sounds like a plan!

32

CAPITAL GROWS TENSE AS INVASION NEARS
'LIKE A CROWD BEFORE THE KICK-OFF'
Grim Days Are Ahead

The tempo of the war is accelerating. Mounting tension among the leaders is the most significant change in Washington and New York. This tension is now reflected in the public. You see it. You feel it. It is like the tenseness that descends over the crowd just before the kickoff of a big football game.

By Roy A. Roberts

San Francisco Chronicle, May 5, 1944

All of America was looking for a decisive turn in the war. The Allied advance seemed to be stalled in Italy. For months our boys were pinned down within spitting distance of Rome. After a change of command and the arrival of reinforcements, they finally broke through the enemy lines.

In the meantime, it was clear that something was

brewing in England. Massive training exercises, some of them producing their own list of fatalities, took place throughout that winter and spring. Something was coming, but exactly what, where, and when remained question marks.

Faye did everything she could to hide her growing pregnancy. She began to wear her blouses untucked, then purchased a few outfits that adjusted to and masked her expanding middle: a suit with a boxy jacket, a wrap dress with an adjustable waist, a two-piece dress with a long peplum that hid a cut out in the front of a skirt, and an all-concealing swing coat. Outside her immediate circle of friends, people thought she'd just been hitting the sour-dough bread more than usual.

June 1944. On the fifth, the Allies marched into Rome. The very same day on the other side of the globe, the US shot down 220 Japanese fighter planes, defeating the last of the Imperial Air Force. Then, shortly before midnight on June fifth, Hannah, still in her dinner-date dress, opened Faye's bedroom door.

"Faye. Faye. Are you awake? Come listen to this."

All three girls remained glued to the radio for the rest of the night. CBS and NBC were both reporting that the long-awaited Anglo-American invasion of Western Europe may have begun. For hours the news was intermittent and incomplete. German broadcasts described bombardment of Le Havre and short-wave transmissions asking civilians to evacuate had been intercepted. Both national networks warned that the Germans might be faking reports as a diversionary tactic, and that the War Department was providing no confirmation.

Several hours later, the invasion was confirmed by a short statement and, after several more hours, a radio address by Ike himself was broadcast.

> *People of Western Europe! A landing was made this morning on the coast of France by troops of the Allied expeditionary force. This landing is part of the concerted United Nations plan for the liberation of Europe made in conjunction with our great Russian allies… I call upon all who love freedom to stand with us now.*

The tide had turned. Fifty-thousand Allied troops landed on the beach at Normandy in the pre-dawn hours to begin the liberation of Europe. Faye could only presume that among these thousands of boys from the cities and farms of America landing on Omaha Beach that day was Technician G4 Steven Connor of Evanston, Illinois.

All-in-all, the news was encouraging. For all the soldiers and supplies that came ashore in France that day, for all the booby traps and choppy water and razor wire and machine gun fire, Allied troops seemed to gain a strong foothold. Wave after wave of landing craft unloaded soldiers and materiel for days and days.

Invasion Extra editions of the newspapers reported that losses were low; our boys were pushing the Germans away from their vital coastal positions. All of San Francisco, and indeed the nation, crossed their collective fingers that the tide of war was turning. Citizens across the US were encouraged to attend the church of their choice and pray for victory. By the end of June, the Allies had secured the stretch of Normandy coast from Cherbourg to Caen and were slowly making their way toward Paris.

While significant progress was made in both Pacific and European theaters that summer, Faye stayed busy in her little office from morning till night. True to her promise to maintain a low profile, she sent a secretary to cover meetings and ate her bag lunch at her desk. Finally, at the end of July, Faye was told she had to take a leave of absence.

"Our company really doesn't have a policy for this situation, but I'm getting pressure from Personnel," Nugent explained, the blush of embarrassment creeping into his cheeks. "We'll give you a furlough without pay. I hate to pull the plug, because you're so productive, but I don't want to have any more lectures. They're afraid you'll set some kind of precedent."

I guess that's the best I can expect.

"I'd like to continue to work, when the baby's old enough," Faye said. "At least, that's my current thinking."

Nugent's face lit up. "We're in no obligation to hold open your job, but I can assure you, we'll work something out if you want to come back—at least for the duration of the war."

So, on Friday, July 28, Faye made sure all her files were in order, gathered her coffee cup and her photo of Steve, and officially started her furlough.

As August began, time weighed heavy on Faye's hands —and her mind. She missed the feeling of control she had at work, as well as the mental stimulation of being around other smart people. Her stomach continued to expand, her ankles started to swell, and her feet disappeared from view.

She waited for letters from Steve that never came. She puttered around the flat, setting up a bassinet in her room and painting an old dresser to double as a changing table. Several boxes arrived from Evanston, chock full of layette clothes, swaddling blankets, and what seemed like mountains of hand-hemmed diapers.

Goodness, thought Faye. *Mother must've put her entire bridge club to work on these.*

As she folded the tiny little nightgowns and hand-knit cardigans and arranged them in the dresser, the reality of parenthood began to set in. Was she up to it? She wished with all her heart that Steve was here with her, to rub her feet and whisper reassurances in her ear. And maybe kiss her neck, right below her ear.

Mid-August turned into late August and Faye's due date came and went. She couldn't get comfortable day or night and burst into tears when anyone asked when the baby was due. Her doctor, a grandfatherly man with thick glasses and a condescending attitude, told her not to worry, that every woman had a slightly different gestation period, and the baby was just getting its finishing touches.

Meanwhile, the apartment was neat as a pin, the layette was all folded and ready, and Faye was going stark raving bonkers. It was a hot day with no breeze, and she knew by nine in the morning that the flat would soon be unbearable in the midday heat.

Fudge and fiddlesticks, I can't spend another day cooped up in this apartment!

She was contemplating how to fill the empty hours until Evie and Hannah got home when the phone rang.

"I have some information for you regarding you-know-who and you-know-what."

While guarded, Madeline's voice simmered with excitement. Faye was thrilled, as it had been months since their last conversation about Jim Wallace.

"Where are you? I'm itching to get out of the house. Can we meet for tea?"

"I'm in Chinatown today, so absolutely! Let's meet at the Red Blossom on Grant in say an hour? Do you know it? It's in the block just behind Portsmouth Square."

"I'll be there!"

Faye laced on her sturdy saddle shoes—the only shoes that still fit, grabbed her summer hat and purse and headed for the door. She set off in a buoyant mood, excited to see Madeline and trying as much as possible to ignore the taut, hefty "watermelon" she was lugging around. She chugged up Nob Hill and down again to Clay, then headed down an incline toward Grant. As she peered over the rooftops to admire the views of the Bay Bridge—*wham!*—she lost her footing and found herself smack on her caboose. She just sat for a minute to regain her breath and collect her energy, when a small crowd began to gather.

"You all right?" The question, from an elderly Chinese lady wearing a purple cotton coat, sounded more like a command. The gathering crowd spoke excitedly in Chinese amongst themselves, and Mrs. Purple Coat scolded them to be quiet.

"You need help." Again, more commandeering than questioning.

"I'm fine," Faye said, although she was not entirely sure. "Let me just sit here a sec."

The group again chattered among themselves while Faye strategized how she would heave her belly onto her feet again, considering the steep incline of the sidewalk. She wiggled one leg, then the other, one arm, then the other.

Yep. All okay. No broken bones or even skinned knees. But how on God's green earth am I going to get on my feet again.

Mustering every ounce of energy, she crooked her left leg under her body and rose to her knee…just as her water broke and went cascading down the street.

She looked in horror at Mrs. Purple Coat, who clasped her hand.

"You have baby."

"I know, I'm going to have a baby. And soon. I need to get to Saint Francis Hospital."

"Ah, good. Saint Francis close."

"Can you call a cab?"

"No cab in Chinatown. Baby coming soon."

The water breaking was followed immediately by a dull heaviness in her lower abdomen. Something like cramps when her "friend was about to visit" only giant-sized.

Oh, God. That must be a contraction. This lady must know what she's talking about. I really don't want to give birth in the middle of the street.

"I think, if I can get to my feet, I might be able to walk. It's not that far. Can you help me up?"

The lady, who still held Faye's hand, began to bark orders at the others in the crowd. After a few minutes of what could only be described as chaos, a well-muscled teenage boy appeared with a kind of cart that the grocers used to haul crates of *bok choy*. Others returned to the scene with blankets and pillows.

"Missus, we help. We take you to Saint Francis."

Considering the enthusiasm of the crowd, the lack of other transit options, and the fact that her contractions had begun to intensify, Faye agreed.

With the help of many eager hands, Faye was situated on the cart, propped on pillows, wrapped in blankets.

"Faye!"

Madeline emerged from the crowd and took her hand.

"Oh, Madeline. I'm so glad you're here! How did you know?"

"This is Chinatown, my friend. Word travels fast. When I heard 'white lady is having a baby in the street,' I knew I'd better hightail it over here."

She turned to the lady in the purple coat and spoke in Cantonese. After a brief exchange, she turned back to Faye.

"Faye, here's the deal. I was going to send for a car, but this is really the best plan, given that you're in active labor and we're just a few blocks from the hospital. I'm going to walk ahead and stop traffic." She paused and looked directly into Faye's eyes. "You and your baby are going to be all right." She ran off to lead the transport team.

The cart began to move, powered by four people and followed by another half dozen. Once they broke the crest of Nob Hill, it was an easy downhill glide about six blocks to Saint Francis. Faye and her escorts rolled up to the hospital's emergency entrance about fifteen minutes later. For the entire ride, Mrs. Purple Coat sat on the edge of the cart and made gentle circles with her work-worn hands on Faye's back.

Madeline disappeared inside, then re-emerged, followed by an orderly with a wheelchair.

"You'll be fine, now," Madeline reassured.

Faye suddenly recalled the original purpose of her meet-up with Madeline.

"But what have you learned about Wallace?" she asked as she was helped into the wheelchair.

"It'll keep. You go have a healthy baby. And don't worry. Even though this is the biggest news of the week in Chinatown, I won't file a story on it."

The events of that afternoon sank into a state of murky restlessness, what the nurse later called "twilight sleep." Faye remembered the commotion of her arrival, but not actually being in labor, although she was somehow sure it was the most intense pain she could imagine. There was a faceless nurse who checked her progress and kneaded her stomach, hushed conversation, a mask, and a frustrating haze that dulled her mind. She thought she heard commands to breathe, then breathe faster, to push, then push harder. That's all she could recall until much later when she awoke, one of very few people in a very large ward.

"Mrs. Connor." A non-nonsense voice pulled her from her semi-conscious state. "Wake up, Mrs. Connor. It's time to meet your daughter."

Daughter! A girl.

She hoped Steve would be happy with a girl. He'd always talked of teaching his son to play hockey and what not, but he rarely considered the notion of a daughter.

"Where is she?"

"Just down the hall in the nursery. I'll let them know you're awake and would like to see her."

Stephanie France Connor entered the world on August 25, 1944, the same day Paris was liberated. It was love at first sight. The enormous eyes that blinked up at Faye held the promise of her dad's coloring and her grandpa's analytic prowess. Faye tried to describe her pink, plump little body, her ten perfect little toes, and her intent gaze that defied her extreme youth in a letter to Steve.

> *She is the most perfect little human being imaginable, and she's so looking forward to meeting her daddy. I'll send a photo in my next letter. I can't wait to get her home, but my doctor says I have to stay here for four days. I hope I don't starve; the food is just horrible. I'd rather they serve us K-rations; at least then there would be no pretense that meals here are anything but what they are—inedible. In the meantime, I hope you know how much I love you and that I will be forever grateful to you for the gift of this perfect child.*

Mother and Pops called every few days for updates, promising to come out for Thanksgiving. Steve's parents called the day after Stephanie was born, requesting photos and a blow-by-blow description of their fourth grandchild. Every few hours, the nurse brought in another congratulatory bouquet and gifts for the baby from her workmates, her extended family and friends back home. The drab corner of the maternity ward was soon awash in a riot of pink and yellow flower arrangements, stacked vase-to-vase on the window ledge.

A steady stream of visitors made the next few days fly by. Faye called them the Auntie Brigade. Midge, Hannah, and Evie all spent their lunch and evening hours with her, passing the swaddled Stephanie around like a football. Even Mr. Dalton showed up, clearly uncomfortable in a maternity ward, but clutching a large bouquet of pink roses that coordinated well with the blush on his face to the tips of his ears.

"She's so beautiful," Mrs. Chu gushed, who dropped by with Madeline. They presented Stephanie with a beautiful jade pendant in the shape of a monkey.

"It's the Year of the Monkey and jade is good luck," Madeline explained, proud of her part in the healthy birth. "People born in the Year of the Monkey are intelligent, witty, and strong-willed."

"I think she started out with good luck, thanks to you and your friends."

"Believe me, you're the talk of the neighborhood—and most likely will be until Stephanie is in college!"

On the fourth day after the birth, Faye and Stephanie were bundled into a taxi for the ride back to Fella Place, Midge riding shotgun to get them settled. The next day the doorbell rang, and the Western Union deliveryman handed Faye a yellow envelope.

33

———

*The Secretary of War asks that I assure you of his deep sympathy in
the loss of your husband, Technician G4 Steven Connor, killed in
action on August 7, 1944, in northern France.
Confirming letter follows.*

—Major General James Ulio

Acting Adjutant General, United States Army

Faye sobbed audibly and endlessly for several days, then settled into weeks of silent weeping. As the reality of Steve's death sank in, grief, like a parasite, consumed her from the inside, leaving her hollow and numb. Steve, her love, her life, was gone. Forever. He would never know his daughter, never realize his full potential. Her heart, so recently filled with joy, now felt vacant. It was a burden to even breathe.

Her friends and flat mates tiptoed around the house, offering tea or sympathy or both. Midge and Aunt Liz showed up regularly to take care of the baby and give Faye time with her own despair.

Madeline Chu would arrive some mornings and sit in the corner of her room, sometimes all day, scribbling on her notepad in silence. Faye, barely aware of anything, explored the depths of her anguish. Seventeen days. That's all the time she and Steve had spent together as a husband and wife. And now she was on her own—not just for the war, but for good—with no one to set her future path. With the polestar that directed her very existence now extinguished, she drifted aimlessly in her grief.

I'm a widow, and I barely knew what it was like to be married.

The progression of European cities liberated by the Allies that autumn—Marseilles, Brussels, Antwerp, Ghent, Luxemburg, the progress in the Pacific, then the entrance of the Allies into Buchenwald—all rang bittersweet to Faye. With Steve gone, her capacity to feel even the slightest bit of elation at the events of the day died along with him.

Faye spent week upon week submerged in despair. It was a chore to focus on the present. She found the routine of feedings, diaper changes, and nap times like a sedative, calming and tranquil, requiring little thought. The tedium of getting through the day dampened her pain and allowed her to—very gradually—reawaken.

Then, toward the end of October, Faye found the reason to poke her head above her grief. The sun was streaming into the bedroom. She had just changed Stephanie, who was now trying to shove her entire fist into her mouth, drooling all the while. As Faye leaned forward, Stephanie's focus shifted to her mom's face. Stephanie blinked her huge eyes—Steve's eyes—then broke into a dimpled smile and a stream of delighted gurgles and coos.

In this most ordinary of moments, Faye experienced the most extraordinary epiphany.

You sweet thing. You know nothing of sadness or loss. Everything for you is new and exciting.

She took a series of deep breaths, each more fortifying than the next. The balance had tipped. Heartache still present, her determination now overshadowed it.

Faye Elizabeth Baxter Connor, you snap out of it. You need to set aside your own grief and be present for this child. She shouldn't have to start her life in sadness.

With that, Faye swooped Stephanie up from the changing table and hugged her close. "Mama's here, Stephie. Mama's here."

Over the next few months, Faye discovered that grief was kind of like the tide. While it never went away, it ebbed and flowed and, in the meantime, life could go on. She settled into an energetic routine with daily walks. Faye pushed Stephanie, bundled up in her pram, through parks, over impossibly steep hills, and along the bay. A favorite excursion was to Chinatown, where Faye reconnected with Mrs. Wong, the lady in the purple coat who helped her get to the hospital. When they stopped in at her produce market for a quick visit and some fresh vegetables, Stephanie would squeal in delight as Mrs. Wong "goochie gooed" in Cantonese.

Sometimes, something—a place, a sound, a smell—triggered a memory and Faye found herself weeping. But each day her soul healed a little more, and she eventually gave herself permission to delight in her child's happiness.

For the preservation of our way of life from the threat of destruction: for the unity of spirit which has kept our Nation strong; for our abiding faith in freedom; and for the promise of an enduring peace, we should lift up our hearts in thanksgiving.

By the President of the United States of America

A Proclamation, Thanksgiving Day, 1944

The Baxters came to visit for Thanksgiving, and the Fella Place table this year included proud grandparents. Midge, Faye, Evie, Madeline, as well as the typical rag-tag assortment of friends and "orphans," crowded shoulder to shoulder in the living room for the third year to break bread and give thanks. And, although this year had brought more than its share of sadness, they found plenty to be thankful for. The boys in Europe were close to crossing the Rhine for the final push to Berlin. General MacArthur had landed on Leyte and the liberation of the Philippines was at hand. And President Franklin Delano Roosevelt, Commander-in-Chief of the US Armed Forces, had just been elected to his fourth term in office.

For most of the afternoon and evening, Pops bounced a smiling Stephanie on his knee. Faye had never seen this bubbly side of her father's personality. Ever. He cooed and chuckled as he held his granddaughter, convinced that her IQ was well above average.

"Pops, she's three months old. The last thing I need is a precocious infant with a swollen head."

"She's going to do great things," Pops announced to the group. "Mark my words, we have a mathematician in the making."

The Baxters stayed for a week, encamped a block away at the Mark Hopkins. On rainy days, excursions to the de Young museum in Golden Gate Park and the Legion of Honor near Baker Beach provided warm, dry places to stroll and visit. Pops insisted on several trips to the local bookstore, which resulted in a sizable library for Stephanie that included *Mother Goose Rhymes, Goodnight Moon, Le Petit Prince*—both English and French editions—and, of course, *Essentials of Algebra.*

The evening before they were to return to Evanston, Evie offered to watch Steph while Faye and her parents went out to a nice dinner at Tadich Grill.

"Fifi, you've done a fine job, but we want you to think about coming home," Pops said after sipping his Manhattan and smoothing the white linen tablecloth in front of him.

"Home? You mean back to Evanston?" Faye could barely think of Evanston without thinking of Steve and teetering on that ever-present crevasse of sadness. Here, her life was hers. There, she'd be confronted by memory after memory.

I'm only now getting used to the idea that Steve's gone. I couldn't bear being in Evanston right now.

"You are our only child, Faye," Pops continued, sensing her hesitancy. "Stephanie might well be our only grand-child. Mother and I would like to know her as she grows up."

"And we'd like her to know us," Mother added. "I'm sure Steve's parents feel the same."

The sincerity in their voices and hope in their eyes tugged at Faye's heart. Was she being selfish? She paused to sip her martini and ponder her response.

"I understand," she said, her voice rich with emotion, "but I feel I am still useful out here. I'm set to return to work in January."

"But who will watch the baby?" Mother asked, clearly horrified at the thought of her granddaughter in a stranger's care. "Your child should be your first priority, Faye dear. Why, I've heard of moms parking their kids in movie theaters while they're at work. Besides," she continued after a sip of her cocktail, "it isn't like you *have* to work, Faye dear. You could move home with us."

Faye sipped deeply from her martini as she carefully formulated her response. She knew this was a sensitive subject for both of her parents, and she didn't want to end their visit on a bad note. At the same time, she felt she could handle both work and motherhood—and she did *not* want to move back to Evanston right now. Maybe someday, but not right now.

"Actually, Liz Bosch asked if she could watch Steph while I'm at work. Her girls are still in Los Angeles for another year, and she's been hankering for another little girl to nurture. She's offered several times, and we've talked seriously about a schedule. The Gregor Corp building is only a few blocks from here, so I can be home in a flash if need be."

The Baxters looked at each other very briefly with apprehension, then shifted their focus to the three huge bowls of cioppino the waiter delivered to the table.

"The Gregor Corp management has been nothing but generous in allowing me a flexible schedule. I'd really like to give this a try while I have a job and they need me. When the war ends, I'm not sure what kind of opportunities there will be for working moms."

"Well, at least think about it," Pops said as he tucked his napkin into his shirt collar and broke off a hunk of sourdough bread, poised to dig in. "You and Stephanie seem to be doing okay here, but I'm sure you could make a fine life just as well in Evanston."

34

Faye's life as a working mother fell into place as 1945 got underway. Aunt Liz would arrive at the Fella flat at six thirty a.m. to watch the baby while Faye showered and dressed for work. Faye would be at her desk by seven thirty, enjoying a few productive hours before the bulk of Gregor Corp employees arrived. She'd leave every afternoon promptly at four, often greeted at the Montgomery Street entrance by Aunt Liz with Stephie bundled up in her stroller.

Liz would catch the streetcar home, while Faye and Stephanie strolled one of many routes back to Fella Place, sometimes through Union Square, sometimes through Chinatown for a visit with Mrs. Wong, always with much excitement on Stephanie's part. It was quite a workable routine, and Stephanie seemed to be thriving.

However manageable things were for Faye in her personal life, she knew that the tide was about to turn on world events. As the spring wore on, Allied victory in Europe seemed imminent. The terrible Battle of the Bulge, the surprise last gasp of Nazi power in the flatlands of Belgium, was finally quelled in late January, clearing the way for an all-out assault on Berlin. From the east, the Red Army marched into Warsaw and saw a clear path to Berlin. In the Pacific, the US took the island of Iwo Jima, where they would establish a base for fighter planes for the coming invasion of Japan. In March, those planes conducted a massive bombing raid on Tokyo, leaving half the city in flames.

Also in March, Faye came home to a package in the mail from the Army Effects Bureau in Kansas City. She stared at the paper-wrapped parcel with trepidation.

Steve's things.

As she held the box, her emotions wrestled with her curiosity. Did she want to open the box, or would she be too distraught? Sure, she wanted to see the things Steve carried with him into battle, but she didn't want to spend the afternoon overcome with sorrow. After a few conflicted minutes, she put the box on the highest shelf in her closet, closed the door and went to fix Stephanie some pureed carrots and rice for dinner.

We interrupt this program to bring you a special news bulletin. A press association has just announced that President Roosevelt is dead. The president died of a cerebral hemorrhage.

Radio Broadcast, April 12, 1945

The news of FDR's passing swept with gale force through the Gregor Corp offices as soon as the news hit the airwaves. He was the only president Faye and her contemporaries could ever remember, right below Almighty God in terms of reverence and stature. It was like losing a beloved and very wise uncle. For the rest of the afternoon, the Gregor Corp staff gathered in little clusters throughout the building, sharing memories and seeking comfort in numbers. More than one bottle of whiskey appeared from various bottom desk drawers, and toasts were made, as both men and women wept. This was a national loss at a time when the end of the war slowly crept into the realm of possibility.

Our troops have crossed the Elbe River and are within sixty miles of Berlin! How could he be dead when the war was almost over? Who will fill the void? Truman? The haberdasher from Missouri?

The president's death brought back the stark reality that Steve was also gone, and Faye huddled in her office for the rest of the day, unable to concentrate. She sipped her paper cup of whiskey and cried for her loss, for the nation's loss, and for the uncertainty of the future.

Both Evie and Hannah showed up at Faye's little office just before quitting time, so when she met up with Aunt Liz and Stephanie in the Montgomery Street lobby, she had the "aunties" in tow. Stephanie, delighted to see her doting housemates, gurgled and laughed. Faye's mascara was long gone, but she again found the resolve to put on a brave face for her baby's sake.

I swear I will not to be the one to bring grief into her world.

Coverage of the Roosevelt funeral dominated the radio and newsreels throughout the weekend. Faye made an extra effort to take Stephanie on a long walk in Golden Gate Park on Sunday, the National Day of Mourning. The magnolias in the Botanical Gardens were in bloom, and they sat and enjoyed the sunshine while Stephanie babbled at the canopy of blossoms.

Work went on as normal on Monday, as Roosevelt

would have wanted. War production, in his mind, was way more important than a funeral, even if it was his own. Employees gathered in the break room throughout the day to listen to burial coverage on the radio, and most everyone wore black. There was a solemnity throughout the company that day, hushed conversations, no chit chat, all business and quiet reflection. While it was clear that the war was not over, all of America felt that some unseen door had been closed and bolted.

~

On May 7, 1945, after the Russians entered Berlin and Hitler committed suicide, Germany officially surrendered. Victory in Europe Day was marked by tumultuous celebrations in London, Paris and New York—and business as usual in San Francisco. The fight in the Pacific continued, after all, and San Francisco felt a connection to all those boys who sailed off through the Golden Gate. The Big Party would have to wait until all the fighting had stopped.

Stores, churches, and businesses remained open, but most bars closed. Like the majority of the city's workforce, the Gregor Corp staff responded to the call to "Celebrate VE Day by Giving Blood," and the lines at the Red Cross blood bank snaked around the building all afternoon.

Never willing to pass up an opportunity to celebrate, the Fella Place sisterhood pooled their ration coupons and bought a nice leg of lamb, baked some potatoes, harvested some spinach from the roof garden, and found a bottle of red from Cresta Blanca Winery out in Livermore.

"Thank goodness the Army made enough raisins in '42 to keep the troops in fruit for the duration," Evie noted. "Otherwise, who knows what we'd be drinking!"

The roast was shared by all the usual suspects, plus a few guests: Evie invited a new friend, Sue Stevens, from her gardening club, a bookish woman in her thirties who taught school in the Inner Richmond neighborhood. Sue had a lilting laugh that rang out frequently during the evening, especially when Evie made one of her corny puns. Midge brought along a new gentleman admirer, a nice-looking man called Joe. Categorized 4-F for his flat feet, Joe had been assigned to the management team at Kaiser Shipyard #3 for the duration. He was quiet, witty, and clearly smitten with Midge.

Midge was quite the center of attention that evening, showing off a bandaged forearm. She'd caught it on a piece of metal as she climbed a ladder down into the hull of a Liberty ship and received eight stitches at the Kaiser hospital that morning.

"Old man Kaiser looks at delivering emergency services like he does building ships: make it efficient and cut out the middleman," she relayed. "I was stitched, wrapped, and back in the Yard in a few hours."

Like all workers at the Kaiser Shipyards, Midge had fifty cents withheld from every paycheck as a contribution to prepaid health services. Kaiser had clinics on site and built a full hospital close-by in Richmond to serve his workforce.

"You'd think they'd give me the rest of the day off, but nope. 'If you can see straight, you can help out inspecting the welds,' is exactly what my floor manager said," Midge reported. "So, I'm on light duty until the stitches come out in two weeks."

"Sounds like you need an extra serving of bread pudding, then," Evie said, serving her up a double portion. "Considering that the war in Europe is officially over, how many more ships will we need? I imagine the Yards will be cutting back soon."

With the party contemplating changes on the horizon, Faye excused herself to put Stephanie to bed. As they rocked, Faye breathed in the baby sweetness of her daughter and gently sang "Swinging on a Star." The baby's eyes grew heavy. Faye kissed her forehead and held her close, marveling at how fast she was growing and how quickly her little sponge of a mind was learning.

"Your daddy would be so proud, Stephie," she whispered.

Steve was on Faye's mind for the rest of the evening. She decided to forgo more alcohol and dancing, instead tackling the pile of dirty dishes stacked on the counter. As she listened to the music and laughter coming from the living room, she felt as if Steve was next to her, dish towel in hand.

"Gosh, I miss you," Faye whispered out loud.

"Ditto, kiddo," he would have said. "You're doing such a good job with our baby, my Faye. Please let her know that I didn't want to die. I was just doing what our country needed me to do."

The tears that started to roll down Faye's cheeks dripped off her chin and popped the bubbles in the dishpan. Not wanting to sink into all-out sadness while she still had guests in the house, Faye caught herself.

Goodness. What a crybaby. Chin up and stop feeling sorry for yourself. You've got a lot to be thankful for, so quit wallowing, Faye Elizabeth Baxter Connor.

With that final bit of self-admonishment, she dried her hands, switched off the kitchen light, and joined the frivolity in the living room.

35

It took her months, but Faye could finally see the bottom of her inbox. New contracts always took priority, so the receipts, shipping manifests, and inventory reports from the beginning of her time away continued to pile up. Though she was tempted to pass the stack on to the clerical staff for filing, her gut told her she really needed to review everything.

And if there's one thing I've learned since I've been in San Francisco, it's to listen to your gut.

She was glad she did. The dozen receipts for ammonium nitrate were all exactly the same: 161 bags delivered. So was the purchase order: 167 bags ordered. She scrutinized the penmanship.

"No, these definitely say 161, so take that, Wallace."

Wallace!

As she remembered that humiliating meeting all those months ago, it occurred to her that she never had a chance to hear what Madeline had learned about the Wallace-

Douglas Chu rift. She dialed the neighborhood news desk at *The Chronicle* and left a message for Madeline to call her back as soon as she could.

"It's really an issue of Cantonese pride and stubbornness," Madeline recounted in the lobby of the Saint Francis later that afternoon. Like many hotels, the Saint Francis had real coffee, and the girls ordered a small pot to share. "I finally got my godfather to fill me in. That's one thing about my people, if one gets their nose out of joint, the entire brotherhood will share the aggravation."

Faye added more cream to her coffee, then said, "Well, I've come across some information that may or may not put Wallace in a lot of hot water, so spill it, sister."

"It has to do with explosives."

Faye's eyes opened wide as she almost choked on her coffee.

"What kind of explosives?"

"Well, that's the issue. My people are experts in black powder, the kind of explosive used in fireworks. Dynamite, too, but mostly fireworks these days. It seems that Wallace approached my father to find people who could work with ammonium nitrate."

"Do you know why?"

"I don't think the conversation ever got to the why. Baba knew Wallace was up to no good and didn't want to get involved. A white man asking the Chinese for help with explosives just sounded too shady. To get off the hook, he explained that there were different kinds of explosives, and black powder was a whole different kind of expertise.

Wallace said some things that were clearly racially charged and that was the end of it."

So, Wallace could have a connection to the missing chemicals. But for what?

"Okay, it's your turn now." Madeline lit a cigarette and settled back in her chair.

Faye looked around the lobby to make sure no one could overhear. She pulled her chair in closer and spoke in a low, steady voice.

"Wallace might be stockpiling explosives. I don't know why, but the receipts clearly don't match the purchase orders—and that's since I went out on furlough last August. He knew no one would be reconciling the accounts while I was gone. It's always six bags short."

"Six bags of ammonium nitrite! How many in total?"

"At least 180. That's like 9,000 pounds."

"Given the right circumstances, that could mean a big kablooey."

"That's what I'm worried about." Faye sipped her coffee. "I need to find out if, and where, it's being stockpiled."

Madeline rolled her eyes. "Faye. Be reasonable. You're a mother, and Stephanie is the most precious baby ever who's already lost her father. Let's just tell the police."

It occurred to Faye that Madeline knew nothing about her OSS assignment or even that Simon Miller was an enemy agent.

Careful, now. She's a smart cookie—smarter than most—so watch what you say.

"It's too early. There are too many questions. We use ammonium nitrate as a blasting agent in our road construction projects, but it's also used as fertilizer. So, it could be perfectly innocent. I've been condescended to enough by people like Wallace, so I need to have my story pinned down to a T," said Faye forcefully. "The shipment comes in by rail in Oakland, and it's held at our warehouse before it's delivered to the job site. The correct number of bags are leaving the warehouse, they're just not arriving at the job site. I checked the schedule, and a delivery is expected at our project in Burlingame on Thursday. No one's going to know if I happen to follow the truck and see where it delivers its cargo. What could go wrong?"

"Well, let's see. An explosive, an unknown plot, a hothead of a suspect, what could go wrong, indeed." She took a deep drag of her cigarette and exhaled slowly. "Okay, sister, let's do it."

"What?"

"Well, look, I brought you some key information, didn't I? I'll come with you. That way I won't be sitting at home worried sick about you. And, who knows, this could really turn into the front-page story I've been looking for."

The Gregor warehouse in West Oakland was a sprawling single-story brick building between Seventh Street and the harbor. The girls sat in Madeline's navy-blue Ford De Luxe coupe outside the main gate. It was just after seven a.m., and the delivery trucks were still inside the gated area. The street at that hour was empty, except for three burly Chinese men sweeping the sidewalk and a vendor—also Chinese—selling snacks from a cart. It was only when the snack cart vendor ever so subtly looked over and nodded at Madeline that Faye made the connection.

Faye looked pointedly at Madeline, who 'fessed up.

"All right! Oakland's Chinatown is only a few blocks away and alerted my network there might be trouble. So, sue me."

"How 'bout I thank you, instead?" Faye smiled. "I must say it's reassuring."

She surveyed the scene for a minute, then quietly opened the car door. "I'll be right back. I know the warehouse supervisor, so I think I can find out what truck is making the Burlingame delivery."

"If you're not back in fifteen minutes, I'm coming in after you."

"I'm counting on it." With that she strode purposefully through the gates to the office entrance, hoping she projected an air of authority to the gaggle of drivers smoking by the door.

"Mrs. Connor! What a surprise. To what do we owe this visit?"

She'd only been to the warehouse a few times before but talked frequently to Mr. Hernandez.

"Good morning, Mr. Hernandez. I hope you don't mind me stopping by. There was a last-minute change in a few of the deliveries, so I want to make sure the correct information got communicated to you.

"We had a call from purchasing late yesterday, so they should be fine." He showed Faye his clipboard. "See Benicia gets 217, not 180, bags of cement and Napa gets fifty bundles of rebar added to their order."

Faye casually took the clipboard from him and scanned the page, as if confirming the changes. She actually looked for the number of the truck headed to Burlingame.

"The PM in Napa was frantic, so I promised to come check personally," she commented.

There it is. Truck number 136.

She smiled.

"Looks all in order." She handed the clipboard back to him. "I also wanted to ask if you have enough drivers for next month. Benicia will be in full force by then, and deliveries will probably be triple what they are this month."

He pondered the schedule on the massive chalkboard that dominated his office. "I think we'll be alright. We can always shuffle drivers if there's a day that's especially busy, but thanks for the head's up."

"Well, you and your team have been doing a great job, but if you need anything I can put in a word with the management team."

"Will do!"

"I'll let you get back to it. Thanks again for the impromptu meeting!"

"My pleasure. Stop by any time."

"I got it!" Faye reported as she slid back into Madeline's car. "It's truck number 136. Trucks are going to start coming out of that gate in about ten minutes, so let's keep our eyes peeled."

"I'm going to tell my posse to stand down, then." She quickly went and talked to the food vendor and was back in the car in less than sixty seconds with a small paper bag, bulging and fragrant. "Uncle Wu gave us sesame balls. He told me we look too skinny."

"Breakfast of champions! I'm starving."

As they munched their *jian dui*, both women kept their eyes glued to the gate, car engine running.

"There it is!" they said in unison.

When truck number 136 emerged, Madeline slid her

coupe in gear and followed it at a discreet distance back to the Bay Bridge. As it merged with other traffic, Faye made sure she had the truck in sight. They tailed it down Mission Street, the most direct route to the South Bay. But as they approached South Van Ness, the driver's arm appeared and signaled a right turn.

"Hmm…that's odd. If he was heading to Burlingame, he would stay on Mission to 101. Be sure to stick with him," Faye instructed.

"So where are you going, Mr. 136?" Madeline whispered, slowing to make the turn.

The truck made its way past the Victorian apartments, fabrication shops, neighborhood markets, contractor suppliers, and corner bars that populated this working-class neighborhood. It turned left onto Grove Street, and immediately pulled into what appeared to be a body shop. As soon as the truck entered the work bay, a portly man in overalls pulled the garage doors down.

"I'll be right back." Faye reached for the latch on her door.

"You are *not* going in there!" Madeline was adamant.

"I just want to look in the window. See?" Faye pointed to the window that was easily accessible from the loading dock. "No one will see me, just a quick peek."

"I'll go. You'd be surprised how invisible my people can be."

Madeline pulled a tatty jacket, an old Fedora, and a well-used broom from the back seat.

"I never travel without my blend-into-the-pavement outfit."

Faye had to admit: her comrade looked pretty anonymous in her shabby garb. Pulling her hat low, Madeline dashed across the street dashed across the street, crept up the stairs to the loading dock, stood on her tiptoes and peered through the window for several minutes. Then, suddenly, she raced back down the stairs and started to randomly sweep the sidewalk just as the garage door opened. The truck emerged and turned east back toward Van Ness. Faye slumped down in the passenger seat as two men exited through the loading-dock door onto the sidewalk. Faye's breath caught.

Wallace! You weasel!

The two men talked for a minute, then Wallace strode off—right past Madeline—and the other man went back into the body shop.

Once she was sure both men were out of sight, Madeline swept her way leisurely back to the car.

Faye bombarded her as soon as she slid into the driver's seat.

"That was Wallace."

"I know." Madeline turned the ignition and calmly steered west on Hayes. "I heard there's something going on at the end of the month. I didn't catch all the details, but they specifically said Opera House."

The two women looked at each other, reaching the same unspoken conclusion. The War Memorial Opera House was currently hosting the United Nations Conference. Representatives from more than twenty nations had been meeting since the end of April to ratify an agreement to ensure world peace. It was just announced that President Truman would attend the signing of the Charter, scheduled for June twenty-sixth. A secret cache of an explosive was being amassed two blocks from the Opera House and the signing ceremony was next week.

"What'll we do?" asked Madeline, knowing the seriousness of the situation. "Go to the cops?"

"I have a contact at the FBI," said Faye. "I have names, addresses, and dates now, so let me start there. And in the meantime, you'd better start making notes. Someone's going to get a nice fat byline, and it sure as shootin' should be you!"

36

───────

The news broke two days before the charter signing ceremony.

"Holy crapballs! Knock me down and tie me up sideways!"

Evie saw the article first. It was on the front page of the *Chronicle*, all but overshadowed by UN news.

"Gregor Corp Execs Arrested; Treason Alleged," she said, reading the headline.

"What? Who is it?" Hannah rushed to look over Evie's shoulder

Evie continued to read, "The FBI arrested two top Gregor Corp executives on suspicion of diverting construction materials for treasonous activities. The two men, Mr. James Wallace and Mr. Herman Smith, are expected to plead not guilty in Federal court today, according to their attorneys. The FBI apprehended the two men at their homes, also seizing files of documents and correspondence. An arraignment is scheduled for next week."

Herman Smith!

When Faye spoke with her surveillance team last week, she'd only implicated Wallace.

Herman Smith must be the high value target they've been after.

And the more she thought about it, the more sense it made. Starting way back at Smith's house party when she stumbled upon his art collection, to the sighting with Red Lips at the Palace…the random signs over the years seemed merely like odd incidents individually but added up to a damning body of evidence.

"Well, I have a strong suspicions that not much work is going to get done at work today," Hannah said. "I'm anticipating a gale breeze from all the flapping lips."

"Who'd a thunk it?"

When Faye finally got the front page she re-read the article, making a mental account of what was *not* mentioned. *The cache of explosives. The plot to blow up the War Memorial Opera House. The averted cataclysm at the birth of the United Nations.*

Turning back to the front page, she spotted the byline for the article: Staff Reporter.

I bet Madeline Chu is spitting nails.

"I was mad at first, but understood their perspective in the end," Madeline affirmed the following Monday as they walked from Faye's apartment to the Civic Center to see President Truman arrive.

"Which was what? To cheat you out of your due recognition?"

"Don't worry. My time will come. I stayed up for two days straight reworking the story with both my editor and legal breathing down my neck. They didn't want to detract from the importance of the Charter signing with news of a thwarted plot. That's why we reported 'diverted construction materials' and 'treasonous activity.' And they didn't want the fact that I'm Chinese and female to detract from the credibility of the article."

"They think no one will believe the cute little Chinese girl?"

"I'm sure there's some of that. But given the hostilities between my family and Wallace, they didn't want any possibility of retaliation. In the end, I agreed with them. I'd feel awful if anything ever happened to my family because of some reporting I did."

"That's understandable."

"At least my editor didn't get credit, which was one of the options under discussion. The good thing is…" She flashed a press pass with a sly smile. "They owe me big, and they know it."

"Is that for today?"

"You said it, sister! A fully credentialed member of the press, covering the signing ceremony. My name will appear with a half dozen others on the front page tomorrow."

"Well get to it, Lois Lane."

As Madeline veered off at Larkin toward the Opera House, Faye joined the crowd on Market to watch President Truman arrive. Streamers and confetti poured from office buildings, Navy bombers flew overhead, crowds five- and six-people deep lined the parade route. The crowds cheered and cheered as the motorcade passed.

A world with no more war. A commitment to resolve international conflicts by diplomacy through a democratic process. The free world was united in its desire for a lasting peace.

It seems too good to be possible.

Some blanks in the Wallace/Smith conspiracy were filled in at the next briefing—or rather debriefing—of her surveillance team.

"At this point, we're just beginning the investigation, so a lot of the story is still unknown. Here's what we *do* know," G-man Paige said. "Jim Wallace isn't so much a Nazi as a nationalist. He'd been active in the America First movement and has a beef with any kind of international cooperation, which is why he signed on to help disrupt the charter conference. He was not the mastermind, merely a patsy."

"The real villain is Herman Smith, who's clearly a Nazi sympathizer," Balboa continued, referring to her file.

I knew it!

"Both he and his wife spent time in Germany in the '30s and were active in the American Bund. Early in the war, they would hold house parties for young military men on leave, hoping to liquor them up and get them to reveal details of their training and activities. We found copies of detailed reports to Kruger, who was their contact."

"Not only was he planning to cause chaos at the Charter signing, but he also seems to have been successful at enriching his own pockets by siphoning off materials from the Gregor suppliers, then reselling them under his own company he'd set up in Nevada," G-Man Paige added.

"So, your instinct about the gravel overages was correct, Mrs. Connor," Dalton said. "Smith had certain truckers on his payroll who would drop part of their load at a yard out in Stockton; then it was transported to Smith's business outside of Las Vegas. There's plenty of construction in that area, so dealing in stolen goods paid him very well. He counted on no one paying attention to the big picture, which worked fine. Until you came along."

"And even for some months after that." Faye tried to keep the I-told-you-so tone out of her comment.

"So, with the help of Wallace, Smith got very rich, and planned to throw the signing of the United Nations Charter into chaos," Balboa chimed in. "They'd already started transferring the explosives to the basement of the War Memorial Opera House, disguised as crates of dinnerware for the reception."

"A desperate last gasp for a defeated enemy—and Smith's entire value set," the G-Man said.

Dalton turned to her and, after a slight pause, added, "At any rate, Mrs. Connor, we are eternally grateful for your efforts in this matter."

Faye flushed with pride. She'd done it. She'd helped save the promise for a free, peaceful world.

And no one will ever know.

37

———————

R ight after July Fourth, Faye was summoned to Mr. Nugent's office, and was surprised to see Mr. Dalton already there.

"Have a seat, Mrs. Connor." Nugent gestured to the empty chair in front of his desk.

This doesn't sound like it's going to be good news.

Nugent cleared his throat and, without making eye contact, began what sounded like a well-rehearsed statement. "As you can tell, the war is about over, and we anticipate the boys coming home. They will need their jobs back."

What he said was no surprise to Faye. She had always intended to work only for the duration, but now that the gig was up, she found herself off kilter a bit.

"And that means, *my* job?"

"You've been such a marvelous asset to the company," Dalton said, who was clearly uneasy with the conversation.

"It's only right. They saved the world. We owe them a future." Another canned response from Nugent.

Like I didn't put my life on the line more than once to do the same?

"I understand, but, with all the reconstruction—not only here but around the world—our business is booming. Aren't there enough jobs for both men and women?"

"Let's think about what you just said," Nugent said, cutting her off abruptly. "Men and women. You really think men and women can work together on a professional basis?"

"But we've been working together for the last three years. And pretty successfully, if I do say so myself."

After exchanging glances, Dalton continued in a sympathetic tone. "Everything's different during war. We are able to bend rules and test limits, because we all have a common goal that takes priority over peacetime paradigms."

"But haven't I been working to your expectation?"

"Expectations be damned!" an agitated Nugent responded. "It's not a matter of performance or ability, but of opportunity. You don't think you could have worked as a married woman or matriculated out of the secretarial pool in peacetime, do you? Even I will have to give up my place, and go back to retirement," he added, as if that would strengthen the argument.

"And I will have to honcho a whole gaggle of rookies, back from the war and ready to raise some hell," said Dalton wistfully. "I can tell you I don't look forward to that at all."

"Anyway, Mrs. Connor," Nugent shifted his attention back to matters at hand, "your contract with Gregor Corp will terminate on July thirty-first. We will pay you through August, as we would like you to stay on and train your replacement."

What?

The ultimate insult. Faye closed her eyes briefly to keep her anger from spilling out and filling the room.

Oblivious, Nugent continued, "If you'd like to use our air transport voucher to fly back to Chicago, that can be arranged. It might make relocating with an infant easier. We feel we owe you that much, for your years of fine service."

Faye didn't hear any of the praise. Her brain had stopped listening as soon as Dalton said "relocating."

Back to Chicago?

Faye was stunned.

I put my life on the line for this company, and now they're showing me the door? Surely there's a way to accommodate the returning men and *the women who have worked for the war effort from the home front.*

"I would like to remind you gentlemen that I am not a married woman. I am a war widow with a young child to support."

"We applaud your ambition, Mrs. Connor," Nugent said without emotion, "but these are policies from corporate.

Dalton, clearly flustered by Faye's intensity, added, "We're just the messengers, here. I'm sure your family will be glad to help out. Your father's still working, is he not?"

So that's it? I'm expected to go back to my father's home and be supported.

Faye knew she'd had a change of heart over the last few years. She'd started off planning to stay in this job only while the war was on. But the more responsibility she was given at work, the more her sense of value increased. She felt strong and consequential, feelings she never knew were so important to her. Now that the reality of dismissal was staring her in the face, she felt indignant and insulted.

After a pause and a deep breath, she said calmly, "It so happens, gentlemen, that I am a capable adult and do not wish to be dependent on my father."

They both looked at her in shock, as if she had blasphemed. She looked from one manager to the other: Dalton wore a sheepish expression, but Nugent remained defiant.

After a lengthy pause, she continued, "What about the girls in the secretarial pool? Will they be pink slipped, too?"

"Those are jobs that are traditionally held by single women, so single women will be permitted to stay at the junior levels. Married women and the girls in accounting are all being given notice. It's only right."

Right? Really?

Faye was suddenly filled with an outrage too intense to contain. She rose to her full height and cleared her throat. Then, very calmly, she spoke.

"Gentlemen, since the risk of me being fired is moot at this point, I want to say something. I readily admit that I am a woman, but I am also a capable *person*. I took on a job, previously held by a man, and did it well—dare I say, better than my predecessor. I have seen a lot of injustice during these war years that I've overlooked for the so-called 'good' of the nation, but I will no longer stay silent. No, gentlemen, it's not right. We women have pitched in when we were needed, and we should continue to be given the same opportunities in the workplace if we want them."

"Now, now, my dear. Please calm down," Mr. Dalton said, clearly wishing the conversation was over.

"I am perfectly calm. I don't expect you to change the way things are. After all, you are only two men in a much larger patriarchy. But I want you both to hear me loud and clear: It is not right."

With that Faye turned on her high heel and left the two of them, eyes wide and mouths agape, to ponder her words.

As news of potential layoffs spread, panic began to grow among the women at Gregor Corp. It was already the beginning of July, less than a month before the terminations would officially begin. It seemed ironic to Faye and many of her colleagues that just when hope had returned to the world that the cloud of war was lifting, they had to deal with a new worry: unemployment. As summer progressed, raw emotions and brittle tempers permeated the workplace, and hurt feelings hung in the air, heavy and dank like wet laundry on a cloudy day.

Faye stayed steamed for days after her conversation with Dalton and Nugent.

At the very least, Dalton should have stood up for me. I'm the one who put my neck on the line and blew the whistle on what could have been a global disaster. And that's the thanks I get?

It was Midge Swanson, of all people—her shipyard-working, sex-loving, straight-talking, independent-minded friend—who helped her gain perspective on the matter.

"For the duration, tootsie…remember? That was the deal," Midge reminded Faye over martinis at Yankee Doodle later that weekend.

"Oh, I remember, but now that the moment is here, I feel taken for granted. I don't like it."

"Look, Faye, these boys saved the world from fascism, and they deserve some payback. I know if Steve and Arnie were still alive, we'd gladly give them our jobs. Everything was different during the war, and now it's going back to normal. I, for one, am glad."

Little do you know, my friend, that I did more than most to save the world from fascism. Where's my payback?

Faye paused to sip her drink, then said, "I have a feeling normal isn't what it used to be."

"Be that as it may, we'll just have to adjust again. I'm proud of the work I've done, but it's kind of tedious. I don't know about you, but I could use a change."

She swirled her martini for a few seconds, then said tentatively.

"Joe and I are getting pretty hot and heavy. I might marry him. I know he'll ask me if I give him any encouragement. He's been offered a job at the Ford plant in Richmond to help transition the assembly line from Jeeps back to consumer vehicles. I wouldn't mind putting down some roots here in the East Bay." She took a sip and added, "And all those boys coming home are going to want to settle down and start families. You'll have plenty of chances to marry again, I'm sure."

Marry again?

Faye hadn't even considered the possibility. Besides, her ability to attract male attention was a big question mark in her mind. "I'm a widow with a child," she commented, as if she had two strikes against her.

Midge plunked her glass down on the bar. "You are a beautiful woman, Faye. And Stephanie is such a peach. I'm sure many men will see you two as a great package deal— kind of a head start toward a storybook family. Or, if not, I'm sure you will be able to find some kind of work when things settle down. They say the switch to a peacetime economy will open up all kinds of opportunities in business and, with your experience, you'll have a leg up."

"Are these seats taken?"

Two men, one in Navy blues and one in civilian clothing, slid into the seats next to Midge. She winked at Faye, as if to say, "watch me get us a free second round" and turned to the lieutenant.

"We've been saving them for some tall, handsome men-about-town. Know any?" she asked in her flirtiest voice.

"Sadly, we're just two broken-down sailors, about to be discharged, looking for a nightcap. We're here to ponder our futures under the influence."

"Ahh, the future," Midge responded, now fully engaged. "My friend Faye and I were just pondering the same thing. I'm Midge," she said, extending her hand.

"Paul."

"I'm Faye," her voice up-beat on the other side of Midge.

As they all shook hands and introduced themselves, Paul suggested, "Let's get some drinks and carry on," he motioned to the bartender. "Bring these ladies another, I'll take a scotch, Jack will have…"

"I'll have a beer." With Jack's New England accent, the word came out "*bee-ah.*"

"You boys on your way home?" Midge lowered her voice to full seduction mode.

"I am home. San Francisco born and bred," Paul declared. "My friend Jack is in town reporting on the United Nations, and he's headed back to DC later tonight."

As the bartender set new martinis down in front of them and removed their empties, Midge said, "Well, we've been here working our hearts out for the war effort, and now we're getting laid off! Whaddya think of that?"

"Why would you lovely young ladies want to keep working? Don't your husbands want to start families?"

"That's not the point," Faye said, ignoring the stereotypical female future Paul had described. "We no longer have the choice. After four years in jobs previously held by men, and doing some great work in those jobs, I might add, it's 'so long, sweetheart. Don't let the door hit your backside on the way out.'"

"We both have places waiting for us in our family businesses, but I feel for ya," Paul said.

"I have often felt that women are getting a bum deal," Jack said. "When we were in the Pacific, we saw women administrators, drivers, mechanics, flight instructors, and nurses who were doing a heck of a job. It would be a shame to let all that talent and experience go to waste."

"Well, here's to you, Jack," Faye toasted. "I hope those sentiments will be the norm someday."

She held up her glass and, just before Jack clinked it, they were interrupted by the hostess.

"Phone call for you, Mr. Kennedy."

"Hold that thought." He flashed a smile at Faye. "I've been waiting for this call from my editor." He grabbed his notepad and rushed off to the lobby.

Kennedy? Jack Kennedy!

Faye and Midge stared at each other, jaws dropping in unison.

Like the rest of America, the girls were intimately familiar with the Kennedy saga. Joe Kennedy, former ambassador to the Court of St. James's and famed isolationist, lost his firstborn in the skies over Germany, about the same time Steve was killed. Jack's sister "Kick" was a war widow, like Faye. Her marriage to a British nobleman had been tragically brief, following a scandalous romance—the Kennedy's were devout Catholic, the Cavendish's Anglican. It had all been in the papers for months last year. It had also been all over the papers the summer before last how Jack had saved the crew of his PT boat after it was sunk in the Pacific.

After a few seconds of very fecund silence, during which the girls' minds were processing the fact that the painfully thin and slightly rumpled young man they were drinking with was Jack Kennedy.

Faye leaned in toward Paul and whispered, "Is that *the* Jack Kennedy?"

"In the flesh." Paul shook out a cigarette and reflected, "I haven't seen him in about a year, so I'm glad Hearst sent him out to cover the conference."

"Are you good friends?"

"We met at officer's school, and we were stationed together in the South Pacific. We had different PT boats. Mine, I'm happy to say, wasn't torpedoed."

"I had no idea that he's a reporter," Faye commented.

"Oh, he won't be for long. He's already antsy in the job. He's been talking about running for Congress next year."

"So be sure to tell all your friends back in Boston that I'm a good guy." Jack reappeared to catch the tail end of Paul's comment. His face broke into a grin—perfect teeth! —that lit up the room. "In the meantime, I just filed my last story of the conference, and I've got a plane to catch. Ladies," he said as he tipped his hat, "it's been a pleasure."

~

"Jack Kennedy. He's a lot handsomer in person, don't you think?" Midge mused.

After finishing their drinks, the girls headed out to the streetcar stop.

"More importantly, I like his views on the value of women in the workplace," Faye responded.

"Well, I know for sure that if it were Arnie or Steve coming home, you'd gladly give up your job for them," Midge pointed out for the second time that evening.

If Steve and Arnie were alive… Faye could finally put the jobs situation in perspective. There was no question that she'd want them—or anyone who'd served in battle—to find employment in the peacetime economy.

Sure, I did my part. But work will help our boys forget what they've been through and readjust to civilian life, and they're going to need that more than me.

This change of heart was solidified when Faye met her replacement, Charles Harriman, an eager, polite young man in his mid-twenties who served in Italy and then Germany. Originally from Kansas City, he did his basic training at Camp Roberts—just like Steve—and knew he wanted to return to the Bay Area after the war ended. He had a slight limp from a shrapnel wound to his left knee, but the doctors told him it would heal with time. He'd fallen in love with an Italian girl while overseas, and now he waited for her to arrive under the War Bride program. He'd already rented a flat in North Beach, thinking the Italian community there would help her feel more at home.

"She should be here next month," he said, eyes glowing with excitement. "You wouldn't believe all the paperwork and red tape we've had to deal with, but it'll be worth it. I can't wait to show her around."

Faye couldn't begrudge this kind, thoughtful, self-sacrificing person anything, even her place at Gregor Corp. In the several weeks he shadowed her, she swallowed her pride and hurt feelings and gave him all the pointers she could.

38

Toward the end of July, when the sun broke clear and strong over the East Bay Hills, the girls of Fella Place headed to the cooling breezes of Baker Beach. They spread their picnic blanket on the sand. In the last month, Stephanie had mastered the first syllable of several nouns. This sunny afternoon, she shrieked "bir, bir, bir" at the sandpipers.

While Evie and Stephie dipped their toes in the frigid surf, Hannah and Faye rubbed their arms and legs with baby oil, stretched out, and felt the sun, like a soft blanket, envelop their bodies from head to toe.

"*Ah.* That feels yummy."

Evie, a manager in a traditionally woman's role, had already been told she would be kept on at Gregor Corp. Hannah, a mid-level accounts receivable clerk, fully expected to be shown the door.

"Where will we be a year from now?"

"I'm heading back to LA as soon as I get the boot," said Hannah without hesitation. "I'm still on the hunt for a nice

Jewish boy in the film industry. Daddy knows someone at Paramount, who says he can hook me up with a production assistant job. Then, it's simply a matter of identifying a victim and making my move." A pause. "What about you?"

"I'm really torn," Faye said tentatively, as if testing some ideas. "I love it here, but I'll have to find a new job. As far as I know, teaching, nursing, and library work are the only options for women outside the secretarial pool. I'm not wild about any of the above. For so long, the war effort has given me a purpose. I need a new one."

"You've got Stephanie."

"I know, but even during my maternity leave I was yearning for something to challenge my adult brain."

Faye had been mulling an idea around for weeks. Since she'd first arrived in San Francisco, she felt guilty for not speaking out more aggressively about the relocation of Japanese Americans. Sure, it was a state of emergency, but she felt strongly that the imprisonment of law-abiding American citizens would fall on the wrong side of history. This had sparked new thoughts regarding her post-war life, and now was as good a time as any to put it out there for comment.

"You know, I've been reading about all the refugees coming to Chicago. I'm thinking I'll go back—maybe not to Evanston, but to someplace in the general area—buy a little place for me and Stephie not too far from my folks and help out the refugee resettlement effort. I'm a really good project manager, and there are lots of aspects of resettlement to coordinate. The end of the war is a new chapter for everyone, and I'd like to help displaced people sort out their lives and find a fresh start."

What Faye didn't share was that the idea came from the last good conversation she had with Simon Miller, when he lied to everyone about working with an international committee for refugee resettlement. That was total hooey, but she'd been intrigued by the notion ever since.

Hannah propped herself up on her elbow and looked at Faye quizzically. "Gee, after all these months of saying you want to stay out here, I'm surprised you're considering a move back home."

"Me, too. But I have to think about Stephie, too, and the pull of home is strong. She should know her grandparents."

"How soon will you leave?"

"Probably as soon as I'm terminated from Gregor Corp. Dalton and Nugent offered to fly me and Steph home, so I'll probably take him up on the offer."

"Let's see—a ten-hour flight or a three-day train trip. Even though Stephanie is the perfect child, she *is* an infant. You'd be nuts not to jump at that."

As promised, pink slips were distributed on July thirty-first. The following week, atomic bombs were dropped on Hiroshima and Nagasaki, and the end was in sight.

39

PEACE!
… Allied Troops Told to Cease Firing
A City Goes Wild—and Nobody Cares

*The end of a long haul came at 4 p.m. in San Francisco yesterday
afternoon and the city went wild. Split seconds after word of the war's
end was flashed from the White House, the celebration began.
Anything that could make noise was blown or pounded or beaten.*

By Charles Rauderbaugh

San Francisco Chronicle, August 15, 1945

The formal announcement of surrender came on a Wednesday afternoon. Just as it had with Roosevelt's death, the news whooshed around the Gregor Corp offices in minutes. Co-workers hugged and kissed, then clustered around the radios to hear updates.

Mr. Dalton, who had stockpiled a case of champagne from before the war, began popping corks. Conversation reflected simple dreams for peace: no rationing, plentiful nylon stockings, long drives in the country for fun. A songfest of victory tunes broke out in the sixth floor conference room and gained enthusiasm as the champagne disappeared.

Evie and Hannah appeared at Faye's desk just before four thirty.

"We're headed out to Market Street to see the celebration," Evie announced.

"I'm due to meet Aunt Liz right now to get Steph. I'll walk over to Market with you. I'd like Stephanie to see history. She's so young, but I still want her to see it."

Aunt Liz was apprehensive about the idea. "The crowds are already forming," she said, waiting with Stephanie as usual in the Gregor Corp lobby. "Celebration or not, the amount of liquor being consumed out there in broad daylight can't be good. I'm headed home to a burger and glass of beer with Henry. That'll be celebration enough for fogies like us."

Faye hugged her tight as she bid her goodbye. "Have a great War's Over evening, then. Tomorrow and Friday are legal holidays, so you can have a nice long weekend with your family."

Aunt Liz knelt and gave Stephanie a kiss on her forehead. "You take good care of your mommy, sweet girl," she said. "Keep her safe and out of trouble."

"Ba," Stephanie said with her most adorable wave.

Then, with a, "See you Monday," to Faye, she headed out the door to the streetcar stop. "If things get too crazy downtown, you girls are always welcome at our place."

The girls made their way a few blocks over to Market Street, Faye pushing Stephanie's stroller along the crowded sidewalk. Stephanie laughed and clapped at the streamers and confetti falling from office windows all along Montgomery. As they approached Market Street, they encountered a solid wall of revelers. Car horns honked, sailors rode atop streetcars and climbed up anything they could, liquor and beer bottles were being passed around and everyone was kissing, hugging, and yelling. The crowd roared as someone started a bonfire in the street.

"There's no way I can navigate through there with the stroller," Faye said. "I'm going to cut up Pine and head on home before things get too crazy."

Hannah nodded, clearly eager to join the throng. "We'll bring you a full report." With a final wave and, "Bye-bye, Pumpkin," to Steph, she and Evie disappeared into the crowd.

The route home took them past impromptu dance parties, crowded bars, and throngs of sailors—all well on their way to falling-down drunkenness, it seemed. All the liquor stores were doing a booming business, and Faye had to divert into the street several times to avoid the crowds of customers waiting to buy more booze. As they turned onto Powell, she encountered a woman—stark naked—dancing her heart out for a horde of appreciative sailors, who clapped and whistled encouragement.

"Oh, for cripe's sake," Faye roared with amusement. It was clear to her that nearly four years of pent-up emotion was suddenly uncorked, and any sense of restraint was being thrown to the wind.

This could get ugly.

"Ipe cakes," Stephanie echoed.

"That's right. Ipe cakes. You tell 'em, Steph."

"Ipe cakes," Stephanie shrieked again, this time clapping her hands and very pleased with herself.

"Well, let's get you some supper, then we'll see about

some special 'ipe cakes' for you, sweet girl. It's a celebration, after all."

Hannah and Evie arrived back at the flat shortly after
midnight. Faye, who had been writing a long letter to her
parents, heard the celebration from three blocks away in
Union Square. Jubilant yelling, air raid sirens, church bells,
car horns all added to the din. At one point, a group of
drunken revelers started to gather in the alley, and Faye
shooed them away.

"That was insane," Evie said, flopping down on the
sofa.

"Things were really getting out of control when we
decided the party was over for us," Hannah confirmed.
"We saw an old man get knocked to the ground when
someone threw a bucket of water from a hotel window! I
would say the vast majority of those punks were too drunk
to walk straight, much less know right from wrong."

"Weren't there any MPs around? Or even regular
police?"

"Sure, but it seemed like they wanted to party, too. We
saw a group of shore police sharing a bottle of something
good while some sailors were breaking a store window in
the same block."

"I don't begrudge anyone a good time, but this was
clearly turning dangerous," Hannah added.

The girls' impressions were confirmed over the next few
days, both by reports in the newspapers and the amount of
rubbish on the streets. Peace was greeted with violence.
Eleven people died, 1000 were injured, and who knows
how many were raped during what the newspapers called

the Peace Riots—all in the name of celebration. With the following week being Faye's last week at work, she was glad to have packing and organizing to focus on while the city around her blew off steam.

For the first time since Faye moved in, the flat on Fella Place was filled with a sense of impending change. Evie intended to stay put, but the other two girls began to sort out their housewares and furnishings. Boxes holding clothes and books were stacked in the corner of the living room, awaiting shipment. Steph was fascinated by all the empty cartons that had suddenly appeared in her domain and had spent the morning crawling blissfully around, moving from one box to another and back again.

As Faye took down a stack of sweaters from her closet, she noticed the long-forgotten parcel from the Army. Steve's personal effects were still untouched in a package that looked the same as the day it had arrived.

Well, I guess this is as good a time as any.

Taking a deep breath, Faye removed the box from the shelf and sat down on her bed. She untied the twine and found a small cardboard box, stamped *Personal Effects* on all six sides. She held the box to her nose and breathed deeply, hoping to catch Steve's scent, like new-mown grass and wintergreen chewing gum. Nothing. After another few minutes gathering her courage, she carefully broke the tape and slowly opened the box.

She was flooded with affection as her eyes fell on Steve's wristwatch. As her eyes began to water, she lifted it from the padding and held it to her ear.

Stopped.

She looked at the face, the second hand frozen and a slight scratch across the top of the crystal. She ever so gently twisted the winding mechanism and, sure enough, the second hand sprang to life.

She watched it tick for thirty seconds, then gently placed the watch on her bed. She unpacked his wedding ring, purchased so hastily that weekend in Monterey, a tin of chewing gum, a picture of herself—pretty dogeared at this point, and the mechanical pencil she'd given him for his twenty-first birthday.

That was a great party.

An envelope had a big red *Undeliverable Return to Army Effects* stamp across the address. Her handwriting. It was the letter she'd written right after Stephanie was born, unopened.

He never knew he had a daughter.

She sat quietly for a few minutes, then lifted his dog tags from the box on its chain. As she stared at the few items on the bed, memories began to swirl like caresses from long ago. Just as her feelings of affection began to turn blue, Stephie crawled into the room, wearing a colander like a helmet atop her unruly curls.

"Mumma!"

"Well, look at you, big girl!" Faye giggled. "Do you have a hat?"

"At!" attempted Stephanie.

"That's right, h-h-h-hat," Faye instructed, emphasizing the *h* sound.

"At."

"Well, let's take that *at* and put it back in the box, you little dumpling," Faye said, lifting Stephanie up and carrying her back to the living room. "That belongs to

Auntie Hannah. The idea is to pack up the boxes, not unpack them."

After dinner when Stephanie was sound asleep, Faye returned once more to Steve's effects. One by one, she placed them in the cigar box that held all the letters he'd written to her. She slipped his wedding ring on her thumb and stroked it softly, tears again blurring her vision. Then, she placed it—along with her own—in the box and gently closed the lid.

The next week turned into a whirlwind of packing, parties and sad goodbyes. Gregor Corp threw a grand "thank you" dinner for all the departing workers, and Faye received a $1,000 bonus check as part of her severance. With her survivor benefits from Steve's death and the money she'd been able to squirrel away from her salary, she was returning to Chicago with a nice nest egg. One of her first orders of business would be to find a broker who could help her make some investments.

On their final evening before their departure, after all the boxes were sealed and Steph was sound asleep, the three flat mates took their gin and tonics up to the roof to watch the sun set. As the fiery orb descended toward the western horizon, it slipped into the fog bank and ignited the entire sky with magenta hues.

"Wow," Evie said. "Look at that. The sun sure is giving you girls a big send-off."

"I've never seen a sky like this in Chicago," Faye commented. "I remember the first time I came up here. I felt so uncertain, like I'd been pulled into an unwanted detour between graduation and marriage. Now I feel ready for anything. Despite it all, I know I can make a good life for me and Steph."

"I believe in you," Hannah said. "And I'm excited for what comes next."

"This may sound cliché, but I think this sunset is a sign of hope—for us and for the world," Faye said, raising her glass. "To the future, ladies."

40

———————

At the crack of dawn on August 23, 1945, two days before Stephanie's first birthday, Faye and Stephanie took a cab over to the Alameda Naval Air Station for their flight to Chicago. Commercial airlines, all nationalized since 1942, were just beginning to re-establish routes and order new aircraft. Faye and Stephanie were scheduled to travel as military contractors on an old DC-3, the work-horse of the war.

Faye planned to stay for a few weeks with her folks while she found a house and a job. She'd already set up interviews with the The Jewish Federation and the United Nations Relief and Rehabilitation Administration, and she hoped to soon find work. Hundreds of thousands of refugees were beginning to pour into Chicago, mostly from Eastern Europe, and her skill set seemed well suited to the effort.

Stephanie became quite the center of attention, the lone child among a passenger roster of mostly men in uniform. They sat by the window of the terminal as Stephanie laughed and clapped at the aircraft outside.

"See the airplane, Stephie?"

"Pane," Stephanie repeated.

"That's right, Pl-l-l-lane. Airplane," Faye pronounced distinctly.

"Pane," Stephanie said again, this time pointing out the window.

As they lined up to board, Faye juggled a squirming Steph plus her trusty net shopping bag filled to the gills with diapers, snacks, and toys. Stephanie babbled with excitement as they waited for boarding to begin, squealing "Pane, Mumma, pane."

"Is your daughter in pain?"

The question came from the tall captain behind them in the boarding line.

Stephanie smiled at him and reiterated "pane," gesturing forward with her dimpled hand.

Faye laughed. "Her p-l digraph hasn't quite kicked in yet. She's actually saying *plane*."

Now the captain was laughing, too. "Sorry, that was an automatic response. I'm a doctor and a cry of pain makes me want to spring into action. Here, let me help you with that bag."

He took Faye's bag, his hand grazing her arm as Steph wiggled to get free. His touch was brief but stirred something yet undefined in Faye.

Desire? Settle down, sister, it's way too soon for that since you know zero about this man. Just because he's under fifty and has a sense of humor doesn't make him your next great amour.

As the three of them settled into a row of seats by the bulkhead, Faye found herself smiling. She and the captain chatted as the other passengers settled in and buckled up for take-off. His name was Roger Townsend. He'd been stationed at Tripler Medical Center on Oahu, a main hospital for the Pacific theater of war. He'd grown up in Chicago and was returning to a staff position at Rush Medical Center. He didn't mention a wife and wasn't wearing a wedding ring.

Stop it.

To interrupt that train of thought, Faye lifted Stephanie onto her lap. "See the bridge, Stephie?" She pointed out the window at the Bay Bridge, looming large on the near horizon.

"Bige," Stephanie answered sleepily, then inserted her thumb into her mouth.

Aunt Liz was a stickler about nap times, and Faye realized it was well past time for her morning snooze.

As her eyes grew heavy, Steph added, "Boat, Mumma, boat."

"Yes, darling, that's a boat, isn't it?"

"How old is she? Eighteen months?"

"Not quite. She'll be a year old in a few days."

"She's really quite advanced," commented the captain. "The typical twelve-month-old is still babbling nonsensical words."

"Well, she's had plenty of attention from lots of articulate adults."

"Still, it's very impressive."

The engine started and began to hum, which sent Stephanie over the edge and off to dreamland. Faye turned her attention back to the window as the plane picked up speed and lifted off over the choppy waters of the bay. As it banked to the right over Oakland, Faye caught sight of a large banner hanging from the Golden Gate Bridge.

Well Done. Welcome Home.

She gazed at the giant black block letters as if they were speaking to her.

Well done, Faye.

She settled back in her seat and stole a glance at Captain Townsend, who just happened to be looking directly at her. He smiled quickly, flushed slightly, and went back to his journal.

How nice. A sleeping child. A handsome man to chat with. This could be a pleasant homecoming after all.

AFTERWORD

As predicted, the post-war years saw a booming global economy and birth rate. Women, like it or not, gave up the jobs at which they had excelled for the duration, embracing their new roles as mothers to one of the largest generations of children in history—The Baby Boomers.

Midge Swanson married Joe and stayed in the Bay Area. She had two sons. One was killed in Vietnam, and one went to UC Berkeley and became an engineer. She divorced twice and married two more times. Her last husband died of lung cancer and left her very well off. She was a major force for the establishment of the Rosie the Riveter Memorial in Richmond, California, on the former site of Kaiser Shipyard #2. At the invitation of Vice President Joe Biden, Midge traveled to the White House in 2014 with a handful of welder-sisters to be honored for her service. When President Barack Obama reached out to shake her hand, she stood on the very tips of her ninety-four-year-old toes and kissed the Leader of the Free World smack on the mouth. She tried to deny this, but it was captured on videotape and broadcast on national television.

Hannah Goldman worked at Paramount Pictures for just a few weeks before she stole the heart of Ben Epstein, a textbook Nice Jewish Boy and newly hired scriptwriter. The two married six months later, bought a house in Westwood —Hannah's father gave them the down payment—and raised three children. Hannah worked briefly at a property management company when all her children were in college at the same time, but otherwise enjoyed life as a Hollywood hostess and fundraiser for Democratic Party and Jewish causes.

Evie South never married, although there were rumors that she and her female roommate were really a couple. She stayed in the Fella Place flat until 1951, when she had an opportunity to buy a little house in Sausalito. She worked at Gregor Corp for her entire career. Although she never made it to CEO, she was promoted in her late fifties to vice president for finance, the token woman to appease the cries for more diversity that began during the 1970s.

Madeline Chu married Charles Liu, whose family was in finance. They were one of the first Asian families to settle in the East Bay community of Lafayette, where they raised their four children. Madeline taught journalism at the local public high school and freelanced stories for regional and national publications. She made the trek to Chinatown every Saturday for *dim sum* with her father until his death in 1973.

After two years of gentle, unhurried courtship, Faye Baxter Connor married Dr. Roger Townsend in a small civil ceremony at Evanston City Hall. Faye worked with the United Nations for two years longer, then quit to have her second child. As a busy mother, she volunteered with various refugee organizations throughout the rest of her life, helping thousands of immigrants from Europe, then Korea and Vietnam pursue their versions of the American Dream. Even after Roger retired, the little flat behind the Townsend's garage was often occupied by a family in transition.

Roger Townsend adopted Stephanie as his own, and it was only as a teenager she learned that Roger was not her biological father. On her fifteenth birthday, Faye gave her the box of Steve's personal effects, told her all about Steve and answered every one of her questions.

Steve Connor was buried at the Brittany American Cemetery, located near the village of Saint James, France. By the time the Army offered a program to repatriate the remains of those killed during World War II, Faye had remarried and didn't want to revisit a dark chapter in her life. So along with markers for more than 4,000 of his fallen colleagues, Steve's stark white cross stands proudly in the countryside of Northern France to this day.

Faye stayed in touch with her wartime friends through letters and occasional visits, but rarely spoke of her time in San Francisco and never told anyone of her OSS service. Once she returned to Chicago, her life was filled to the brim by the present—her work, her marriage, her children, and her community. The confidence she discovered during the war propelled her forward—out of an excruciating sadness to a place in which love and contentment were second nature. She vowed, early on, to never retreat. And so, as her new life gained momentum, the time spent in San Francisco faded into the far corners of her memory, like the fog that disappears with the warming sun.

This is a fictional story set against the context of real events. It is intended to provide a realistic picture of life on the San Francisco home front. The eviction of the Japanese American community, the return of the *USS San Francisco*, the visit of Madame Chiang Kai Shek with the banquet at the Palace Hotel, the United Nations Conference, which was indeed covered by a young JFK, and the Peace Riots on VJ day are all actual events. The internment of people of Japanese heritage remains a black mark on our domestic policy; many of the evacuated families never received their property back after the war.

Espionage networks, such as the Duquesne Spy Ring, successfully placed enemy agents in key positions in the aviation, utilities, technology, and engineering sectors in the US in order to gather intelligence for the Reich. Sabotage targets were intended to cripple the US economically, and included aluminum factories, railroads, bridges and hydro-electric plants. The attempt to disrupt the signing of the United Nations Charter is entirely imagined.

The appearance of Midge as a ninety-four-year-old on national television was inspired by an actual event. A former shipyard welder, Phyllis Gould, fought for years for Federal recognition of women workers, which finally came on March 31, 2014, with the assistance of Vice President

Joe Biden. Phyllis and five of her fellow "Rosie the Riveters" appeared on ABC News the following day (find it on YouTube).

My thanks to the many people who inspired and supported me during this process:

Ann Haggardt, who lived in the Bay Area during the war and generously shared her time and stories, and her grandniece Heather Golbienko, who introduced us. At the age of ninety-eight, Ann was one of my first beta readers and provided many fascinating details about her wartime experience. She passed on in 2021, and I am fortunate to have met her.

I am grateful to the The Rosie the Riveter National Historical Park, which houses a wonderful archive on the home front and pays tribute to women who worked in the Kaiser shipyards. University of California has an extensive oral history archive that provided me with first-hand details of that time period.

Thanks to Colleen Edwards, who was so insightful with her comments and generous with her time, to Rosalind Jackson, Janet Greenlee, Katherine Edson, Julia Curry, Cheryl O'Connor, and Heather Jackson for the many hours of reading manuscripts and sharing ideas, and to Terri Pyer for her thoughtful and thorough review. Thanks, as well, to my editor Laura Taylor, the Acorn Publishing team, and to my fellow authors Anna Wilcoxson, Laura C. Rader and Thomas Wing for their comments.

When my mother-in-law, Dorothy Jackson, passed away in the 1990s, detailed stories of her time in San Francisco during the war years perished with her. I am thankful for the little bit she told me about her experience. I also thank my late father, Dean Taylor Edson, for stories of the Pacific theater from 1944 through 1946 while he served with the 29th Engineering Topographic Battalion. Lastly, I am eternally indebted to George Jackson, who has inspired and encouraged me from the first time we met in the summer of 1972.

QUOTATION CREDITS

Page 38: From *San Francisco Chronicle* ©1942 Hearst Newspapers. All rights reserved. Used under license.

Page 121: From *San Francisco Chronicle* ©1942 Hearst Newspapers. All rights reserved. Used under license.

Page 251: From *San Francisco Chronicle* ©1944 Hearst Newspapers. All rights reserved. Used under license.

Page 304: From *San Francisco Chronicle* ©1945 Hearst Newspapers. All rights reserved. Used under license.

ABOUT THE AUTHOR

Lynn Marie Jackson has spent many years engaged in the creative process, working as a marketing strategist, copywriter, podcast producer, blogger, and novelist. Raised in California and Washington, DC, she is a long-time San Francisco Bay Area resident. When not writing, she's on the hunt for inspiration; she can be found hiking new trails, visiting museums, or exploring any place well outside her comfort zone.

For more, visit LynnMarieJackson.com